The Tainted Wars
Unworthy

W. J. Grupe Jr.

Twin Pines Publishing

All the characters in this book are fictitious, and any resemblance to actual persons living or dead is coincidental

ISBN (Hardcover) 978-1-952662-05-8
ISBN (Paperback) 978-1-952662-04-1
ISBN (Ebook) 9781952662-03-4

For Kris and Will.
Your ability to be exactly who you are, no matter what,
is a constant inspiration to me. Thanks for keeping me
young.

The Tainted Wars

Unworthy

Prologue

I FELT IT ONLY fair to bring you up to speed on what's been going on. You needn't have read the journal that came before this, titled Awakening, I will cover the main parts below. However, if you would prefer to start from the beginning, feel free. I'll wait.

My name is Christian Bateleur, and I am a Bishop. Not the kind you're thinking of. I don't wear a tall hat or carry a staff, and it's not a religious thing. I have supernatural powers supposedly derived from God with which I do battle against the Tainted. So, I guess it is a religious thing.

The Tainted are immortal beings who, according to legend, were Satan's revenge for being cast out. There are eighteen that we know of. They are the puppet masters for most wars and large-scale human-caused disasters. They are bad enough by themselves, but like anyone with power, they have a following. Besides the normal paid armies, there are the Afflicted, people who've had their mind manipulated by one of the Tainted. These are unknowing pawns and in extreme cases puppets who are completely controlled. The side effects of being victimized in this way mimicked the symptoms of Schizophrenia. It also causes the person to emit an aura that creates intense feelings of sympathy in anyone near them. I had met one of these victims, her name was Denise Ellery.

The next step up is a Converted, normal humans who derive power by drinking the blood of people who have betrayed personal oaths. Demons are created out of Converted who have undergone ritualistic torment for years until they relinquish their soul to the darkness. They are extremely rare and nearly unstoppable.

Six months ago, I was just your ordinary retired Army Ranger. I owned a small heating and cooling business named after the Miser Brothers from one of my favorite Christmas shows. It all changed when my best friend, Jackie Townsend, tricked me into attending my cousin's wedding. Something about that priest had me out of my pew and in line to take communion. This was something I had never done before since my mother, who championed my religious education, died just before my first communion. That ceremony kick-started my supernatural engines.

Afterwards, I got a visit from Amram Hager, head of the New York Covenant of Bishops. Hager is a British Hasidic Jew that looks past retirement age and lives to point out my flaws. He informed me that my mother had been part of this secret war and apparently died in battle. The powers I inherited from her are passed down from parent to first-born child. He introduced me to the fantastical world I was now part of, and the team who were to become my new family.

John McCaw also has military training, is a mechanic, engineer, and weapons expert. Soon-Li Yuan grew up and trained together with my mother. She can out code some of the best hackers in the world and is one of the foremost experts in hand-to-hand as well as edged weapons combat. Tira Gupta is a medical doctor, psychiatrist, research scientist, yogi, and all around badass. Finally, there is Jelena Torres, Marine sniper turned mercenary after an injury led to an honorable discharge. I hired her as the first non-Bishop to work for our side in all of history, shortly after she tried to kill me.

So, new superpowers, kick ass new team, all should be right with the world. The problem is typically Bishops start their training around the age of ten. Being twenty-plus years behind in my training and having a rebellious attitude against anything having to do with faith, I was having difficulty connecting with my gift. Those times it did work I ended up performing acts that had either not been seen since the days of Jesus Christ, one of the more famous Bishops, or had never been witnessed ever.

Last November we had a run-in with Baldemar, one of the worst of the Tainted. He had orchestrated a domestic terrorist attack in the middle of Manhattan. A total dick move. We prevailed but many lives were lost. During the final battle, I performed several more acts thought to be impossible. It created a small but palpable rift between me and the other Bishops. Like trying to be friendly with someone holding a grenade with no pin. Instead of staying and continuing my training, I left.

With Jelena by my side, I moved to Miami. Hager connected me with the Covenant down there. Her and I, along with her son, Enric and Mother Janice all moved in. Things seemed to be going okay. The Covenant head gave me an assignment to track down a new drug that was popping up down here. I got the feeling it was busy work to keep me out of her hair. That is until one night at the warehouses by the docks…

Chapter One

THE RAIN HAMMERED ON the roof echoing through the spacious Range Rover Velar. I thought back to the asshole sales agent that had guaranteed me that outside noise would never penetrate the double insulated interior.

"Bullshit," I responded to the blatant lie I was told two months before. I stared out the windshield at the warehouse and shook my head. This was ridiculous.

"What's wrong now, grumpy?"

I looked over at Jelena Torres in the passenger seat. She was short compared to me with long black hair, pronounced eyebrows and full lips.

"I feel stupid."

"More than usual?" Her accent gave her sarcasm a sharp edge.

"Look at this." I waved my hand at the windshield.

"What's the matter? Big bad Bishop is afraid of getting a little wet?"

Yup, that's me, Chris Bateleur, Bishop. I'm not sure I really liked the title. After a childhood of playing Dungeons & Dragons, a person with supernatural powers derived from religious connections was a cleric. Period. I'm pushing for a name change.

"The whole scenario. We are sitting in a car, watching a warehouse on the docks in a rainstorm. If I had a sports jacket with rolled-up sleeves, and your hair was teased up to the moon, we would be every eighties cop show."

"What's with your eighties obsession?"

"It's not an obsession, it just happens to be the best decade for movies and music."

"Whatever, old man."

"We are almost the same age."

"Then why are you so crotchety?"

"I'm not…" I took a deep breath, trying to calm myself. "Remind me again why I let you tag along?"

Jelena made an annoyed sound. "Because you need someone to watch your back and keep you out of trouble. Plus, you were going close to Disney and I've been promising Enric a trip." She lifted the book from the armrest between us. "And explain this."

"What? You have a problem with poetry?"

"It's in French, and it's like a thousand years old."

"It's only 16th century."

"Yeah, only." She waggled the book. "Why the hell are you reading this?"

"It was one of Jackie's favorites."

Jelena crossed her arms. "You know she's gay, right?"

"I'm aware."

"Which means she's not having sex with you."

I frowned at her. "I'm not trying to have sex with her."

"The way she looks, everyone is trying to have sex with her. Hell, I'm trying to."

"I'm not." No, seriously, I'm not. Well, not anymore.

"Okay sure. Then why the book?" She held it up as if it were empirical evidence.

"Research. The author had many of the same symptoms as Denise. Also, some poems have similarities with what we know about the Tainted. She was a fan of the poems before all this and made the connection afterwards. I'm trying to see if anything in there makes sense."

"And?"

I adjusted myself in the seat. "I'm hopeful. There is a section in here that hints of a way to kill one of the Tainted."

"I thought that was impossible."

"Not impossible. Just never done before."

Jelena tossed the book in my lap. "Same thing." She pulled up the hood of her parka and took her sniper rifle case from the back seat. She grabbed the door handle, paused and looked back.

"Let me tag along," she said, as if it were the stupidest thing she had ever heard. "Like I gave you a choice." She opened the door. "I'll tell you when I'm in position."

She slammed it closed again, and I cringed.

"It's a new car, you know!" It was my first new car ever. Not counting my work van. An Econovan. One side painted with a tropical scene, the other a frozen tundra. The Miser Brothers were engaged in a pictorial battle on the hood and rear doors. A Luxury car it was not, but thinking about it made me smile. Then I remembered someone else was driving it.

I left Miser Brothers Heating and Cooling behind with the rest of my old life. I hadn't seen Jackie, my childhood best friend, in over a month. She came for a visit shortly after I got settled in Miami. She dragged me along to club after club as if this was her second home. My ears were still ringing from that weekend.

I checked the time on the heads-up display then turned on my coms unit. Killing the ignition, I put my hood up, and got out. "I'm going in."

"I'm not set yet."

"I'll be fine."

The drug dealer I harassed, a guy by the name of Skinny, pointed me toward this warehouse. I assumed the name was ironic based on his keg sized belly. He said this was where the shipments were coming in. If there was a Converted involved, they would be here.

I walked nonchalantly towards the entrance gate, the rain sounding twice as loud slapping against my waterproof hood. The security booth was outside where the guard on duty could check people in before allowing them access to the property. I could have snuck in, but I really didn't feel like playing a muddy version of hide-and-go-seek. Instead, I walked up to the booth. The guard opened a little square in the Plexiglas door. Apparently, he wasn't thrilled about the weather, either.

"Yeah?" He was a big guy. Not big as in round, big as in, I pick things up and put them down. The one thing this monster couldn't put down were his arms, which were the size of legs jutting out at an angle. His tone suggested he was not expecting to use the phrase 'sure go right in' anytime soon.

"Hey Arnold, I'm here for the drugs."

"What? What drugs? Ain't no drugs here."

He was obviously not waiting for his big break in acting.

"Oh, good they are here. Can you buzz me in?"

I pointed in case he forgot where the button was. He looked down, confused. For a second, I thought he might comply with my request. He came back to himself before fully succumbing to my charms.

"Do I need to come out there?"

"I rather you didn't, Lou. I don't feel like dragging your wet, gargantuan body back into the cramped booth after I knock you on your ass."

It took him a second to figure out that I was insulting him. His face contorted into what I imaged he considered his mad face, but it came across more constipated. The Hulk opened the door to his tiny house, and I reached for my gift. Its soft glow lit the horizon of my mind. Power flowed through me. I became acutely aware of my surroundings, as though someone switched the lights on in a dark room.

The guard took one step out of the booth. I took one step towards him, lashing out with both fists and a lick of power. I struck him in the chest with the fast staccato rhythm of a drumroll. The so closely timed strikes caused his heart to skip a beat and his breath to leave him. His boots hydroplaned on the wet asphalt, and he fell backward into the booth. I leaned in to look at him. The guard, stared at me with wide eyes. He clutched at his chest as he struggled to inhale.

"See, wasn't that easier?"

He looked around the booth for his dignity.

"No, that's alright. I've got it."

I grabbed his legs and shifted him into the cramped space. Then I flipped him over. Still struggling to inhale, he gave little resistance as I zip tied his hands in back of him. For good measure, I put on a second one and contemplated my work. I grinned madly as I added another. Then I leaned down next to his head and spoke with a Boston accent.

"He can't with three on him. Not with three."

I added two to his feet and then hog-tied him. I took his radio with me, since that's what they did in the movies and closed the door on him. A decent start to my first solo mission.

The gate was still closed. I didn't know if there was a motion sensor in the warehouse, but I didn't want to take the chance. Plus, it was only like ten feet with barbed wire and not really preventing my entrance. I used some of my gift for an enhanced jump and launched myself over the fence. I misjudged the amount of power needed and sailed a little too high. I landed hard and slipped just like my buddy in the security booth.

"I really need to practice more."

I only hoped that Jelena didn't see it. She would never let me live it down. The ex-Army Ranger, superhero klutz.

"Nice move." I could hear Jelena's laughter over the com.

Oh well. At least I remembered to reinforce my back before I landed on the pavement. No need to waste my reserves on healing. I dusted off my pride and made my way to the warehouse.

It wasn't large compared to many of the others that filled every space around one of Miami's many industrial complexes. In fact, it was its size that made it so inconspicuous. Wedged in between the massive on-line giant, the top selling electronics retailer, and an iron supplier that shipped out more raw materials in one day than I had seen in my entire life.

This short, square, tan building with a low-pitched roof was ringed by a high fence. It could accommodate four tractor trailers, nothing compared to the monolithic buildings its neighbors put up. Those could handle ten times the volume. This one had several skylights but few windows. I saw cameras in strategic locations. Safe to assume they had motion sensors. Even doorbells did these days. They were easy to avoid when I could blur past them. I headed straight for the front door.

In hindsight, this may not have been the best plan. But in my defense, I had just recently come into superhuman powers that I had been wanting to play with. I mean, come on, what kid at heart didn't want to play Superman? Plus, it was night. How many guys could be hanging around in there? I snapped the door handle off, using more pressure than the man of steel would use in the old black and white series. He always made it look like they were made from rock candy. This one might have been made from stale taffy. Maybe not as elegant, but I was in.

I walked into a small reception area with a few rickety chairs, a table, and an empty water cooler. The door on the far side led to a hallway with a row of tiny offices. Each had just enough furniture to not call it empty. In the first office, a window looked in on the reception area. A shotgun leaned up against the folding table just under the window.

"Not very welcoming."

I made my way down the hall to the door that I assumed led into the main warehouse. In the old days, I would have used tech to verify the number of combatants, room layout, egresses, and choke points. Now I just used my gift to enhance my senses. Sound and smells that were muted became amplified. I could make out the sounds of a small group of people in the warehouse. The smells made me wish I knew how to enhance one sense at a time.

"Overwatch, can you see anything in the warehouse?" I asked.

"Negative. There are no windows. Thermals show a group of people but it's hard to distinguish how many, or if they're armed. I suggest backing out until we have more intel."

I considered this but I was getting impatient with our lack of progress. If the stash here was half of what Skinny implied, it would be a big step to cutting off the distribution.

The problem with vanquishing a couple of demons single handedly, it made you cocky.

"I'm gonna take a peek."

"Not a good idea."

I stepped up to the door, putting a light touch on the knob. I tried it and found it unlocked. "It's all good. I'm just gonna sneak around the warehouse and find the drugs before anyone notices me. No sweat."

I pushed the door open, and a loud buzzing sounded in the

warehouse. The cat was already out of the bag so I continued in trying to look like I was supposed to be there.

Seven men and a woman stood together in front of two trucks. There was a raised office accessible by a stairway, lit from within though seemingly empty. Otherwise, the warehouse was empty.

All the men carried various assault rifles, or submachine guns, which, thanks to my noisy entrance, were all trained on me. The woman carried no weapon but gave off a more dangerous aura than the men. She looked me up and down and said, "Who the fuck are you?" It wasn't what she said that gave me a little shiver, but the way she said it. She said it lovingly like an entomologist finding a new species of caterpillar. She looked to be Japanese but that was mostly a guess.

"Did you guys not order the stripper?" I casually approached the group of people and tried another excuse. "Would you believe this is a case of a wrong address?"

One goon lifted his rifle, but the woman put a hand on the barrel and lowered it. She leaned forward and whispered in his ear. My senses were in high gear now that I had walked into the middle of a shit storm.

"Only a complete idiot would burst in there without backup." I tried to push Jelena's berating to the background so I could focus on the woman in front of me.

"Right now, he just walked in on people holding guns. If he is a cop and you shoot him, we all become accessories." She cooed the words as she caressed the steel of the rifle.

The man nodded, but she wasn't done yet.

"If you move again without my permission, I will feed you to Krissi."

The goon went three shades paler and the woman smiled ear to ear. I only knew two women with that name and they were both from seventies sitcoms. Neither one filled me with dread. Now if she'd said Alice…

The chastised guard stepped back, and the woman whom I so shrewdly identified as the one in charge approached me like a snake hypnotizing its prey. She performed the catwalk strut so quickly towards me I was amazed she didn't trip. Stopping well into my personal space she scratched a fingernail down my pectoral muscle.

"Can I help you?" She looked up at me past long eyelashes.

If the stance was supposed to throw me off, it worked. Almost. Luckily for me, my sarcasm takes on a life of its own.

"Yeah, I'm looking for the rave. This woman at the bar told me it was here, but now I'm thinking that she was just blowing me off."

"There is obviously," she fanned her fingers out to indicate the surroundings, "no rave here."

I gave the aw-shucks motion with my fist. "I knew it. Only phone numbers on TV start with 555."

"I am sorry for your inconvenience, mister?"

"Tully, Louis Tully."

She hesitated only a second, then continued with her marketing script.

"Mr. Tully," she practically whispered. "I'm afraid we are very busy and I am going to have to ask you to leave."

"You're saying you don't know Krissi?"

All eyes focused on me, some registering shock, others fear. The woman in front of me narrowed hers.

I held my hand up about shoulder height. "Short woman, purple hair, multiple piercings." Everyone relaxed. "And a tattoo on the back of her neck." The playful scratches she had been performing on my chest developed into an annoyed tapping. I estimated my host was at the end of her patience. Time to kick it up a notch. "I think it was a Bishop."

Her eyebrows twitched, letting me know I was in the right place. But otherwise, the rest of her remained calm.

"You know, the chess piece."

No response, at least not to me. She cocked her head as though she was listening to something else. Then she stepped back away from me.

I tried to reengage her. "I'm sorry I didn't catch your name."

Again, no response. No witty banter. No threats. What ever happened to playing to the tropes? She just stood there, staring at me. It was making me kind of uncomfortable. While she was saying nothing, everyone else's body language was giving me all kinds of intel. One guy even chambered a round. Amateur. I didn't think I could hold the staring contest for much longer without saying something cliche.

The door opened to the office and another woman emerged. She was also Japanese, or just really into their Kimonos. The entire outfit was various shades of red. Even her skin tone had a pronounced red tint as though she had bathed in blood. Her hair was divided and twisted into five horns making it appear as if she was wearing a disturbing looking crown. She just stood there at the railing looking down at me. The other woman looked at the newcomer then back at me narrowing her eyes as again though just given information she didn't like.

"Chris, you have incoming. Get out of there. I say again, evac." Jelena said.

I perked up my enhanced hearing again and caught the sounds of pre-breach activity.

I took in the overall scenario, smiled and said, "saved by the bang."

I tried to keep it in, I really did. The breaching charge became a period to my sentence, and a flood of officers poured into the warehouse from different entrances.

"DEA! Everyone on the ground!"

Pandemonium ensued; rifles being waved around, and goons being thrown down on their stomachs. The unnamed woman and I never moved. She never even twitched again. I just smiled down at her. Until we were both dragged to the floor. When everyone had been secured, everything quieted. Footsteps reverberated on the concrete floor echoing around the open space like gun shots.

They came to a stop in front of my face, which was currently pinned to the dirty floor. She started tapping her foot.

I tried to say, "at least someone knows how to play their role," though I'm not sure how much of it got past my smushed face. The owner of the shoes crouched down in front of me and I strained my peripheral vision to get a look. If I wasn't physically restrained, I would have done a double take. Hazel-green eyes stared back at me, framed by wavy black hair. She wore a jeans, a gray sports jacket and a white V-neck tee shirt.

"Hey there, John Wayne."

I tried to reply, but was, again, prevented.

"I just wanted to congratulate you."

Nodding was apparently not an option either.

"You got here just in time for the bust." She did a slow clap, then brushed the hair out of my face. "No, no. Don't speak. We'll talk real soon." She stood up. "Get CSU in here."

I was cuffed and as they lifted me to my feet, giving me the opportunity to take a final look around. The woman in red was gone.

Chapter Two

I T WASN'T MY FIRST visit to this side of the interrogation table. The first time, an MP was on the other side, and the issue was more of a case of what I didn't do. This one resembled the one we had cuffed Jelena to back in November before she transitioned from prisoner to team member. A large ring was bolted to the middle of the table. The cuffs threaded through it were attached to my wrists. Most Bishops can manipulate locks with their gift and unlocking these would have been no problem. But that would have been kind of a giveaway. I figured I would play along for now.

There was no-one on this side of the two-way mirror, but I was sure I was being studied like new bacteria under a microscope. I'd been sitting there for the better part of two hours, presumably so I could make myself nuts dreaming up the worst possible scenario. Had it been last year—hell, even six months ago—I would have. Much had changed in such a short amount of time.

The agent from the warehouse walked in with a folder and laptop. She smiled, as though this was a job interview.

"Good morning. Sorry to keep you waiting."

She sat down and placed a bottle of water in front of me. Then she opened the file and flipped through it, not looking at me. I guessed I was supposed to start the conversation. Ask for a lawyer. Claim innocence. Instead, I took the time to admire my host.

Now that I wasn't lying flat on the ground, I noticed she was shorter than I had thought. Not too much over five feet. The black wavy hair was natural, or she was one of the few people I knew that also dyed her eyebrows. Her eye makeup was subtle except for the winged eyeliner.

I always liked that. A crucifix hung on a delicate chain, around her neck. She finally looked at me. That feeling came over me like when someone catches you watching them, even though we were the only two in the room sitting at the only table facing each other. I felt myself blush and cursed my lack of coolness.

"Christian Bateleur."

"It's Chris."

Her eyes lifted, and I smiled at her, hoping to disarm her a little. Her gaze returned to the papers in front of her.

"I am special agent Marie Valentini of the DEA. Are you new to Miami?" She had a slight southern drawl, like she was a transplant. I couldn't pin down from where.

"No, I have been here before."

"How long have you been here this time?"

I tilted my head toward the folder. "What does it say on the paper?" She regarded me again.

I leaned forward trying to peek. "I don't want to get it wrong."

"Where do you live, Mr. Bateleur?"

"New York. That should be in the file. And it's Chris, remember."

"Where are you staying while you are in Miami?"

"With a friend. That's an awfully thick folder to not include any of this information."

"How long have you been in Miami?"

"A few weeks."

"Plan on staying much longer?"

I smiled, "Just until we're done talking."

"Cute, I meant Miami."

"No specific plans."

"Why were you in a remote warehouse in the middle of the night?"

"I needed to use the bathroom. It looked like a nice clean place."

"You didn't get thrown out of a window, so how 'bout we try that again?"

My heart fluttered that she had caught the reference and gave one back. "Just because it's been used before doesn't make it invalid."

We were playing cat and mouse, both of us trying to be the cat.

By the way her ears raised when she smiled, she was enjoying herself.

"Where were you coming from?"

"A party."

"You went from a party to the industrial area of Miami?"

"Yes."

"Why?"

"I was going to another party."

"In a warehouse?"

"You know one of those underground parties."

"Must be really underground if the only way to get in is to hogtie the guard and scale a ten-foot barbed wire fence."

"In my defense, I really had to go."

"Were you looking for a bathroom or a party?"

"Preferably a party with a bathroom."

"I thought the best thing about being a man was the ability to go wherever you wanted."

"That would be illegal."

"Assault, battery, criminal trespass, breaking and entering are all okay. But urinating in public, not so much."

"There's a level of decorum one must hold oneself to."

"Mr. Bateleur."

"Chris."

"Unless you can provide a reason for being there other than a full bladder, we're going to add interfering with a federal investigation and conspiracy to the charges. It will turn this into a federal issue and bump everything up to felonies."

I took a second then I nodded and leaned forward, motioning her to do the same. She rolled her eyes but complied without getting too close.

"What time is it?"

She looked at me, her expression telling me to get to the point. I raised my eyebrows. She picked up her phone and told me. I nodded.

"In about thirty seconds, your phone is going to ring. At that time, I will be accepting your apology as you're releasing me."

Picking up my bottle of water, I tried to lean back in my chair, forgetting that I was cuffed. I covered as best as I could, going for an air of mystery. Special Agent Valentini's expression went from skeptical to curious as a response to my body language. I am a big believer in the fake it till you make it philosophy. We both watched the phone as the seconds ticked by.

Three-and-a-half hours later, I was still cuffed to the same table. This time, however, I had a full bladder. Damn water bottle. The chains weren't long enough for me to reach my mouth, so I had to lean down and tilt my head to the side to drink. It was not comfortable or very accurate. I had a feeling agents on the other side of the two-way mirror were making fun of me. Her phone had never rung. Worth a shot. It would have looked awesome if it paid off.

The door opened, and Adam entered. He was a Bishop from the Miami Covenant and the prettiest man I had ever seen. He had fair skin, high cheekbones and unusually long eyelashes. I knew some guys that didn't need to shave often, but this guy must have used a straight razor and a magnifying mirror to get that close. He wore a well-tailored jacket over a white shirt and tie, jeans and loafers with no show socks. Either that or he wasn't wearing socks, a thought that made me a little squeamish. The door closed behind him, but he didn't sit down.

"Mr. Bateleur?"

"Chris."

I looked towards the two-way mirror. Adam shook his head.

"I told them I was your lawyer. No one is monitoring."

"In that case, what took you so long? You were supposed to call over three hours ago."

He gave me a questioning look, but decided he didn't care.

"They are processing you out."

A knock came to the door, then opened before we could respond. An officer walked in with a set of keys and unlocked my cuffs. I was disappointed it wasn't Marie. I opened my mouth to ask where she was, but Adam interrupted.

"Mr. Bateleur, please say nothing further while we are in the station."

They guided me out, more like hurried. No one attempted to intercede, nor did anyone apologize. It wasn't as enjoyable as I pictured. We exited the building and found Marie leaning up against the central metal stair railing, arms folded, and she still had a smile on her face.

"Hello again Mister… Chris."

My scowl must have done its job.

"My client will not be making any statements at this time. If you have questions, you can direct them to my office."

"Hello, Special Agent Valentini." She hadn't asked me to call her Marie, yet.

"Looks like your timing was off."

"Better late than never."

"Did you ever use the bathroom?"

"Not yet, and it's getting a little uncomfortable."

"Shame. Last chance to get something off your chest. Anything to say?"

Adam tried once again to dissuade me from opening my mouth. Bless his heart.

"Yes, as a matter of fact there is."

Adam shook his head.

"Who allowed someone to put up that ugly gray building within sight of the LoanDepot stadium? Luckily it was off season, it practically ruined my pilgrimage. If you are looking for a crime, that is what I would focus on."

"I'll keep that in mind. Anything else?"

We stared at each other for a few tense seconds. Several stupid responses bounced around my head. I settled on, "I'm still waiting for that apology."

She kept up her eye contact for another second or two, then pushed off the railing with her hips. She walked up to me, touched my biceps, and leaned in. I felt a rush of warmth where her hand rested. She spoke softly but didn't whisper, "It's not how long you wait, but who you're waiting for."

Then she walked off. Her words sounded familiar. I looked after her, willing her to turn back. She didn't. As I descended the steps, I nearly bumped into Adam.

"Done?" he asked in a clipped voice.

"Unfortunately." I looked back longingly.

"When I said don't talk to anyone, that was clear right?"

I regarded Adam. "Did you have breakfast?"

"Mr. Bateleur…"

"Chris, for Christ's sake."

Adam made a face.

"Sorry. Bad habit."

"I'm not insulted. That just sounded like a tongue teaser for a moron."

I thought about it and realized I could not argue. "So, breakfast?"

"I'm supposed to bring you right back."

"Yeah, but… breakfast!"

He walked away down the stairs, shaking his head.

I followed quickly behind him. "And that bathroom thing wasn't a joke, either. I can't be having a serious conversation with Ima without coffee and a bio-break."

Adam looked like a bobble head going the wrong way.

"What were you thinking?" Imaculada Rosita Castillo made me feel like I was being scolded by my sixth-grade schoolteacher. Adam refused to stop for breakfast but at least he let me use the bathroom before being given the riot act.

I shook my head. "I know. Ima bad boy."

Adam sighed from the corner of the room behind me where he stood at parade rest, hands behind his back feet shoulder width apart.

"Why would you go in alone?" Ima asked.

"I figured if I found the drugs, I could call in the cavalry."

"And?"

"I didn't get the chance."

"Why am I not surprised?" Ima did not sit behind her desk while she berated me. She preferred to be up close and personal. Ima was tall, and it was quite effective as she stared down at me, her green eyes shining, black, gray streaked hair pulled back into a ponytail. She didn't tower over me, but she made me feel short. Was there a height requirement to be a Covenant head?

"Mr. Bateleur…"

"Chris."

Ima ignored I had spoken.

"Amram seems to hold you in high regard."

I smiled at that. Although my relationship with the man who introduced me to this world had come a long way, I couldn't imagine Hager talking me up to anyone.

"Though to date, I have not seen evidence of anything to warrant it."

My smile disappeared.

"I know you're new to your powers, but I would expect you to show more restraint than our teenage students."

"I think you are overreacting a little. It's not like I boosted some liquor and got drunk in a parking lot while performing tricks for my friends."

"No, you broke into a drug dealer's warehouse alone, impeded an investigation, and got yourself arrested. Which was lucky, or you would probably be dead."

I flipped a hand. "I had everything under control."

Ima stared down at me another few seconds for good measure, then stalked back to her minimalist desk. The loose robes that covered her from wrist to neck to ankle flowing around her. The décor was all wrath of God depictions which was giving me a subliminal message. I looked to one side at a painting of Sodom and Gamora and shivered.

The Miami Covenant resided in a converted church. Not one of the old-style stone ones with a gothic theme, this was more like a budget church. Everything was nice, but minimalistic. They still held mass in the front section. The back was all Bishop central.

The door opened and Jelena marched in, positioned herself between me and Ima's desk, her eyes shining, her lip a thin line. Then she drove her fist into my gut. She was subtle and quick enough for my gift not to kick in. I didn't quite double over, but she had a hell of a punch.

"You idiot. How am I supposed to cover you if you don't listen to me?"

"Nice to see you, too." I grunted at her.

"Mrs. Torres, we are in the middle of something, if you would kindly wait outside."

Jelena didn't move, just continued to stare at me eye to eye thanks to my somewhat hunched position. Whatever issues I had with authority, Jelena had them tenfold. Much of it may have stemmed from the fact that her last boss tried to blow her up.

"Mrs. Torres." Ima didn't raise her voice, but the tone demanded attention.

Jelena pulled her death stare away long enough to glance over her shoulder.

"It's Miss." She gave me one last pointed look before briefly acknowledging Adam, then marched out, slamming the door.

"I won't debate the rationale of keeping a military sniper as your backup, however while you are here, please do your best to control her." Ima took the top page from a pile on her desk and started scratching at it with a pen.

After I could take a deep breath, I replied, "If I kept her chained up, she wouldn't be much of a guard dog."

I caught Adam trying to hide a smile. So did Ima.

"Discipline needs to be observed. As a former military man, I'm sure you can understand."

"Not wanting to blindly following orders is why I am no longer a military man."

Ima watched me, her pen hovering above the paper.

"But I will talk with her."

She inclined her head and continued her scratching.

"So, were you able to salvage anything from that debacle of a mission?"

I nodded. "Before the DEA so rudely interrupted, I was having a pleasant chat with one of the women in charge. I didn't get her name, but she definitely knew who we were."

"That doesn't quite narrow things down."

"I got one name. She mentioned feeding one of her thugs to Krissi."

Ima's pen stopped, but only for a second.

"Was there a second woman, Asian?"

"Yeah. That one was a little more dramatic." I described the woman in red.

Adam let out a slow breath. Ima silenced him with a look.

"I'm guessing you know them."

"We have run across them in the past. Nothing for you to be concerned about. I appreciate you looking into this for me, but we will take it from here."

"I'm kind of invested now, and I would like to see things through."

"Admirable, but unnecessary. These are low-level operatives who don't rate our concern. We will leave them to the DEA."

"Did you hear me say that they know who we are?"

"You didn't even get a name. How could you deduce that?"

"Their reaction to the word Bishop."

"Do you just go announcing our organization to anyone you see?"

"I was a little more subtle than that."

"I'm sure."

"I think this is more than a low-level operation." I pushed.

"Is that what your keen investigative experience has led you to believe?"

"Listen, I may—"

"Mr. Bateleur, I know you were somehow helpful with the incident in New York. However, you are out of your depth with the Miami drug cartels."

"I thought they were low level."

Ima looked up from her paperwork again.

"Stick to sightseeing while you are here. Enjoy a vacation, go to a club. We have enough of them."

"I'm not on vacation."

"You are now. Dismissed."

"Ima, I didn't come here to sit on the bench."

She didn't respond but motioned with her pen. Adam took the cue and touched my arm. I didn't move right away, deciding if I wanted to continue this battle or come back when I was better armed. I looked at Adam, indicating that his hand was unwelcome. He removed it and I walked out.

Chapter Three

JELENA WAS LEANING UP against the wall outside of Ima's office, arms crossed. Above her hung rows of pictures with small plaques under each, a memorial for fallen Bishops. Her head covered the most recent. She gave my escort a passing glance before refocusing her stink-eye on me.

"Adam, I guess I owe you five bucks since he survived. Double or nothing for the next time out."

"You won't be able to make your money back. She benched him," Adam replied.

"Okay then, ten bucks says he doesn't stay benched. The only thing he is better at than almost getting killed, is finding trouble."

"You're on."

I crossed my arms. "I'm not sure which is worse, that you are betting on my demise or that my overwatch is betting against me. Seems like a conflict of interest."

"Hey! I'm a professional." Jelena objected. "Plus, there's no sport in letting you die."

"Great."

She pushed off the wall and stepped in front of me. "But the next time you don't bail when I say, I will shoot you myself." She jabbed her finger into my chest to drive the point home. It hurt.

"Point taken. I promise I will make sure I get into a situation where you can save my life with a well-timed sniper shot."

She nodded, then stepped out of the way. I started walking, and she kept pace taking the opposite flank from Adam.

"Did you happen to bring back my car?"

"Yeah. When I saw you get arrested, I got out of there and called Adam."

I stopped and faced him. "Why did it take you so long to get to me?"

He hooked a thumb back the way we came. "She wouldn't let me. Said the time in jail might be good for you."

"That was a dick move."

"She's my mother," Adam said.

"What I mean is—"

"Relax. I don't disagree."

"What's our next move?" Jelena asked.

"First things first."

"So, coffee?" she guessed.

"Damn, straight. Followed by pancakes and a nap. Take the day to hang with Enric. Maybe get some rest. We're going out tonight."

I started walking away.

Jelena asked, "where are we going?"

"Clubbing," I called back.

I woke up at around dinner time and jumped in the shower. This was where I did some of my best thinking. That evening however I wasn't thrilled with where my mind was going. I kept hearing both Ima and Jelena's voices in my head telling me how stupid and useless I was as a Bishop. Those weren't their exact words but that was what I was hearing. My ego took a hit. I stuck my head under the stream trying to wash away the unwanted thoughts then shut off the water.

I toweled off, and dressed. Grabbing my notebook off the desk I flipped through it to my last entry. A list of clubs.

Before I went to sleep, I reviewed the recording I made of the "interview" with my informant, Skinny. Along with the warehouse he had dropped the names of several night clubs where the drugs were being distributed. It was the suggestion to go to a club that reminded me of them.

"Thanks Ima."

I pocketed the notebook and left the compound.

The semi converted church sat on a decent sized piece of land with several structures. The resident building contained dorm rooms eerily similar to the ones I had just vacated back in New York. It had a gymnasium with all the same kinds of equipment, though laid out differently, as if the Covenants both used the same interior decorator.

Down the street I stopped in my new favorite gastro pub, Chi-Chi's. It was named after the owner, Norma. I didn't get it either and she wouldn't explain it, just laughed it off. However, Norma, or Chi-Chi, served the best empanadas I've ever had. I am a sucker for a good empanada. I texted Jelena to let her know where to meet me.

"Chris!"

Norma came around the counter when I entered and planted a kiss on my cheek. She was in her sixties though had more energy than Enric on a sugar high. She pulled me into a booth as she started calling back for my regular order.

"No beer," I told her. "Just water tonight."

"What? Beer is practically water." She had an accent derived from her Cuban ancestry and colored with thirty years in Brooklyn. Kind of like a Spanish-Italian-English accent. She recognized my New York accent, which is what spurred our new friendship.

"Not the kind you serve."

A devilish smile cut her face, and she yelled back the adjusted order, "Grande Agua. Wasa problem? Still a few days before lent."

"Going out tonight. Hitting a few clubs. A wise man once told me, 'hydrate before you medicate'."

"Pah, sounds like an amateur to me."

I would have argued, but I had a feeling that Norma was a card-carrying member of the beer is for breakfast school of thought. These were people who believed that water was for growing vegetables and cooking pasta. I can't hang.

"What club?"

I showed her the list.

"Looks like fun, maybe I should tag along."

"I think Chester would get jealous."

"As long as I bring him the bread, he doesn't care what made the dough rise."

"You are bad, Norma."

She giggled behind her hand. A worker brought me my dinner, and I immediately dug in. The juices flowed down my cheek as I savored the spicy carnitas filling.

"So, you are going by yourself?"

"No, famous guys like me always have an entourage."

"Smart ass."

"I thought you said I had a nice ass."

She smacked me, almost knocking my Grande Aqua out of my hand, with a big smile on her face. I ate the rest of my dinner and continued my gratuitous flirting with Norma while Chester looked on in gleeful anticipation.

Jelena arrived with Adam following close behind. I guess we had a chaperone for tonight. Norma usually gave her a stink eye, but today she was all smiles. I'm not sure what changed, but I wasn't about to jinx it by saying anything.

"So, where are we going?" Jelena asked.

I showed her the list.

I could see recognition in her expression but didn't let on. "Impressive. You ready, or are you still fluffing Norma?" Jelena hooked a thumb at our host.

I wasn't sure what that meant, but apparently Norma did and gave her a playful nudge that nearly threw her off her feet.

"You are very naughty." Norma told Jelena then patted me on the shoulder. "Chris, have a good time, but be careful. Sometimes I am seeing the drugs around there." She blew me a kiss and waved at the others as she moved back behind the counter. Crossing the threshold put her back into boss mode, and she launched into a tirade at the kitchen staff in Spanish. Or was it Italian?

I got up and threw money on the table. "Come on, before she grabs a rolling pin."

It was almost one in the morning. The Blue Martini was the last on the list. It was on the second floor in the corner of a set of buildings. The only entrance was up a flight of stairs and across a footbridge that overlooked the courtyard. I questioned the logic of this design for a bar. Despite the parapet, I could see intoxicated patrons taking a header to the pavement below.

"Stop being such a killjoy," Jelena rebuked. "I think it's cool." She grabbed Adam by the wrist and dragged him ahead. He looked back at me as though pleading for help.

Jelena approached the guy working the door, hooked a thumb backwards and bounced in, Adam in tow. I reached him a few seconds later.

"Girl said you were her uncle, and you would pay the cover charge for them."

"Of course she did."

I handed over the money and walked in, shaking my head. That joke was getting old. For me at least. This whole night had been torture for me. I don't do clubs since I'm not fond of crowds. Wiggling myself into the middle of a packed dance floor to grind on people I've never met just doesn't appeal to me. Tack on music so loud that conversation is nearly impossible, and drinks that cost as much as lunch from a street vendor back in Manhattan, you have created a Chris proof environment. Give me a quiet bar any day. The worst part was, so far, we had absolutely zero leads.

I pushed my way through the blue tinged throng of people thanks to the lighting. It surprised me to recognize the song that was playing, Give up the Funk by Parliament. Three separate people tried to pull me into the fray, and I extracted myself, miming the need for a drink. I finally made it to the relative safety of the main bar and was shocked to find a corner stool just vacated by a woman in a painted-on dress dragging her friend onto the dance floor.

I confess to using a little enhanced speed to help claim my spot. I surprised the guy who almost sat on me.

"What the… dude, not cool."

"Don't worry, you will reach some level of cool when you grow up." I like to be supportive of the younger generation when I can. They can be very sensitive.

"What? Are you starting some shit?" The guy was obviously trying to put on a show for his date, who apparently left her house in her nightgown. The music changed to Celebration by Kool and the Gang.

"Danny, this is my jam," his date said and dragged him towards the floor.

"Yeah, hurry along Daniel-san before Mr. Miyagi makes you sand the floor. With your face." I tried to restrain myself, I really did. He gave me a look, but luckily, he found his companion's assets more interesting than getting his ass beaten in public. It was a good decision.

It was seventies night, according to Tony the bartender. We had been there about an hour. I was enjoying the music, which to my amazement was not too loud, but the investigation was once again coming up empty. I had been people watching in the extreme. Using my gift to focus in on one monotonous conversation after another, trying to find a drug buy. Instead, what I got was a litany of bad lines and drunk talk.

"Hey, do you come here often?"

"OMG, I am so trashed right now."

"I've got an apartment nearby with a killer view."

"This is my jam, come dance with me."

The only thing I had found was a headache. The few times I had seen Jelena and Adam they seemed to be enjoying themselves. I'd, however, had enough. Time to find them, and bail.

"Tony."

He ignored me.

"Cashing in already?"

This was the third young woman that approached me. I was one of the oldest people in the club that wasn't attending a corporate happy hour trying to recapture their youth. I guess that made me a target. Miami. I swiveled in my seat to let her down easy, not something I am used to. She was not what I expected.

"Agent Valentini?"

Chapter Four

H ER JEANS, TEE SHIRT and sports jacket were replaced with a purple, chiffon, sleeveless dress that shimmered in the blue lighting. She had freed her hair from the ponytail and it danced about her shoulders. I gaped openly, knowing what I was doing but unable to stop.

"Marie."

"Huh?"

"I'm off duty. Call me Marie."

I tried, but nothing was coming out. The stool next to me freed up, and she slid onto it. No one fought her for the spot. A queen taking her rightful place.

"What are you doing here?" I finally found my voice.

"Getting a drink."

That wasn't what I meant, but let it go. "Good luck with that. It is impossible to get Tony's attention."

Marie wiggled her fingers next to her face and Tony reacted as though someone blew a whistle. Current conversation forgotten, he crossed the bar and slid up in front of her.

"What can I get for you?" The question was innocent enough. The way he said it was anything but.

"What kind of Prosecco do you have?"

"Tell me what you want. If it isn't here, I will go get it."

"Thanks, but I need a drink now. Just tell me what you have." She gave the bartender a sweet smile, and he rattled off a few names.

Marie made a face. "Can you make an orange-tini?"

"Vodka, triple sec, and orange juice, right?"

She nodded. "And get my friend whatever he's drinking."

I waggled the bottle as a reminder of what he'd been serving me all night.

"Really?" Marie said after the bartender stepped away to prepare our libations.

"What?"

"I didn't peg you as a fan of the mass-produced flavorless piss water."

"Ah-ah." I pointed at the label. "Light piss water."

"You on a diet?"

"On duty."

"That's no excuse to drink crap beer."

"I need to blend in."

"Try seltzer with lime. Everyone will assume you are drinking a G and T, and it tastes better than that swill."

I looked at my drink, then back at Marie, who was watching the bartender as though he was looking after her children. Her logic was solid. Dammit. I hated feeling like an amateur. You'd think I would be used to it by now.

"First time on security duty?" she asked, still monitoring the bartender's progress.

"Huh?"

She looked back at me. "You're a bodyguard, right?"

"Why do you say that?"

"Remember that file?"

"The one with no information in it?"

Our drinks arrived. After she had settled up with Tony, we clinked glasses and took a sip. She was right. It did taste like piss water.

"What's an Army Ranger doing installing ACs?"

"I also do heating. Why does everyone forget that?"

"I thought that was a cover," Marie continued as though I had not interrupted, "but no other agency will admit to you being on the payroll. That leaves black ops…" Marie hesitated briefly, looking for confirmation.

"I've logged many hours in Black Ops on PlayStation. They were all good but, two is my favorite. I got to seventh prestige on that one."

"Or private security. So, I figure you tired of the grind and contacted an old army buddy that hooked you up with a security gig in sunny Miami."

"I like your version better. Let's go with yours."

"So, who's your client?"

"Madonna."

Marie gave me a face. She had a lot of those.

"No really. She's incognito. Cleverly disguised as a 62-year-old woman. You would never recognize her without the coned bra and blonde ponytail."

"So, you're not going to tell me why you're here?"

"Well I could, but…"

"Let me guess, you'd have to kill me."

"No, I was going to say you'd have no reason to talk to me anymore."

She kept up the "you're an idiot," stare for a good three seconds. "We are people of action. Lies do not become us."

The quote from one of my favorite movies practically smacked me into shocked silence. Not only had she caught my reference yesterday but she was throwing out lines of her own. I had never met a woman who didn't find my habit annoying to some degree much less participate. I was about to say something when the song changed. September by Earth, Wind and Fire.

"Ohhh, I love this song. Come on, I wanna dance."

Marie grabbed my shirt and pulled me off the stool. Only the long-necked bottle of my "beer" kept it from spilling all over me. I set it on the bar before she guided me into the mass of bodies overloading the floor. People parted for us like grease for a drop of dish soap, creating a void for our passing. She stopped nearly dead center, spun around and met my gaze. Then she started moving.

My skills were limited to Dance Dance Revolution, again on the PlayStation. Without an avatar guiding me, I felt like I was flailing around like a sock puppet being electrocuted.

Several couples were getting extra friendly with each other, especially one that looked like it was time to retire to the hotel room. We worked it for another two songs. Me smiling like a fool while Marie was outright laughing. I assume it was at my expense, but I didn't mind. The sound of her laughter was worth it.

Something tugged at my attention, and I glanced to my right. The overly affectionate couple had apparently skipped the getting a room part. The guy had his female dance partner supine on the floor, partially on top of her. A few of the onlookers cheered them on like a bunch of elementary school kids on the playground. Something didn't feel right to me, besides the obvious lack of decorum. Then I saw her struggling. If this whole scenario was consensual at first, it no longer was. I was just about to intervene when a good Samaritan stepped in.

"Hey, buddy. How 'bout you get a room?" I guess I wasn't the only one thinking it.

He was ignored, and the woman's struggles became more frantic. I started towards them as he tried again to get the molester's attention by leaning down and tapping him on the shoulder. The guy's hand shot out like a snake and backhanded the Samaritan, who flew back ten feet into a small crowd that toppled like bowling pins. I picked up the pace as two more guys tried to haul him off the woman, who was now screaming. It looked like they were trying to lift a car instead of one slight framed guy. Before I got to them, Marie ran past me, gun in hand.

She jammed the muzzle against his head. "Federal Agent, freeze right fucking now."

I slowed to a stop as it appeared there was little I could add at this point. The other two guys that had been trying to help backed away as well, no doubt wanting to avoid being in the line of fire. The couple on the floor were facing us, so I could see the rage that pained his face as he lifted his head. Whatever this guy was on, it had him in a frenzy.

His hand moved at blazing speed, grabbing her wrist and slamming it on the ground. I could hear the bone snap over the pounding of the music, but maybe that was just my imagination. The gun skittered away, and the crazed maniac lifted himself onto his knees without the use of his hands.

The shock of the inhuman movement froze me in place, just for a heartbeat. It was enough. Marie's form was curled forward, face scrunched in torment as she cradled her shattered hand. He grabbed her by the throat as the woman still trapped under him pounded on his chest. In one movement, he threw her twenty feet across the room, where she smashed into the nearest wall. She crumpled to the floor, unconscious.

"No!" I yelled, drawing the thing's attention. He was no ordinary man, but neither was he a demon. Something in him recognized me. Or rather, what I was. There were too many cellphones around for me to go full on Bishop mode, but I needed to do something. The thing still sat atop the woman who had gone still. I was about to go for a diving tackle, hoping to dislodge him from his perch, when he solved the problem for me.

He lifted off one knee and planted his foot. Never taking his eyes off of me, he grabbed the woman by the bust of her tight-fitting dress and launched her underhanded right at me.

Time slowed as I kicked in my blur. I jumped backwards at high speed just as she was going to bowl me over. I timed it almost perfect. Almost. I caught her midair, and she caught me in the nuts with her elbow. We slid to a stop just short of the large window that looked out onto the catwalk. The woman scrambled off me and headed towards the exit, somehow reconnecting with the family jewels.

"You're welcome," I croaked as I crawled to my feet, resting my hands on my knees like a bored right fielder.

The… thing was standing and sizing me up. I fought to find a word for what he was while I checked that my manhood hadn't done a frightened turtle impression. Quality names that would rival any creature from the Tremors franchise started running through my head. Horny Man, Inappropriate PDA guy, Mississippi. Not the state, or the river, the guy from Rio Bravo. Why does my brain do this in moments of stress?

Losing his victim must have transformed his lustful mood into fury. I thought I could hear his teeth grinding as he stared at me, practically foaming at the mouth. Then he attacked, running at me in a wild-eyed frenzy. He may have recognized me as a natural enemy, but he didn't know what he was up against.

I slipped back into a deeper stance. When he collided with me, I used his momentum against him. Grabbing his shirt, I pivoted and, with some added holy strength, tossed him upside down through the window. His head cracked on the railing, spinning him into a belly flop onto the concrete below. I hopped over the sill, crunching my way over broken glass to look down on where it landed. I watched for movement. There was none.

I braced myself for the wail of the dying. It's what I call the feeling I get when I am forced to kill. More than a feeling really. As if every loved one–past, present and future–were all crying out for the life lost. It normally overwhelmed my senses. This time I felt nothing. Like his mortality had already been lost.

I looked back to the window where the patrons crowded around, trying to get a glimpse of the carnage below. "Make a hole!" I yelled as I jumped back through. Running for Marie, I had to focus, so I didn't blur where everyone could record my superpowers for posterity. A few people were more concerned with her injuries than seeing the gory scene. I dropped next to her and checked for a carotid pulse. It was weak and thready, but it was there. And it was all I needed.

"Step back please," I asked those who were trying to help.

"Dude, this woman needs a hospital."

"You a doctor?"

"Premed student."

"Then step back, Doogie."

He raised his hands and stepped back.

I made sure no one else was touching her. I wasn't sure what would happen, and I didn't want to find out. Then I pushed my gift into her. The pained look she had, even while unconscious, faded and her breathing became regular. Her eyes opened and a heartbeat later she shot up, groping for her pistol.

"Easy. It's over."

She relaxed for a moment, then her eyes widened again. "Where's my gun?"

I pulled it out from under her. "I think you landed on it."

"Thank God for that."

"Uh, yeah."

"What happened?"

"Psycho public rapist took a header out the window and decorated the cement with his face. Hey, that name was pretty good."

"What?"

"Forget it. Listen, I think you just got your bell rung, but Doogie thinks you should get checked out. It may not be a bad idea."

"Who?"

I stuck a thumb towards the guy I was talking about. "He says he's a premed student, but I think he just wanted to perform an internal on you."

She looked at me with a strange expression on her face. "Are you ever serious?"

"Yup. Super Bowl, March Madness and the playoffs."

"Not the World Series?"

"Nah, we're usually out of it by then, so it's just a matter of drinking, playing the spread, and rooting against Boston."

"How long are we going to be stuck here?" Jelena lamented.

"Why are you complaining? You guys missed all the action. Where the hell were you two, anyway?"

"Sorry, the only spot at the bar was taken by an ex-couch potato trying not to stick out like a middle-aged white boy in a sea of millennials on break. We were keeping watch at the other bar."

"There's another bar?"

Jelena rolled her eyes and shook her head. Adam was looking at his shoes, keeping silent.

We had been sitting at a table in the corner for well over an hour while Marie, the dancing DEA agent, conducted interviews. Jelena had tried to sneak off once, but a burly uniformed cop gently explained that she still needed to remain. By which I mean he put a hand on her shoulder. She nearly took his head off, and it took three of them to coax her back to her seat. I smiled at the memory.

"What?" Jelena squinted in my direction, her mouth becoming a thin line.

I raised my hands, proffering my innocence. I was the boss in this relationship, wasn't I?

Marie finished up a conversation with two cops and approached us at last. "You two are free to go."

"About fucking time. Another minute and I was going to add some of your uni's to the road kill outside." Jelena stood up, grabbing Adam by the arm and pulling him towards the exit.

"You're not even going to wait to see what happens to me?" I called after her.

"If you can't handle one DEA woman in a pretty dress, you're already beyond help." She didn't look back. Adam did. I wasn't sure if the look he gave me screamed I'm sorry or help.

"Friend of yours?"

"I guess you could say that. She watches my back."

"Brave man."

"She grows on you."

Marie took a second to consider that, or me, or maybe just the cosmos. She was staring at me, though. "Come on," she said.

"Where are we going?"

"Coffee."

We sat at a twenty-four-hour diner that made me think of the one we had visited back in November. It had the same modern version of a fifties vibe, clean with excellent coffee. Marie being across from me was helping. I liked the way she pushed business talk to after her first sip or two of black gold. She took milk in hers, but I guess no one's perfect.

If John, my newest and oldest Bishop friend, was here, I'm sure he would have her eating out of his hand by now. He had a way with women that I just couldn't comprehend. Conversation just flowed from him like syrup over a stack of pancakes. Sweet, smooth and women couldn't help but to dig in. Me, I couldn't start a genuine conversation normally. Sarcastic response, no problem. Random movie quote, got it covered. This woman was intelligent, tough, and gorgeous. What the hell did I have to offer her? I don't consider myself good looking–despite last night's contradiction–didn't have a fancy job, at least none I could speak of. What would she even be interested in talking about? The only thing coming to mind was the weather or …

"Good coffee." She beat me to it.

"Yeah," was all I could think to add. She moved and her perfume wafted over knocking out any remaining brain cells working on a response. I took another sip.

Marie considered me for a minute. I could feel the sweat trickle down my back as she stared at me from over the coffee cup she held in both hands, elbows resting on the table.

"What's your deal?" she finally asked.

"How do you mean?"

"I'm trying to figure out your angle."

"My angle?"

"You're good, I'll give you that."

"Uh, thanks?"

"You have this clueless routine locked down."

So, not only was I acting clueless, I wasn't even doing it convincingly. Wonderful. "I'm not sure what you mean."

"See? Locked down. Like you just happened to be in a club where another drug related incident went down."

"That was drug related?"

Marie shook her head, causing her earrings to jingle alluringly.

"I thought you just said it was?"

"Oh, it was."

"But you shook your head."

"That was for your act, not the question."

I wiped a hand over my face and took another big sip of coffee. "Do me a favor. Let's assume I'm as clueless as I appear and as innocent as I keep telling you."

Her eyes narrowed.

I tried a different tactic. "How about you just tell me what' s going on?"

"I cannot discuss an ongoing investigation."

I considered that. She brought me to this diner for some reason. I figured it was to read me in on what was going on. I just had to give her the right opportunity. "You think I'm a suspect, or somehow involved, right?"

She didn't agree, but neither did she dismiss the idea.

I pressed on. "Okay, fine. So let's say that I am involved, that I have an angle. Let's say I have some valuable information that will help your investigation along. Maybe we help each other."

"If you say quid pro quo, I'm dumping this coffee in your lap."

"I wasn't going to say it."

She gave me a look.

"Okay maybe, but I would not have called you Clarice."

Her look didn't change.

I held my ground. But hell yes, I was going to. Instead, I said, "How about it?"

"Information flows one way."

I almost growled but took another sip of coffee instead. "How about you give me the Saturday Evening Post version to see if it triggers a reaction from me? Maybe I give something away."

Marie's eyebrow raised. She took another sip, then put the cup on the table. "About six months ago, a strange robbery took place. A guy walked into a custom tailor and demanded he be fitted for a suit."

"That doesn't sound like a robbery."

"At gunpoint."

I thought about that for a second. "Doesn't it take a few days to make a suit?"

"Like I said, strange. Turned out the guy was high."

"On what?"

"Ecstasy." Marie ran a finger over the top of the coffee mug.

"I didn't think it had that effect."

"It doesn't."

"Then why do you suspect it was that?"

"He had nothing else in his system, and when he came down, he couldn't even remember how he had gotten in jail. That was the first reported case that we know about. Since then, incidents have been escalating. We believe the pills are laced with something, but we haven't been able to find the source." She took a sip of coffee.

"The warehouse bust the other night?"

"Clean, no drugs anywhere. It was a good tip too. At least we believed it was. We can't identify the compound being used. Whatever it is, causes people to lose their inhibitions in a very dark way. Like all their desires have become somehow—tainted."

My eyes went wide before I could stop them.

"I knew it. You know something."

"No, I—"

"Bullshit. What is it?"

I tried to think of something, anything. "I really don't have any information."

"What if I drag you back down to the station?"

"How did that work out for you last time?"

Marie's face darkened.

I took another sip to give me a second to think. "I can help."

"Good, help. Tell me what you know."

"I don't have any information, but I can help you investigate."

"Yeah, that's what I need, the investigatory powers of a guy who fixes boilers. Thanks, but no thanks."

"These people are dangerous."

"What people?"

I really need to learn to keep quiet. She repeated the question, and I took another sip of coffee to give my mouth something else to do.

"Listen Mr. Bateleur, I am a trained federal agent. I deal with drug dealers all the time. I am more than capable of taking care of myself."

"Is that what you were doing in the club?"

Marie's cheeks colored, and she unconsciously grabbed her wrist. She picked up her purse from the table, opened it and ripped out a ten-dollar bill flinging it down.

"I'm going to tell you this once. I don't need or want your help. Stay out of my investigation, Mr. Bateleur." She stalked out of the diner, practically ripping the door off the hinges. I thought the old-fashioned bell was going to be torn from its mount.

"It's Chris," I quietly called after her. I looked around to see who may have witnessed the exchange. Then I drained my coffee and shook my head. "I really am an ass."

Chapter Five

"WHAT'S... UP, CHRIS?"

"Good Morning Jelena. Are you out of breath?"

"Is that what you called to find out?"

"Exercising?"

"I was in the middle of none of your damn business, and I'd like to get back to it."

"It'll have to wait. We need to go back to the club see what we can find out now that the cops are gone."

"Now?"

"Now."

She rattled off a string of curses in Spanish. I'm pretty sure she said something vile about my dog.

"Give me ten minutes."

It took her fifteen, but I was not about to highlight the discrepancy. I handed her black coffee. She grabbed it and took a big sip. I could almost feel the hot liquid burning her trachea. She didn't even blink and headed for the door.

"Good morning to you too, and you're welcome."

"It was a great morning till you came along. Coffee doesn't make up for it, but at least I don't want to kill you anymore. Just beat the shit out of you."

"If I had left without you, what would you have done?"

"Killed you."

"No matter what, I end up with the same result."

"Sucks to be you."

We walked in silence to the parking lot where my SUV waited. Adam was leaning on the hood, arms crossed, sipping from a similar cup to the ones in our hands. His hair was not as quaffed as normal, and he looked to be wearing the same clothes as yesterday.

"How the hell did he know we were going out?" I mumbled under my breath.

Jelena shrugged and took another sip of coffee.

"We are just doing some sightseeing," I called out to him as we approached. "Nothing official on the agenda."

He nodded. "Let's go."

"Are you sure you want to waste time with us? I'm sure Ima has a list of chores for you."

He looked from me to Jelena, who was uncharacteristically quiet. "How about we cut the bullshit?"

We stared each other down for a few seconds.

Jelena shook her head. "How about you guys put the measuring sticks down and we just go?"

The ride to the club this time was imbued with an awkward silence. I would chalk it up to being the morning after a late night, but it felt like there was more to it. We got out and made our way to the entrance. I stopped in the middle of the courtyard and contemplated the spot where the maniac had landed last night. The mark of another failure. My screw ups were piling up and I needed to figure a way to do this job. I was sure if any other Bishop was there, they would have disabled him without killing him.

"Are we doing this or what?"

I looked up at Jelena, not realizing that I had been entranced for more than a brief second. She stood several yards away, arms folded, foot actually tapping. Adam stood close by her.

"Yeah, sorry." I caught up to them, then took the lead again.

"What's the problem?"

"Nothing."

"Bullshit."

"You know you really need to work on your language."

"Don't change the subject. You froze over where the body landed. You took out two demons, and a psycho rapist has you queasy?"

"Two demons?" Adam asked in a voice that would have been appropriate while asking how many elephants I kept in my trunk.

Jelena dismissed him with that sound she liked to make and a flick of her hand.

I shook my head. "It's not like that."

"Then what?"

I glanced back at the two. Jelena was in attack mode as usual, and Adam was quietly enjoying the show.

"Forget it. I'm not talking about this with you."

"Why, because I'm not a Bishop?"

I stopped and met her gaze. "You're not insulted. You're just being an ass."

She tried to hide her smile, but it cracked through. I walked away, but she grabbed my arm.

"Okay, I'm screwing with you, but I want to know what's going on."

"You won't get it."

"Why not?"

"Because no one does." I continued walking. Jelena kept pace, Adam right behind.

"You are not the first to be affected by taking a life. If it doesn't affect you in some way, you have other issues."

"This is different."

We reached the entrance, cutting off further conversation. A crew outside was already repairing the window. The bouncer from last night who had been covering the door was absent. We walked in with no one stopping us. Inside, employees and contractors were bustling with cleanup and preparation activities for tonight's crowd. The bartender who had mostly ignored me was going over paperwork with a woman behind the bar. She had straight black hair that cascaded to her open backed shirt.

"Bar's closed. We open at four."

I put on my best creepy voice. "We… we are… not thirsty."

Everyone stopped and looked at me, even Torres.

I huffed. "No one gets me."

"Wait." The bartender pointed at me. "Gina, that's the guy from last night. The one who took out the crazy."

The woman shifted her attention from her tablet to me, her eyebrows coming together.

"Let me guess, the good Samaritan wants a reward?"

"I'm no expert on biblical references but, wouldn't that negate the whole idea?" I looked to Adam for confirmation, but he wasn't playing.

"Then you're suing the bar. That's why you brought your lawyer with you."

Jelena arched her back. "Call me a paper pushing professional liar again, and you'll be the next one going through your brand-new window."

Gina's eyebrows looked like they were about to migrate down her face and become a mustache.

I placed a hand on Jelena's forearm. "I think she meant Adam," she tensed up more at my touch.

Adam just grunted at that.

To the manager I said, "I don't want anything. Just a few minutes of your time."

She watched me for another second, then nodded. We followed her to a table and sat. We were still in view, and the bartender was not so subtly keeping an eye on us.

"My name is Chris Bateleur, and this is Jelena Torres, and… Adam." I extended my hand.

She contemplated her options before taking it. "Gina."

She had a firm grasp which radiated confidence.

"What brings you back so soon? Shouldn't you be sleeping the night off?"

Jelena snorted. "I wish."

I tried to ignore her. "I was looking for some information."

"Pertaining to?"

"The guy from last night."

Her eyebrows started their southerly migration again. "What about him?"

"I was hoping he paid by credit card."

"I turned it over to the police. I couldn't give it to you either way."

"I'm just looking for a name."

She considered that for a second. "Why? You're not with the cops, that much is obvious."

"Let's just say I'm a concerned citizen."

"Forget it. You're probably his dealer and want to get your stash back before the cops connect the dots."

"I look like a drug dealer?"

"It's an equal opportunity profession. Didn't you see Breaking Bad?"

I thought about a different approach. "Do you remember the bath salts epidemic a few years back? People were tripping majorly with them, running around naked and doing all kinds of crazy stuff. There's a new drug out there and it's ten times worse."

Adam shifted in his chair.

"I'm not after anything besides finding a way to stop it."

She shifted her gaze between the three of us.

"I'm sorry, but there is nothing I can do." Gina got up without shaking my hand and walked towards the back, where I assumed her office was.

"Well, this was a blatant waste of time. You couldn't just let me stay in bed?"

We got up and started for the door.

"Chris."

I looked around, thinking it was meant for someone else. The bartender was looking right at me but didn't give any sign that he was the one who had spoken. I went over anyway resting my arm on the bar and saying nothing.

"I know that woman who was attacked. Marguerite. She's a regular. A little flighty, loves to flirt. She comes here to dance. Occasionally she will leave with someone."

He looked anywhere but at me. I let him get there by himself.

"Gina's a good person. She's just worried about liability."

He finally met my gaze and slid a napkin across the bar. He placed a glass on top, filled it with seltzer and added a lime wedge.

"Mags didn't deserve what happened. Whatever Gina says, you drink free as long as I'm here."

He nodded, putting an emphatic period at the end of his statement. I echoed the gesture, then picked up the glass and the napkin and took a long sip. I placed the glass back down. The condensation from the heat of the day rolled slowly down until it met with the shiny surface of the bar.

"Thanks," I said, and left.

Jelena fell in step beside me.

"Anymore worthless endeavors on the docket for today?"

"Not completely worthless."

I held up the napkin. On it was written a name. Matt Holland.

"Come on, Adam," I said, holding out the napkin. "Try being something other than a shadow."

We were back at the Range Rover. Adam stood facing me with his arms crossed, staring at his shoes. Jelena stood between us and off to the side.

Adam shook his head. "Imaculada wouldn't approve."

"What would she approve of?" I replied. He didn't respond. "This is what she asked me to look into."

"That was before you literally crashed an ongoing DEA investigation."

"This time is different."

"How?"

I had no idea. I'm good at instant sarcasm, not logical arguments.

"Because you are here to make sure he behaves himself," Jelena finally added to the conversation.

Adam looked at her—stared was a better word—then plucked the napkin from my hand. He walked a few paces away, pulling out his phone.

"About time you spoke up," I said, once he was out of earshot.

"What?"

"You're much quieter when he's around."

"Fuck you."

"See, that's better."

"Maybe I was trying to decide if you had a point, or were just being stupid again." Jelena gave me a half smile.

"How is Enric?"

"He's good." Her face relaxed and her smile widened. "Mom has been acting as a home schoolteacher. She's actually great at it. We set up a little desk in the kitchen that acts as his official learning center. She says he's like a little sponge."

I smiled back at her and said, "That's great." Not quite knowing what to say next.

"We still want to get him back into a regular school once things settle down a little, so he can interact more with other kids."

Settle down. Was that really an option for the future? I honestly couldn't see a path to relaxation anymore. She could have been able to work her way back into normalcy. Find someone that made her happy and gave Enric a father or another mother. Could I? Knowing about this secret war? A war that had been fought since practically the beginning of time. No end in sight. Could I marry, knowing what that would mean for the other person? For my first born who would inherit my powers. The consequences were worse if I didn't. One less Bishop family to take on the fight once I was gone.

Adam walked back over, still talking into the phone. "Thanks." He ended the call and handed back the napkin. Under the name in black ink was an address.

"Nice handwriting," I said.

He grunted.

"I think the response you're looking for is thank you," Jelena chided.

I nodded. "Yes, what she said."

She drove her fist into my kidney.

"Thank you." I coughed out. "I was going to say it."

"Why are you such an ass?"

"Why are you so violent?"

"Come on. I'm driving. Adam, take shotgun. You get in the back seat until you can learn some manners."

"Hey, aren't we forgetting who the boss is around here?"

"Imaculada," they both said in unison.

"But it's my car."

Chapter Six

WE ARRIVED AT THE address. It was a high-end apartment complex on the corner of Northeast Bayside and Northeast Eightieth Street. There were multiple buildings, the lower third of each was painted a different color than the top two-thirds. There looked to be about twenty floors each with a balcony strategically placed, so that residents were never staring at their neighbors.

I leaned forward from the back, feeling like I wanted to say, 'Are we there yet?' Instead, I said, "what would you call that color combination?"

"Periwinkle and cream," Adam replied.

"Really?" I shrugged. "How are we getting in? This is the type of place that is not a fan of random people snooping around a man's apartment. I'm sure no one has notified them of Holland's death. See, this is where we need our own badges with our own acronym. Like Brothers of Bishops."

Jelena looked in the rearview mirror. "BOB? Really? Is that the best you can come up with?"

"I can get us in," Adam said.

"Tell me you can Obi-wan them and you'll be my new hero," I said.

Jelena huffed. "Let's go before he quotes the movie."

"You're not going," I informed her.

"The hell I'm not."

"You need to keep an eye out."

"Bullshit. You never listen to me, anyway."

"He's right." The look she gave Adam made me nervous for his health. "The cops should be here soon to perform a routine check of his residence," he continued. "We need someone to watch for them."

"And what is your title?" I added.

"Ass kicker."

"No, you were supposed to say…"

"I get it. This time, listen to my warnings." She flipped the earpiece over her shoulder and I barely snagged it out of the air. I almost had to use my gift but didn't want to give her the satisfaction.

Adam and I got out, and she peeled away before I got my door closed.

"What's eating her?" I asked.

He shrugged and walked towards the entrance. I followed after a few steps.

He glanced back. "Keep up."

"What's the rush? It's not like Holland's going to be home soon."

Instead of answering, he stopped until I caught up, then started walking again. As we got close to the doorman, he cocked his head towards me and mumbled, "Stay close. Keep walking and don't talk."

"Why…"

He silenced me with a look but didn't slow. The doorman didn't look at us. We walked through the automated rotating door without him ever acknowledging us. In the lobby, the man at the front desk picked his head up from his computer, looked past us at the door, shook his head and went back to what he was doing. We entered a small alcove where the two elevators waited out of the view of security. I opened my mouth to ask what the hell was going on. Adam shook his head as he pushed the call button. A whir sounded deep in the walls. After a few seconds, the doors opened, and we stepped in.

"Okay, we're clear."

"What the hell was that?"

"My specialty. I call it slipping."

"Slipping?"

He nodded.

"Did you just make us invisible?"

"No. More like gave them a blind spot for us."

"And we just slipped by."

He met my glance.

"That is friggin' awesome. You've got to teach me that."

Adam smiled. The doors opened, and he exited. I followed.

"No, I'm serious. How do you do that?"

"It's kind of hard to explain."

"Try."

Holland's apartment was at the end of the hall. Adam walked up and tried the knob, which was obviously locked. He looked at me, and motioned to the door.

"Seriously? You can make yourself invisible, but you can't unlock a door?"

"Telekinesis was never one of my talents."

"I thought everyone could do it at that level."

His face darkened. "Not everyone."

I crossed my arms. "I'll open the door if you show me how to be invisible."

"Forget it. I'll just break it down."

"Yeah, I'm sure Ima would be fine with that."

He stared at my shoes, then flipped a hand towards the door.

"Thought so." I stepped up and twisted the knob. The door opened. "Show off."

"Not really. It's the one thing I can do consistently. I practice a lot."

The apartment was charming. *Was* being the operative word. It had a great deal of space, tall windows with a beautiful ocean view that could be seen from inside or on the balcony. The furniture looked to have been chosen for their aesthetic value rather than comfort. That was before stains and scratches ruined them. Detritus littered every surface. Much of it was bottles of liquor ranging from beer to sake. All empty.

"Gloves," Adam said.

"You think? I'm a little skeeved just walking around in here."

"I meant to eliminate fingerprints."

"Oh, right."

I took the pair of latex gloves he held out.

"Do you have any color besides purple?"

His looked told me he did not.

"Did someone beat us here?" I asked. "It looks like the place was tossed."

"No, this was done over time."

"How can you tell?"

"This, for one." He pulled a yachting magazine from between the couch cushions. "I recognized the cover. It's from three months ago."

"That just creates new questions."

"Like?"

"Where do you dock your yacht?"

"I just like the articles."

I snorted. "How does that tell you that this occurred over time?"

He walked over to a corner of the living room that was set up like a shrine to a boat. Holland had decorated several shelves with nautical theme baubles, a few trophies, and a framed magazine cover picturing an old sailing vessel. The title of the article was "Immaculate Restoration." A rack of magazines sat on the bottom. Adam pulled out the far right copy, looked at it and showed it to me.

"So?"

"It's from four months ago. Neatly filed. What ever happened to this guy, it started three or four months ago."

I'm not sure if his logic made any sense. He could have been looking for an article during a drinking binge and just not put them away. I wasn't looking to argue, so instead I said, "I'm checking out the bedroom."

It was down a small hallway across from an enormous bathroom with a double sink, standing shower, and a whirlpool tub. The disarray from the living room and kitchen continued into the master suite.

Clothes ranging from suit pieces to sweatpants to clubwear lay strewn about. In the corner, a wicker hamper stood empty. One side of the bed had been deeply slept in. Comforter pulled back, bottom sheet dislodged from the mattress on one corner, pillow half out of the case. The other was still so neatly made, my drill sergeant would have been proud. A gleam of metal was visible from under where the covers draped onto the made side.

I stepped up to the bed, carefully avoiding used tissues like land mines on the floor. Pulling back the comforter revealed a picture frame face down. I flipped it over. The photo was of the psycho rapist in his Doctor Jekyll days. Clean shaven, in a clean suit, and posing with a beautiful blonde woman whom he was clearly in love with. The photographer had captured the mood. A moment frozen in time. In the bottom corner was a separate picture of just their two hands promptly displaying a large diamond ring.

"Find anything?" Adam asked from the doorway.

I flipped the picture to him.

"They look happy."

"Looked," I corrected.

"Yeah."

"Did you catch the date?"

He looked back down. "Six months ago? That is a fast drop into *this*." He waved a hand around to point out the chaos of the room.

"We need to find the fiancée. She may have some insight."

"*We've got company,*" Jelena announced over the coms.

"Understood. How much time do we have?" I replied.

"*Five minutes, tops.*"

"Quick, we need to find a name," I said, and pulled open drawers, immediately regretting it.

"We can just check his social media."

"You couldn't have suggested that a second earlier?" I closed the drawer.

"What did you find?"

"You don't want to know."

Adam shook his head and threw the picture back on the bed. "Let's go."

"*Too late.*"

"What? That was never five minutes."

"*Maybe they called ahead. Two cops and the CSU techs walked right into the elevator.*"

"Shit, we need to get out of here."

"Balcony," Adam said.

"What?"

He didn't wait to hear my argument, just headed for the sliding glass door, pulling me by the arm.

"Why are we going out here?" I wasn't quite dragging my feet, but I wasn't going quietly into that good night, if you know what I mean.

"Just come on." He opened the door and pushed me through. Following me out, he closed the door again.

"Lock it."

"Wh—"

"Just lock it."

I stared at him for a second, then with a mental tug, did as requested. The click was audible, and Adam moved away to the railing. The patio was nice, if you like that kind of thing. There was a comfortable seating area with a high-end grill at one end and a potted plant at the other. This was the only area untouched by the chaos of the apartment.

"Good, this side is clear," he said.

"Clear?"

"We can hop down from here."

"We can do what? We are ten stories up!"

"You know, a controlled drop?"

My expression told him just what I thought of his idea.

"You've never done a controlled drop?"

"I've never had the need."

"But you've had training on them. It's a standard exercise."

"I was kind of rushed through basic training. Did you ever see Spies Like Us?"

"What does that even mean?"

"It means the furthest I have ever jumped was when I was chasing a helicopter and that didn't work out so well."

"Chasing a helicopter?"

"Story for another time."

Adam shook his head. "Okay, short version. You know how you turn your molecules hard for defense?"

"I guess."

"You guess? Who the hell trained you?"

"Get to the point."

"Just do the opposite."

"Do nothing?"

"No!" The sigh he let out could have blown me over. "Make your bones hollow. Make your skin like paper. Picture yourself as a leaf drifting down from a tree, the fruit of a dandelion drifting on the breeze."

"That's not how physics works, and what the hell is the fruit of a dandelion?"

"You know the white puffballs."

"Are you friggin' kidding me?"

"How can you not know how to do this?"

I didn't need to hear this. I knew I was woefully inadequate. "Show me."

"How will that help?"

"Trust me."

"*Boys, you are running out of time*," Jelena urged.

"Just go, I'll be fine."

He looked at me, clearly unconvinced.

"We don't have time for this. Just go."

He nodded, then sprung over the balcony, catching himself on the other side. One foot holding him in place, one hand effortlessly holding the railing.

"You sure?"

"Go."

Adam let go. I watched him fall, and my stomach pulled into my chest. He didn't drop like a stone, nor did he float on the breeze. His suit jacket billowed, fluttering as he descended. He landed, tucking into a roll. Dusted himself off and looked up. I stepped back from the edge.

"See? Easy," Adam said over the coms.

"Yeah sure," I said, mostly under my breath.

I looked over the side again. The ten stories seemed more like fifty. I

heard a knock at the door, followed by the typical police announcement.
"Shit."

I climbed over the railing, perched out of sight from inside. Closing my eyes I sought the calm meadow, and it appeared quickly, the
glass like lake shimmering next to it. I could feel the grass tickling
my ankles, the breeze rustling my hair. When I first started using my
powers this place used to be inhabited by a dragonfly that would guide
me wordlessly. At least that's what I imagined it was doing. It hadn't
been around for a while, not since Thanksgiving. Even without that
spirit guide, this part came easy. Doing something intentionally with
my gift was another matter. Okay, light as a feather. Skin like paper.

Nothing.

The door to the apartment opened.

I squeezed my eyes shut tighter, as though that would make it better.
Think, damn you, think.

"Not think. Feel," Adam's voice said in my ear.

I hadn't realized I said that out loud. His words clicked something
in me. I felt my skin, the muscles under it, the density of my bones.
I pushed at it, shifted the molecules. At first I pushed them together,
and I felt my weight increase, pulling at my grip on the railing. Then
I pushed in between them, spreading them apart. The pressure on
my fingers waned. I forced in more space and I felt almost buoyant.

I opened my eyes to the ground looming below. The logical part
of my brain reminded me that weight had no effect on a falling body.
I felt gravity retaking it's hold. Weight may not but drag did. I envisioned myself as lightweight but vast, a parachute catching the air. I
could hear someone at the sliding door. It was now or never. I let go.

I started dropping. It wasn't the thirty-two feet per second per
second Newton identified as gravity's standard pull. It still felt too fast.
I pushed in more space between the molecules and I slowed more.
A rush of excitement flowed through me. I had done it. Something
completely new, and on purpose. I wondered how light I could make
myself and so added more space. My descent slowed to a crawl two
stories from the ground. I felt like a kid at Christmas. Then I started
drifting.

Okay, too much. I tried to ease back on the space, increase the density slowly. A big gust came off the water, blowing me sideways several yards. The alley that led to Holland's view was short. If I kept drifting at this rate, I would be in public view in seconds. A predicament that was kind of hard to explain. The gust increased again and, in a panic, I pulled back too hard. I dropped like the proverbial penny off the Empire State Building. I hit the ground fast and hard. The wind had me driving in on an angle and went ass over elbows like I tripped trying to steal home.

I came to a sliding stop feeling like a Raggedy Andy doll. I rolled over, spitting out dirt and grass and trying to take stock. I didn't think I had any broken bones, just some scrapes and bruises.

"That was the worst impression of a soccer slide I have ever seen."

I looked up with an acidic response locked and loaded. I stopped short when I looked into Marie's eyes.

"Oh, hey Marie. Funny meeting you here." I hoped I didn't have any visible scrapes. She had too many questions without her watching scratches from my face plant heal themselves. I did attempt to clean myself off, unsuccessfully. The grass was still muddy from what I assumed were the morning sprinklers.

"Yeah, I was going to say the same. What are you doing here?"

Well at least she didn't ask why I was floating. "Me? I'm just out for a jog. What are you doing here?"

"Out for a jog?" Marie and Jelena said in unison. Jelena added some colorful fringe.

"Yeah. Don't you jog?"

"You're thirty miles away from where you're staying."

"Wow, I didn't think I jogged that far. And anyway, how do you know where I'm staying? Are you following me?"

"Jogging in the grass between two apartment buildings?"

"*Okay, tell her…*" Jelena started.

"I saw a duck."

"*That's it. You're on your own.*"

"A duck?" Marie actually crossed her arms.

"Yeah, it was stuck in the fence near the water." I continued as though my words were not the most ludicrous thing anyone had ever heard.

"Where is the duck now?"

"It got loose and flew away."

"Let me make sure I understand. While you were thirty miles out on your morning jog, in jeans, you noticed a duck stuck in the fence two hundred feet off the street."

"It was making a hell of a racket."

"I'm sure it was."

"Kind of sounded like Donald in one of his rages."

"Donald?" Marie didn't make it sound like a question. More an expression of the level of my idiocy.

"Definitely not Daffy. He has a more refined way of expressing himself."

Marie let out a very long sigh.

"*I'm not bailing you out again.*"

I almost told Jelena she didn't bail me out the first time, until I realized it was Adam speaking. Also, I wasn't supposed to be talking to anyone else.

"So, you're saying you were not trying to gain access to Matt Holland's apartment?"

"Who?" I tried to look confused.

"The guy you killed last night."

"Oh, you mean the drugged out attempted rapist I defended myself and you from?" Shit, she got my defenses up. Oh, she was good.

"Po-tay-to, po-tah-to."

"Have you ever heard anyone say it the other way? I mean, other than when using that expression?"

"Stop avoiding the question."

"What question?"

"Were you trying to break into Matt Holland's apartment?"

I looked around. "Why, does he live around here?"

"You know he lives in this building."

"Why would I know that?"

She put a hand on her hip. "Because I got a call from the manager of the Blue Martini."

"Really. Called to thank us for our services?"

"She told me you were inquiring about my perp's name."

I crossed my arms and rubbed my chin. "And did she tell you she gave me the name?"

"No. She refused you."

I flipped a hand. "See. So how could I have been trying to get into an apartment for a man whose name I didn't even know?"

She cocked her head, her curly black hair bounced.

"*That's it. She knows you're lying, but can't prove it,*" Adam said. "*You need to keep her off balance. Ask her out.*"

"What?" The word slipped out before I could stop it.

Marie's brow furrowed. "What, what?"

"*Trust me,*" Adam continued, "*she's interested. I can see her eyes dilating from here. Just do it.*"

"What…" Was I really going to do this? "Are you doing for dinner?"

She had the same reaction I did to the idea.

"Are you asking me out?"

"No."

"*Yes.*"

"I mean, yes."

Marie's eyes squinted. "What are you up to?"

"Okay fine, here's the truth."

"*NO!*" Both Jelena and Adam yelled in my ear at the same time.

"I did go to the bar to find the guy's name. The manager wouldn't give it to me, but the bartender did."

"Okay, good. Why?"

"I figured this was the next place you would go. I wanted the chance to bump into you so I could ask you out."

Marie's stance relaxed a little.

I started pacing. "I was walking around trying to come up with a good reason I was here and not thinking of anything. Then I saw the duck…"

"Wait, the duck was real."

"Of course the duck was real. What idiot would make up a story like that?"

"*Good question.*"

I ignored Jelena and plowed ahead. "By the time I got to the fence, I saw the police cars and was afraid I missed you. I ran back and hit a patch of mud, and…" I stopped pacing, looked at her and waved my hands to highlight my appearance. I gave a big dramatic sigh. "It was a stupid idea. I just thought we had a connection last night at the club. Before all this crap started." I moved to walk away. "Forget it. I'm sorry." I didn't have to fake the embarrassment. This entire encounter had my face feeling like I had a fever, and I was sweating like I did jog thirty miles.

"Wait."

"No, it's fine. I know it was probably really creepy. I'm not good with this kind of thing." I kept walking hoping I could get out of there with some piece of my pride left.

"Freeze!" The command in Marie's voice surprised me. I stopped moving and even put my hands up a little.

"*Oh well. You almost made it out.*" I don't think Jelena really believed that.

"Okay," Marie said, simply.

I waited for her to cuff me, but I didn't hear her move. I looked back to see what she was doing. She stood there, arms akimbo.

"Okay, what?" I asked, a little afraid of the answer.

"Okay, I will go to dinner with you."

The shock must have been plain on my face.

"You can put your hands down now."

I did so.

"I thought you were going to cuff me."

Marie's eyes danced on top of a demonic smile. "Let's see how dinner goes first."

Chapter Seven

"A DUCK?"

"Seriously Jelena, can you just let it go?" I asked for the third time in as many minutes. "Just concentrate on driving. You almost hit another pedestrian."

"What I don't understand is how you went from such a lame excuse as a stuck duck to an almost genius level lie that actually got you a date."

I shook my head. "Just forget it."

"Come on, who knew you could make up stories like that?"

I chose not to reply.

"He didn't make it up," Adam said from the back, as he ended the call he was on. I actually got to sit in the front of my car.

"Do we have an address?" I asked, ignoring his statement.

Jelena didn't. "What do you mean, he didn't make it up?"

"I just sent it to the GPS."

"Good. Jelena, let's go."

"Holdup. We are not going anywhere until Adam spills."

"How about we don't and say we did?" I rubbed at my shoulder that had taken the brunt of my recent fall and for some reason still hurt.

"How about we stop off at the nearest Junior High so you can drop off that expression?" Jelena looked at Adam through the rearview mirror.

"I am guessing the 'story'—" Adam actually used air quotes. "—slipped so easily off his tongue because everything he was saying was the truth."

I rested my forehead on my fingers and shook my head.

"No shit? For real, you have a thing for the DEA agent?"

"Marie," I corrected, then silently cursed my stupidity.

"Ma-rie," Jelena dragged the name out.

"Can we just go, please?"

"Of course. Next stop, druggy's fiancé."

It was another fifteen-minute drive to Holland's fiancé's apartment. The quick trip was made longer by the need to stop and buy clean clothes for me, and unbearable thanks to Jelena's constant teasing. I'm not sure why it bothered me. So, I was interested in the DEA agent that arrested me. Why was I being so sensitive about the whole thing?

I knocked, and after a few moments, a woman answered the door. She had straight brown hair with blonde highlights pulled up into a ponytail. The sweats she was wearing were clean, but well-worn and slightly baggy.

"Good afternoon, I'm looking for Blair McKenna." I could have skipped the introduction. By her red-rimmed eyes and runny nose, I was sure I had found her.

"That's me, but this is not really a good time."

"Yes, I'm sorry for your loss."

She looked up, confused. I presumed she had just been told recently.

"Are you working with the police? Joyce said she spent an hour with them."

"DEA actually." I had engaged my enhanced senses to see if I could deduce anything of use. Instead, I heard Adam groan softly behind me. I think Jelena giggled. "And Joyce would be?" I continued.

"Holland's mother," Adam offered, playing the role despite his misgivings. What a trouper.

"Ah, yes, of course," I said, as though just recalling the information. "Would it be okay if we asked you a few questions?"

"I guess. Come in."

We followed her into the second pleasant apartment I had been in that day. The decorating style had a very similar feel to Holland's. Minus the boat shrine. We sat on a couch while she curled up in an oversized chair. She didn't look at us. Her gaze was fixed on an open photo album on the glass topped end table.

"You were engaged to Mr. Holland, correct?" I asked, struggling to figure how to start this conversation. My instincts wanted me to launch right into the actual questions—what drugs did your dead ex-fiancé use, and where did he get them from? But I knew from experience that was not socially acceptable.

She nodded, never taking her eyes off the pictures.

"How long?"

She shook her head. I was getting frustrated. I didn't know the right questions to ask, nor how to dance around the point from this side of the table. The adage goes fake it till you make it, but I wasn't even sure how to do that.

"How did you two meet?" Adam interjected.

She looked up at him. "At a benefit we both went to. Well, he attended with his firm. I was one of the coordinators."

"Very nice. Black-tie affair? Everyone dressed to the nines?"

"Yeah." She gave a small, sad laugh. "All except for Matt. He was a last-minute fill in and didn't get the memo. He was wearing a gray sports jacket and no tie." Tears rolled down her face. She wiped them away with a tissue from the dwindling box next to her.

"It's what made me notice him. He didn't care that he stuck out like a sore thumb. He wasn't cocky, or defensive, just let it roll off him."

"What were you raising money for?"

Blair paused for a second, staring out into space. "A drug rehab center."

Okay, now we were getting somewhere. I opened my mouth, wanting to get to the point. Surely we had danced around enough. Jelena put a hand on my leg.

"Who?" Adam asked.

I wasn't following his question.

"My cousin." Blair swallowed hard. "She was more like a sister."

"Is she still with us?" his voice changed in pitch. Almost sounding like a whisper.

She shook her head.

"How old?"

"Twenty-four."

"I'm very sorry."

She nodded.

Adam plucked another tissue from the box on the table and handed it to her. "College?"

She nodded again. "She took some ecstasy that was laced with fentanyl."

"I'm sorry."

"When did it start with Matt?"

She looked to the window and the view that lead to more pleasant things. It took her a while to answer. So much so that I thought she hadn't heard. Adam waited patiently. I wanted to scream.

"I think it was the night of our engagement party. About six months ago."

Adam's head pulled back. "That quickly?"

"I wouldn't have believed it possible if I hadn't seen it for myself."

"I'm sorry to ask you this, but when did you break off your engagement?"

"Three months ago."

I expected a gloating look from Adam, but it didn't come.

"Because of the drugs, or for other reasons?"

"At that point, it was many reasons. All caused by the drug use."

"And he had never used drugs before?"

"No. He had a hard and fast rule against it."

"What changed?"

"He had too much to drink. His friends had something they were popping out on the balcony and they talked him in to trying it."

Adam shook his head.

I wanted to ask what the problem was, but I was supposed to be up to speed. Adam stood, walked around the table and kneeled before Blair. He took her hand and she looked down at him. "Do you know where he got the drugs from?"

Her expression shifted from sadness to rage, as though flipping a switch. "Josh." She growled the name.

"Was that the friend that talked him into trying it that night?"

I asked.

Blair directed her venom at me. "Some friend. Are we done here?"

"Do you have Josh's information? I would like to have a conversation with him."

"So would I. With a softball bat."

Chapter Eight

"THIS IS A BAD idea," Adam said.

The dealer's location could have been out of a movie set. It was a low-rent apartment building where tenants didn't blink at the coming and going of shady characters at odd hours. They were on the top floor of a five-level complex where individual units were accessible from the outdoor walkways. It was on a one-way service road for a four-lane highway bridged by a pedestrian walkway less than a block away.

"You've said that every time. Not every plan is bad," I responded.

"No, just yours."

I shook my head and keyed the coms unit. "Overwatch, status?"

"Two minutes."

Great. I thought I sucked at conversation, but when Adam and I were alone he was a functional mute. I could last a few minutes, though. Right?

The seconds ticked by. We stared out the windshield, the equivalent of watching an elevator floor indicator. I searched for a topic and settled on old reliable.

"Did you catch the game?"

"No."

"Not a football fan?"

"No."

"Any other sports?" Hell, I can relate to pretty much anything that has a ball in it.

"Hockey."

Of course. "You're kidding?"

He shook his head.

"You live in Florida."

He nodded like I was looking for clarity.

"Do you mean field hockey?"

He shook his head.

"Do you guys even have a hockey team?"

"Panthers."

"No shit. So Panthers fan."

"No."

"I'm in place," Jelena said over the coms.

"Thank God," I said, getting out of the car. "Sitrep."

"I've got two heat signatures. Curtains are closed so I can't verify the target."

"Good copy."

"Why do you guys talk like that?" Adam asked.

I was about to explain the history of military radio linguistics, then thought better of it. "Habit."

We crossed the parking lot and climbed the stairs. My plan was simple. We were going to pose as DEA agents to get the information we needed. You know, offer him a fake deal to get at the supplier. We knocked, expecting to hear the hurried sounds of drugs being stashed. Instead, what we received were steady footsteps.

"One person approaching the door. The other is on the couch," Jelena informed us.

The lock clicked, and the door opened a sliver. The man on the other side was well groomed and wearing a suit. I was getting a little disappointed at the lack of adequate tropes.

"Joshua Devonport?" I asked.

"Yes?"

"We're special agents Ryder and Allen." I felt Adam turn and look at me, but I pressed on. "We're DEA and we have a few questions."

The reactions I was expecting included surprise, fear, and anger. Josh expressed none of them. Instead, he quirked an eyebrow and asked, "Are you sure?"

"Of course I'm sure." I went on the offensive. "We believe you are holding with the intent to sell. If you cooperate, I may talk to the DA, but the longer you jerk me around, the less likely that becomes."

Josh's expression never wavered. I held mine out of sheer will despite the growing bubble of doubt at the back of my skull. He pulled the door all the way open.

Marie sat on the couch, drinking coffee.

"Are you still sure?" Josh asked, a smirk splaying across his face.

"Agent Ryder, I presume," she asked. "And you brought your lawyer."

"Told you this was a bad idea," Adam said.

"Care to come in?" Josh stood back to give us room to pass. I didn't see any other alternatives, so I entered.

"Oh good, I was hoping you'd be here. I had some ideas for dinner." I was already screwed, why not play confident?

"Would you care for coffee? Marie had me put on a full pot when you guys pulled in."

"Sure love some," I replied with the most positive voice I could muster. Adam shook his head.

"Also," Marie interjected, "could you ask Jelena to come down from her perch? I don't enjoy having a sniper rifle pointed at my head."

I stared at her for a second, contemplating my next move. She smiled at me. I sighed. "Jelena, stand down. Bring it in."

"Why? What's going on?"

"Ima ratted us out."

I assumed Josh was just a DEA agent in a terrible disguise. I was wrong.

"You went to the Feds yourself?" Adam asked from the next room. I was in the kitchen getting coffee. I mean, hell, he made a fresh pot.

"Yeah. The drugs were a side business, to keep friends supplied for parties. I keep this apartment for the occasional buy, and one or two other things."

Yeah, I could guess what those were. The inside of this place was in direct contrast to the exterior. Modern though comfortable furniture, large screen TV, fully appointed bar that could have accommodated two bartenders. He built a bachelor's paradise like Semmi from Coming to America. The coffee maker alone gave me percolator envy.

"How's the coffee?" Marie stepped into the kitchen area. While not secluded, we had a modicum of privacy.

"Good to the last drop."

I expected her to be angry. After all, I had lied to her multiple times and, to deflect her ire, I asked her out. I mean, I wouldn't put it that way, but I'm sure she would. Isn't that how these things are supposed to go? Boy meets girl, boy pisses off girl, girl has sex with boy's best friend, who is also a girl. Maybe that was just me. Marie, however, was smiling.

"Took you long enough," she said.

"Jelena made us stop for lunch."

"I thought you were the boss."

"What gave you that idea?"

"She defers to you."

"Ha. Jelena doesn't defer to anyone."

Marie cocked her head, and one of her little earrings did a dance. It sent a distracting flush through me. "You don't see it do you?"

"What?"

"If you haven't figured it out, I'm not giving you the answer."

"Typical."

"So, where are you taking me for dinner?"

I choked on the sip of coffee I was taking. "You still want to go?" I said once I could talk without spitting on her. "I figured you'd be pissed at me."

"For what?"

I didn't want to say, hoping that she hadn't made the connection.

Her smile disappeared. "Because you have been feeding me a line of bullshit that could fertilize Central Park?"

I wondered if I could make a career out of being wrong. "I don't know that—"

"How about because you are trampling all over an investigation I have been working on for months?"

"I wouldn't say trampling—"

"Or maybe when your ludicrous story about a stuck duck didn't work, you tried to distract me with a dinner invitation?"

I think I opened my mouth, but nothing came out. If I made any sound, it wasn't coherent.

"Apparently I can throw you a little." Her smile reemerged, and I started breathing again. "The truth is, you're the first interesting guy I've met in a while. At least one that didn't end up in a cell."

"The night is still young." I dislodged my tongue from my tonsils.

"Can you tell me the truth about one thing?"

"It depends."

She nodded. "Why are you involved in my case?"

I thought for a moment before I replied. "At first, to be useful. Though in hindsight, I would say it was an activity assigned to keep me busy."

"Ms. Castillo?"

"Who?"

"Imaculada Castillo."

"Oh, Ima. Yeah."

"So, you work for her?"

"No, I wouldn't say that."

"Would she?"

I gave her a sideways glance. "Possibly." I took a sip of coffee. Damn, it was good. I looked at Marie again. She appeared to be waiting for something. Oh, right, the case thing. "Before, this was just to prove something. Whether to myself or some mysterious they, I couldn't tell you. But after that guy in the club… I don't know, Marie. I just can't let this go. Something bad is going on. I get this feeling like I'm the only one that can stop it."

"You?"

"Yeah."

"The AC guy."

"Heating and cooling."

"It still doesn't place you on the front lines in the drug war."

"Let's just say I have a unique set of skills that can be useful in certain circumstances."

"So most men believe. How about Imaculada?"

"What about her?"

"What gives her the right to order you on or off an ongoing DEA investigation?"

"You tell me. You're allowing it."

"Not by choice. The higher ups have instructed me to treat you like a consultant."

I wasn't surprised. The Tainted worked through corrupting people. Many of those held senior level governmental offices. Those that we were able to help, usually supported our operations either because of appreciation or fear of what we knew about them. "Cool. Do I get a badge?"

"You get a leash, a short one."

"Not really my thing. Cuffs are okay though. Ooh, can I get a pair of those?"

Marie poured herself more coffee. "I said before that you were interesting, which doesn't equate to usefulness. That remains to be seen." She put a drop of whole milk in the coffee, barely enough to color it. She faced me. "You may follow me around like a little puppy. Don't speak to any suspects without my approval. In fact, don't do anything without checking first."

"I thought you were kidding about the leash."

Marie raised her eyebrows over her coffee mug, held in both hands as she sipped. She walked back into the living area without a verbal response.

I shook my head at her back. I was out of my depth again. The last verse of Harry Chapin's Taxi ran through my head. A smart man wouldn't allow himself to be leashed. A wise man would have let the DEA handle this and left to get a beer. I just followed her with a nagging feeling this would not turn out in my favor.

"So, this is supposed to be a party?" Jelena asked.

"Not a party, just a few people over," Josh explained.

"Are we just supposed to hang here and pretend to be partying, while you make a buy?"

"Yeah. I do it all the time. Take some company along to get more product for a party."

"Like a beer run?" I offered.

"Exactly."

"But this time we'll put a tail on the courier," Marie added. "Follow him back to the source."

"And a room full of people won't spook him?" Jelena asked.

"Shemp? Nah. We do this a lot."

"Shemp?" I asked. "That his actual name?"

"Just what I call him cause of the way he parts his hair."

I took two beers and sat on the couch and handed one to Marie who sat on a chair next to it. A small table separated us that made a convenient beverage resting place. We had to dump our coffees to better align with the party atmosphere. Neither of us were happy about it.

Jelena and Adam were at the opposite end of the couch, pretending to be a flirtatious drunk couple. When I mentioned that the show could wait since we weren't currently being watched, I thought she was going to cut my throat. I was just trying to save her the discomfort. Me as well. Josh was in the kitchen putting together a platter of crudités, which is a word I hate. Why can't people just say veggies? Either way, I would have preferred cheese.

I held my bottle out to Marie and we clinked. We each took a sip.

"Isn't that better than the swill you were drinking last night?"

"Much."

Someone knocked on the door. Josh came out of the kitchen holding a plate of cut vegetables—no, I'm not using that word again—and wearing an apron, further skewing my vision of a drug dealer. He shifted the plate to his left hand and opened the door which blocked our view.

"Hey, you're not Shemp." They were the last words Josh would ever say.

A shot rang out like a cannon. Cut broccoli, carrots, and celery flew everywhere, and blood spewed out from the gaping hole in Josh's back. Time lurched into slow motion just before his body hit the floor. The guy standing over him held a Desert Eagle immediately identifiable by its huge outline. He was a big guy, completely bald, wearing a well-tailored suit. He started firing again once the doorway was clear. I leaped off the couch, tackling Marie, taking both her and the chair over. As soon as I had her covered, I tried to move into defense. The blur had taken hold instinctively, but I had to shift talents consciously. Not something I was good at under normal circumstances.

I think it was the need that helped. I needed to be bullet proof to protect Marie. My body alone would not stop the massive slugs that were coming our way. I felt my skin tighten kind of like a sunburn. Gravity took a stronger hold on me, and I adjusted myself to ensure I wasn't crushing her. The first three shots wailed into my back, starting low and ending on my right shoulder. Despite my iron-like skin, the pain from each blow screamed through me. Like a spiderweb starting from the impact point, then radiating out. I jerked with each hit.

There was a heartbeat of a pause and the hand cannon started roaring again. It was only then that I remembered Adam and Jelena. Looking over my shoulder, I saw him in basically the same position, protecting her. Three more shots slammed into Adam as I watched. Ricocheting into the wall, into the couch, and breaking a lamp. Out of nowhere, Jelena pulled two pistols and started firing back blindly around both sides of him. I heard the shooter's footsteps trailing away, and I finally looked down to face Marie.

Our noses were inches apart, and I had to lean back so she didn't look like a cyclops. She stared at me, eyes wide, and it took me a second to realize why. She had felt the bullets hammer into me, witnessed my reaction to each as I lay on top of her. As far as she could tell, I had just given my life for her. Then I really freaked her out by getting up.

"Are you guys okay?" I asked Adam and Jelena.

"I'm not a guy," Jelena said. "Chauvinist much?"

"I'll take that as a yes."

Adam just nodded.

I looked down at Marie, who just stared at me. She also had gotten her gun out but hadn't let off any rounds. "You good?"

"Yeah, but…"

"Great. Adam, stay here."

I started towards the door, cringing at the pain pulsing through my back.

"Where are you going?" Jelena asked.

"After Curley," I yelled back as I ran through the door and leaped over the railing.

"Chris!" I heard Marie yell, only then remembering that average guys didn't jump from a fifth-floor balcony. Oops. I landed on a car. Not on the roof with a dramatic explosion of glass. That would have been cool. No, I landed on the hood of a friggin' minivan, which I bounced off like a rag doll. The fall didn't cause any damage, but it too stung like a bitch.

"I've got to be doing something wrong."

I picked myself up in time to see the shooter jumping into a car. A guy in the back seat aimed down the barrel of an assault rifle. I wasn't confident about defending myself against that. I didn't even get the chance to curse before a hail of bullets came down from above, tearing into the car. I looked up to see both Marie and Jelena competing at putting the most holes in the Mercedes.

The hit squad didn't waste any more time as they put the car into reverse, spinning the tires. I realized they would disappear before we could catch up with them, so I took off at a run.

With Marie watching, I couldn't slip into a blur. I might explain away things up to now, but I didn't think I could talk my way out of that one. The hotel was on a one-way street, and I cut across the parking lot and leaped the small fence, using the straight line theory to my advantage. I caught up to them and jumped for all I was worth. It was an epic fail. Jumping onto a moving car looks a lot easier on TV. I hit the roof and rolled off the other side and into a bush.

I watched as they tore off down the street, then banged a quick left at an overpass. When their intentions dawned on me, I smiled. I picked myself up, literally dusted myself off and started sprinting again, this time towards the pedestrian walkway. I didn't need to put on any extra speed, but I had to put some energy into calming my breathing once I reached my destination. A couple of kids were walking towards me from the other direction. I hesitated, but there wasn't time to let them pass before I put my plan into action. The fence that protected people from themselves and flying debris curved inwards to dissuade anyone from doing what I was about to attempt.

Still in mid-run, I jumped up, spring boarding off the left side and adding a little gift to the vault. I grabbed the top and hauled myself over. I might get the hang of this Bishop thing.

"Dude, that was sick!" one kid said. The other had his nose in his phone and had missed the Olympic acrobatics. He caught on though, and aimed his phone up at me like an extension of himself. Oh well.

The car was accelerating down the on-ramp and heading towards me. I aligned my position with the lane as the kids pretended they were Spielberg. As I stood there, poised to leap into oncoming traffic, I could only think of those ridiculous TV shows where some genius in this type of situation would calculate the speed of the oncoming car, the height from the jumper's position to the top of the car, the rate of a body falling, wind speed. All of it accompanied by little white chalk angles and calculations. My ass. When my gut said jump, I jumped.

But not before turning to my combination audience and film crew.

"Don't try this at home."

Chapter Nine

THIS TIME, MY LANDING was much more cinematically sound. I wondered if the kids had captured it. If so, could I get a copy? Knowing what was coming from the previous failed attempt, I was more prepared. I landed on the trunk. The impact, along with the added weight from the density of my enhanced skin, caved it in. I dug my hand into the metal roof tearing it into a handhold. The shock wave from my landing caused the rear of the car to buck like an angry bull. Inside, the hit squad was thrown around. We serpentined until the driver got control again. The goon in the back seat locked eyes with me through the rear window, then picked up his assault rifle. I punched through and ripped it out of his hands, throwing it backward.

It occurred to me after releasing it that it may not have been the best plan. I jerked my head around, trying to figure a way to pull it back. It arched towards another vehicle, closing in fast. A hand reached out of the window and snatched it out of the air. Jelena's face appeared.

"Seriously? Any little kid could have picked this up."

I shook my head and focused on not dying. Making another handhold in the roof, I swung myself up and smashed feet first through the back window. The passenger in the back immediately started whaling on me and the shooter from the apartment aimed his monster pistol. I jammed my foot against the front seat, wedging the shooter against the dashboard. The guy next to me produced a knife. I caught his hand before he drove it into my chest.

"Ease up, Buffy."

I twisted his wrist, hearing a popping sound, and he dropped the weapon. A quick elbow to the face and one bad guy was out of commission. I was distracted enough, however, to miss the driver pulling a gun and shooting the only thing that was in his view. My leg.

Pain bloomed as the bullet tore through my calf, painting the door with my blood. I pulled back my leg protectively, releasing the shooter from being crushed. He whipped the gun around the seat again and I grabbed it just before he fired. In closed confines, the sound was even more deafening than in the apartment. The heat of the barrel burned my fingers as the slide tore into my flesh. The bullet ripped through the backseat two inches from my shoulder.

I ignored the searing pain in my hand and throbbing in my leg, which was mixing with the burning and itching that accompanied rapid healing. My only thought was disarm. I balled my other hand into a fist, placing the knuckle of my thumb under my index finger, causing it to point up like an arrow. The Phoenix eye, as this strike was called, could inflict extreme pain or death, depending on where it was focused. I aimed it at the inside of his wrist.

He screamed and let go of the Desert Eagle. I put my foot over the pistol to keep track of it. Two things happened at the same time. The shooter aimed a second pistol around the other side of the seat, and the driver brought his weapon to bear as well. I bailed.

I went into a blur and launched myself backwards, out through the shattered back window. Pain screamed up my leg, pulling my focus. It hadn't had time to heal. I maintained the blur and grabbed the handhold I had created on my way in. Since I couldn't blur and protect my skin at the same time, the flesh in my hand ripped as the jagged metal bit into it. I pushed the pain back out of the way. In the words of Jesse Ventura, 'I ain't got time to bleed'.

The momentum swung me up onto the roof of the car in time to hear a flurry of bullets tearing the backseat apart. For a second, I wondered if they had bothered to avoid hitting their compatriot. I didn't spend more time or energy on it. My aim now was to not fall off the speeding car.

The wind was stealing my breath and stinging my eyes. I knew from every movie I had ever seen that the guy on top of the car always got shot at through the roof. My chances of escaping unscathed were slim. My only saving grace was since I blurred out, they had no idea where I was. Time to act.

I let go of my handhold and planted my foot, preparing myself for an epically stupid move. Pushing off, I slid to the front of the car. I tried to engage my advanced awareness, to slow time from my perspective, but nothing happened. I slid down the windshield at full speed. My hand clawed for purchase and barely grabbed the edge of the hood. I was able to add strength to the grip with my gift and my body whipped around. I was facing the two goons again, who were still looking for me in the back seat.

I cannot tell you how much pleasure I got out of their shocked expressions as they turned to see me kneeling on the hood. I really wanted to wave, but thought better of it. Instead, I threw a blessing enhanced punch at the windshield blowing through it like sheetrock. I grabbed the steering wheel and yanked it to the side, taking the car off the road. It bounced and bucked as we jumped the shoulder and started driving on the grass, then collided with the one thing Florida had in excess, a palm tree.

Luckily for me, it wasn't a direct hit. We smashed into it on the driver's side, which launched me just clear of the tree. It gave me just enough time to protect myself before I landed. Well, I guess crashed was a better word. I tried for a superhero landing. I pivoted, attempting to slow my momentum by tearing up vast swaths of grass and dirt. Instead, I felt like a water skier skipping across the lake.

Finally flopping to a stop on my back, I lay there in the warm evening looking up at the sky, feeling like I just went ten rounds with Mike Tyson. I reached up to check if both ears were intact.

Why I was suddenly feeling pain when using power enhanced skin was a mystery. I had to say; I wasn't a fan. It was a clear night, and I gazed at the moon, not wanting to move just yet.

"Chris!" Marie's voice held an edge of panic.

I didn't move my head to look. The pain still radiated everywhere. She slid to a stop next to me.

"Chris, can you hear me? Oh, shit!"

I realized that lying there, unmoving, staring straight up, I probably looked dead. Oops. I blinked, forced myself to turn and look at Marie.

"Five more minutes, Mom?"

She stared at me for a few seconds, not quite getting it. I smiled at her.

"Are you fucking kidding me?"

"No," I struggled to get into a sitting position. The pain was deep and I was practically drowning in it. "I really could use a few minutes."

"You could have gotten yourself killed."

The cloud that had worked its way between my ears from the pain was dissipating making it easier to string coherent thoughts together. "There were several active shooters on the loose. I was supposed to just let them go?"

She was examining me still unconvinced that I was not near death. "We were right behind them in a car. They weren't going anywhere. All you did was put yourself and every other car on the road in danger." She found my bloody hand and yanked it up for inspection causing me to fall back to the grass.

"Ow."

She wiped the blood and didn't find any cuts. "Whose blood is this."

"Not sure."

She huffed before continuing her assessment. "What the hell is this?"

"What?"

"There's a bullet hole in your pants leg and it's covered in blood, but your leg is fine."

"I was a little busy trying not to die. I can't recount every moment like a narrator."

She slammed my foot down. "Nothing hurts?"

"Everything hurts."

Marie stood up, dusted off her pants and said, "good!" She walked away and I'm pretty sure the grass wilted around her foot falls.

I sat in the police station on one of those hard wooden benches that reminded me of a church pew. The irony of it was not lost on me.

I rubbed at my palm, which had healed over completely. There was no scar, no knot of tissue just below the surface. It was as if nothing had happened. Except for the pain. There was a deep ache in my palm, radiating into my fingers. Flexing them caused shock waves to my elbow. It was the same in my leg. I thought back to when a demon threw me across a city street into a brick wall. That had been about equivalent to being hit by a truck. I healed from those injuries without this lingering pain. What the hell was different now?

I still felt sore from the bullets that had ricocheted off my back too, although it was hard to distinguish that feeling from the trauma of belly flopping across the grass on the side of the road. Maybe it was something to do with the bullets. Were they made of some kryptonite like material that affected my powers?

I looked over at Adam sitting next to me. His thumbs flew over his phone's small digital keyboard. He looked unaffected by the activities of the night if you looked past the bullet holes in his suit jacket.

"Any residual issues from that Desert Eagle?"

"No." He never looked up from his phone.

"Yeah, me neither." I tried not to stretch out my back.

Marie came down the hall and sat down next to me. She lounged as much as the bench would allow, resting the back of her head against the wall and closing her eyes.

"Tired?"

She reopened them. Her head lolled so she could stare at me silently.

"Okay, stupid question."

She returned to her semi relaxed position.

I tried again. "I'm also guessing you didn't get any information from the goon squad."

"What rank did you reach in the Rangers?" she said, her eyes still closed.

"Private second class. Why?"

"I just assumed you were a captain."

"Why would you... oh. Obvious. Funny."

She smiled at her own joke.

"Then you've got nothing."

Her head rocked microscopically. "They are taking the phrase 'you have the right to remain silent' literally."

"Of course." I looked over at Adam for a little moral support, but he still had his nose in his phone. I tried again. "Any other info?"

"Ballistics are back. They confirm the Desert Eagle from the car as the one used to kill Josh. Big shock there. The fingerprints did not come back with any hits. None of them had any ID. The plates were not associated with the car, both were stolen."

Marie rubbed her temples. "These people act like hardened killers. One came to the door and murdered a man in cold blood, then attempted to kill four more." She paused for a few seconds. "Another, looked like a typical soccer mom, but drove the get-away car like a NASCAR driver while a battle was going on inside. I can see one of them not having a record, but all of them?"

I thought about that for a minute. Something she said was itching in my mind. A familiarity that I couldn't quite pinpoint. I ran through it again and something clicked. I sat forward. "All of them?"

Marie nodded. "None of them have records."

"No. I mean, all of them are keeping silent?"

"Yeah." She looked at me again. "Why?"

"They didn't say anything?"

Marie shook her head. "Nothing at all. That was the weird thing. Just stared out into space. I almost felt bad for them."

"You what?"

"Felt bad for them." Her own statement confused her, like she didn't realize she was having the emotion until she put it into words.

It pulled Adam out of his trance as well. We exchanged glances, then we both looked at Marie.

"I need to talk to them," I said.

"You can't."

"He needs to."

She looked at Adam. "It's not that easy. I would need to get authorization from—"

"Get it."

The intensity of Adam's words looked to grab hold of Marie. She locked eyes with him, both of them staring right past me.

"Okay." She got up and walked to have what her expression told me was a very unpleasant conversation.

I didn't know how he got her to agree so quickly. I was about to ask when he stopped me with a finger as he put the phone to his ear. "It's Adam. I need you to make a phone call." He got up and walked out of earshot.

"I don't know how this was approved." We stood at the door to the interrogation room. Marie was spitting mad. Apparently, the main reason she asked was because of her confidence in the lieutenant saying no. No matter what half the cop shows say, consultants do not question suspects. Not ex-cops, not private eyes, and certainly not writers. What the hell is that about, by the way? Yeah, you don't need any official training, you just need to make shit up for a living. Only a writer would think a writer is qualified to solve crimes.

"Don't make any deals with him." She jammed a finger at my chest. "I'll be watching." She walked into the adjoining room where Adam and Jelena were already waiting. I took a deep breath. This was not something I was looking forward to. The last time I had a conversation like this, the ending was less than optimal. There were no glass coffee pots in there or anything else that could be used as a makeshift knife, but I had a feeling I was still going to be on the losing side of this conversation. I opened the door and walked in.

Josh's killer was sitting at the table which was bolted to the floor, staring forward at the large mirror. They'd handcuffed him to a bar that spanned the table. It gave him some freedom while keeping his hands in view. I sat down opposite him. He didn't react. No twitch, not even a change to his breathing. I blocked the view of the mirror, but I don't think his eyes even refocused.

"Your fingerprints didn't provide us with a name, and you refuse to provide one, so I'm just going to call you Curley."

No reaction.

"It has nothing to do with your bald head. They nicknamed the guy we were expecting, Shemp. You get it, right?"

He didn't even blink.

"I get the feeling that you aren't in charge. Not in control of your own actions, if you will. I've experienced this before. Her name was Denise. He forced her to do things she didn't want to. It made her psychotic."

I was dancing around the subject. Name dropping with all the ears in the other room was a poor plan, but the puppet master wasn't taking the bait. I stood up and walked around the table.

"I would like to speak with the person in charge. Is that something you can arrange?"

I stopped behind him, watching his expression through the mirror closely. His gaze was still not in this universe.

"The person I really want to talk to is…" I leaned down next to his ear. "… Baldemar."

In the mirror, his focus shifted to me instantaneously.

Chapter Ten

"**N**OW THAT WE HAVE that settled, you can stop with the statue routine. Let's move on to the marionette show." I sat back down and faced him again. He had returned to staring into oblivion.

"I have many words for you. Most of them are four letters. I knew you were a coward, but I didn't think you were so much of one that you couldn't even talk through someone else."

It took a second. Then his entire posture changed. His shoulders pulled out of their hunched position, his neck stretched to its full length. Despite my height advantage, he looked down at me. I waited for the haughty singsong voice that sounded like he should be in Die Hard. The first one. Don't get me started on the sequels.

It wasn't Baldemar that spoke next. Nor was it Curley, or whatever his real name was. The voice was distinctly... female.

"He is a coward, as are most men."

"How so?" I had no idea who I was dealing with, but I needed to figure it out. The only way to do that was to keep her talking.

"Most men are very brave when dealing with those weaker than themselves. But when they come up against actual power..." Her voice trailed off as though reliving a fond memory. I shivered internally and tried to keep it there. I'm not sure I was successful.

"I hate to disagree, but I have seen a man of small stature, light frame, and mild-mannered take on two armed men defending an old woman he didn't know."

"Yes, yes, there are the odd exceptions." She waved the comment away. "Just as there is the odd woman who will take advantage of those weaker than her."

"The odd woman?"

She looked at me like she forgot I was there. "Who are you to know of our presence?"

"Just another fly in the ointment."

"You are no Bishop, that is obvious."

I tried not to cringe at the blatant reference to our secret organization. "I'm not even a deacon."

"How then, do you know that name?"

"Let's just say I like to stay informed. Wait, why am I not a Bishop?"

"I make it a point to know my enemies."

"The art of war?"

She inclined her head. "Have you studied it?"

It was my turn to nod. "Written by a man." I couldn't resist the jab.

"Only a fool dismisses wisdom based solely on prejudicial biases."

"The broken clock hypothesis?"

She didn't respond.

"A drug dealer? A little too on the nose, don't you think?" The Tainted were all basically supernatural addicts whose drug of choice was suffering.

"Men and their vices. They almost make it too easy, but I found a way to challenge myself."

"How is that?"

"Would you like me to hand you the answer?"

"If you wouldn't mind."

"I think not."

"Come on. What can I possibly do to stop you? Monologue a little, you know you want to."

She didn't take the bait.

"Okay, let me try to put some pieces together. You are looking for a way to spread fear and misery. Why not go with a tried-and-true method of hooking people on a highly addictive drug? The crack of a new generation, if you will. So you find yourself a chemistry teacher with a mobile home and set him to work."

The man puppet raised an eyebrow.

"Or her. Sorry. Eventually you come up with this new recipe for a really pure batch, but it needs a secret ingredient. Something to give it that extra kick and make Huey Lewis proud."

"Very good."

"Pretty slick right?"

"Yes. You gave yourself away beautifully, Christian."

I was about to complain about people not adjusting to my preferred name, then I remembered she was not supposed to know it. Or me. What just happened? I tried to come up with a reply, but she had put me off balance.

"Yes, I know who you are, what you are. I have to say I was expecting more. I will give you credit for not falling victim to the most classic blunder."

"Never get involved in a land war in Asia?"

"See, you can't help yourself."

"I'm not following."

"Yes, I know. Let me spell it out for you. Usually, the quickest way to get a man to admit to something is to tell them it is not so."

"You said I couldn't be a Bishop."

She nodded. "Instead, I accomplished what you were trying to get me to do. Talk. You showed me your nature in two minutes."

I felt myself sliding down a ravine, unable to stop. I had to keep her talking while I floundered for a handhold. "How so?"

"In our conversation, you referenced or quoted one movie, one television show, a song, and a commercial, of all things."

"The commercial could have been a fake of an ad within a movie."

"And your true self is revealed. Not the next new thing. Not a new thing at all. A recycled poor replication of legend, without the capacity to even use new dialog. Go ahead attempt to say something that is not a derivative of someone else's imagination."

Quote after quote came to my head, and I threw them away disgusted at my lack of originality. I literally stammered, unable to get any full words out.

"One last question as you stand there, debating your worth as a person."

My mouth hung open.

"Have you ever heard of time released capsules?"

The Tainted faded away. Her presence must have been holding the man together. Now released, the drug coursing through him took hold.

It was like watching Bruce Banner transform. She was right I really can't stop. His muscles undulated under his skin, fueled by biochemical reactions they were never supposed to experience. His veins distended. I stood up fast, the chair under me sliding back against the wall.

"Chris, get out of there!" Marie's voice sounded strained through the intercom. I thought her idea held merit. Let this guy tear the room apart. What did I care? As that thought was still forming, Curley ripped out the bar, securing his cuffs, then grabbed the table and hurled it. Not at me, but at the door. It collided with an explosive sound, mangling it beyond use.

"I'll just stay here then?" I could have gotten out. Hell, I could have gone through the wall, but that would have left an exit for the hopped-up psycho marionette. Instead, I just stared down my opponent and nodded. "Cage match it is."

Chapter Eleven

DESPITE MY BRAVADO, THIS would not be a cakewalk. I was pretty sure I could pull out a 'W' without too much trouble… under normal circumstances. I couldn't, however, pull out the big guns with the captive audience on the other side of the two-way mirror, not to mention the cameras. My opponent didn't give me much time to plan. With a roar, he ripped the chair off its bolts and lunged at me.

He swung it like Reggie Jackson aiming for the fences, my head playing the part of the ball. I dropped under and came up swinging, but I aimed much lower. I was looking to put him down fast and wasn't worried about being called out for hitting below the belt. Forgive the mixed metaphors. It did nothing. I take that back. It lined me up squarely for his back swing and allowed me to migrate analogies to tennis.

The chair took me across the side a split second after I put up my protection. I flew halfway across the room and into the metal table, making a man-sized dent. That was going to be hard to explain away. I looked pointedly to where I believed Adam was. I couldn't play superhero while on Candid Camera. In answer, I received three clicks. I looked up at the camera and made a silent prayer that it was now off. And if it was, so were my gloves.

I closed my eyes and reached for the image of the glowing sunshine over a meadow by a lake, and found it waiting. The lake had pulled back from the shore as though a severe drought had affected it, but the water was still shimmering in the light. I opened my eyes and climbed to my feet.

The hulkinator had paused, reveling in the damage he believed he'd caused. My standing enraged him more, and he ran at me, swinging the heavy metal chair like an axe. I reached up and stopped its descent in one iron hand as if that proverbial axe impaled itself in a mighty oak. He tried to pull it back, but my gift held it as tight as hundred-year-old bark. He started yanking at it in a mindless frenzy. No longer worried about me, he just needed to get his weapon free. "Hey!" I yelled.

He stopped and stared at me, frothing at the mouth.

I poked him in the eyes and smacked him in the face. I couldn't help myself. The guy went completely insane, but never let go of his grip. I pulled the chair towards me, dragging the wild man with it. I let loose a palm strike to his sternum. It was his turn to fly across the room. He had a softer landing on a sheetrock wall with metal studs that crumpled like an accordion. I tossed the chair behind me out of his reach as he extracted himself.

I slipped down into my lowest stance that looked like I was riding an invisible horse. Far too low to be of any use in fighting, but I was going for dramatic. I rotated my fist and waved for him to try again in the best Bruce Lee impression I could muster. I wasn't overly concerned about my improper position. After all, I had a distinct speed advantage. Right?

He slipped into a blur, hitting me with a chest level tackle, driving me once again back into the table. I didn't have time to brace myself consciously, luckily my instincts compensated. He fell on top of me and began whaling away on me as I covered vital organs. I felt each punch he landed as though I had no protection at all. Had I not been sure that my iron skin was in place, I would have sworn that my ribs were cracking.

Somewhere in my pain addled mind, I realized the table I was leaning on was pushing on me. Help was trying to get to me, but barging into a scenario they didn't understand would only make the situation worse. I wasn't fully grasping what was going on, but I had a better chance of battling it than they did. Their only options were overwhelming him with tasers, or guns. The pummeling I gave to his nether region would have incapacitated a eunuch. I didn't think a few bullets were going to slow his drug induced hysteria.

Wait a minute. Drugs. This guy wasn't one of the Tainted. He was exhibiting enhancements that mimicked their power through some drug. I may not have understood it, but I knew paramedics gave overdose patients Naloxone to counteract the drugs. Could I replicate that with my gift? I didn't wait.

In between his battering, I reached up and grabbed either side of his head. I tried to push my blessing into him but felt a resistance. The act itself shocked him into inaction, which gave me a second to think. I wasn't sure what was wrong. Something was telling me that this was still possible. The guy was coming back to himself, so I had to take action fast.

Pushing didn't work, so I tried the opposite. I opened myself up. I still don't know how I did it. Like the first time I meditated with Hager, instincts took over. Images flooded my mind. I was hovering high above a lush garden that extended as far as I could see in all directions. Sparkling streams wound in spidery patterns around the thick foliage, converging finally to a central pool. A murky sludge creeped in from all sides along the water lines. Where it passed, the greenery withered. With every foot it progressed, it picked up speed. I got a distinct feeling that if it reached the center pool, it would be bad. Like cross the streams bad.

Suspended over the oasis, I struggled to find a solution. What could I do from up here? Nothing. I needed to, what? The crud intruded, speeding up as it moved. My hesitation gnawed at me. My Ranger Instructor from training screamed in my head. *You failed Ranger. You couldn't make a decision.*

My resolve hardened. I looked down into the shimmering pool. The trunk of a tree whose branches were quickly dying. I dove, the conscious decision having spurred the action itself. I rocketed down at high speed, faster than gravity's pull. My personal Tower of Terror. I hit the water headfirst, not bothering to lead with my arms. I submerged without a splash and came to an abrupt stop in the very center. The consistency was thicker than water, viscous. Treading was not needed to stay in one spot. Like a piece of fruit suspended in a Jell-O mold. Now that I was in, I could feel the drug. The alien presence. The Taint.

It was Tainted. I could feel the wrongness of it. Not simply a makeup of chemicals designed to dull your perception or cause hallucinogenic sensations. I didn't know how they did it, or how I was going to stop it. I felt the pressure of its migration as though it was forcing the soul's purity into a central point. Trying to expel it, as a teenager would an errant whitehead. There was danger in that pressure I could sense as well. A tsunami approaching the coastline.

Something tickled my memory: an article I had read in Popular Science about a theory to use acoustic gravity waves to reduce the energy behind tsunamis. There were two problems with this solution. I didn't have AGWs, and this was not a tsunami. But I may have something better. Coursing through this man's veins was a derivative of the evil that Bishops fought against since the beginning. What pulsed through mine was the pure essence of what the Covenant stood for.

The pressure increased. A small cloud of blood from my nose plumed in front of my face. I pushed all thoughts aside. I reached out with my senses, trying to find the encroaching poison. It was easy even for a new Bishop with little training. Now how to deploy my gift?

I'd used it to enhance myself. I'd pushed it into others to help them heal. Now I was trying to use it like Iceman stopping a natural disaster. Even if that was an option, there were too many tendrils at which to point my hands simultaneously. I closed my eyes which was weird because I already shut them on a different plane. Shaking my head, I tried to focus, picture each vein of death as it creeped forward.

I pulled my gift around me, focusing it into a beam of power aimed at one of the black lines. I wasn't sure how I did it and I tried not to think about it too much. Where the beam impacted, the taint shrank back like grease atop a pool of water when soap is added. Encouraged, I aimed a second beam, and the blackness reacted the same way. I had found a solution. Streams of light shot out from me at different angles lacing into the blackness again and again. Each time one touch the infection, it cringed back as if struck. It wouldn't take long before

I ran out of energy. Before the multiple lines of white-hot power radiating from me drained me to the point of exhaustion. That was obviously not going to work. I had barely pushed back a quarter of the invading tentacles.

Maybe I was using too much power in each beam; employing a sledge when only a ball-peen hammer was needed. I started again, this time with a lighter touch. The sludge reacted as before, if not as quickly. I started multiplying the beams again, pushing back the evil. The tension against my temples lightened. I made it nearly three quarters of the way before having to stop. My supernatural muscles gave out.

When I released the rays, the taint pushed back. Hard. The pressure in my head slammed back in place and I doubled over with the pain. The dribble of blood running from my nose increased to a steady flow. My eyes were squeezed shut so I couldn't see the rivers of black bearing down on me, but I could feel them. Tickling the edges of the pool, oozing its way in.

There was no time left. This man was about to succumb to the tidal wave of evil and I was sitting in the middle of it. I had a choice. Try to pull out, not that I was sure how I even got in here, or stay and fight against the imminent danger that I had failed against twice. So, no actual decision necessary. The question was how. Splitting my blessing into streams of light was taking too much time and concentration. Plus, I wasn't sure how far back the blackness went. Even if I could separate the focus enough times, would I have enough strength to push it all the way? Somehow, I doubted it.

I felt beaten. Exhausted. A life teetered in the balance, and I wasn't able to help because of my inexperience. Why didn't I stay in New York and continue my education? No, I had to run off like a spoiled child. Abandon the first family I had experienced in years. Leave Jackie, and Father Murphy to go to Miami of all places.

The taint flowed into the central pool. Heavier than the clear essence in which I floated, it sank to the bottom. A snake-like coil curling up at the bottom. A shadow filling up the pool of light. Light...

I pulled my power around me again, but instead of aiming it, I let it radiate out of me. The darkness shrunk against the glow of my blessing. I drew in more power and the light flowing from me grew brighter. The shadowy ooze pulled back out of the pool. I took a deep, slow breath, then dug deep into myself and dipped into the well of power that hovered over the horizon in the calm place of my mind. It was like plugging a light bulb into a nuclear power plant. My back arched, head tilting back. The surrounding glow escalated into a ball of radiance burning like white phosphorus.

The taint didn't merely recede; it fled. A high-pitched wail emanating from all around followed the retreat. I floated up out of the pool, rising back up to where I had appeared. My light bathing the distance. I watched as the taint withdrew, and as I felt it dissipate, I released myself from another person's essence.

I opened my eyes in the real world. I still held the man's head in my outstretched hands. His eyes were open. The madness was gone from them, as was the Tainted one. In its place was confusion, shock, and fear. I released him and he staggered backwards, practically falling into the corner of the room. His eyes bulged, then he turned and vomited. A thick black sludge poured from his mouth as though he had ingested a gallon of crude oil. It came out in a violent flow, more than I felt was possible for his body to hold. After what felt like an eternity, he gasped for air. He looked at me, blackness dripping from his mouth, and said in a voice strained from exertion, "I'm sorry."

Then he collapsed.

Chapter Twelve

THE DEA OFFICE WASN'T actually in Miami, but a little town called Weston in Fort Lauderdale. I guess the party city held too many distractions. I bore you with these little details because the hospital they go to when a prisoner falls ill is, wait for it, Miramar. Granted, it's the wrong Miramar. It's not in California and they are not launching Navel Aviators every two hours, but still, Miramar.

I watched the large man's unconscious form lying in bed from my folding chair next to the window. They'd cuffed both wrists to the reinforced sides. We were in a small private room. He hadn't moved for the few hours that spanned since his collapse, other than the rise and fall of his chest from his ragged breathing. He sounded like a twenty-year smoker with a severe case of emphysema.

The demons had left him, and his body was attempting to recover from the massive strain that was put on it. There were no actual demons this time, just a supernaturally enhanced drug overdose. Yeah, that was *much* better. Officer Jason Ciullo sat in the other corner, watching the latest zombie spinoff on his cell phone. He was stationed in the hospital for just this scenario. Well, maybe not this specific set of circumstances. Any prisoner must be accompanied by a police officer at all times, even during surgery. Apparently, Jason filled the time by binge watching television series that have been milked to epic proportions.

I tried to engage him in conversation once. When he talked, he whistled through his teeth like a cartoon character on any word that included an 's' or 'c'. I thought it was a joke, and after the last twenty-four hours of stress, succumbed to a fit of laughter. It was not. Needless to say, the officer stayed quiet after that. It left me alone with my thoughts and a background accompaniment of moaning undead.

My thoughts weren't really thrilling me either. I came to Miami to help, and instead I was doing a great impression of bumbling detective. I was trying to own this new life I had fallen ass backwards into, and instead I was tripping over my own feet. One big problem was my lack of investigative experience. The books I'd been reading gave me a baseline but applying them was like driving a golf ball. Knowing the mechanics was not enough. You need to develop muscle memory. Right now, my mental muscles were atrophied and sore from their new workout regimen.

Marie walked in and looked towards Officer Ciullo. "You can take a break Jason; I've got you covered. Need my cuffs?"

"Yeah, thanks," Jason replied with a little whistle while putting his phone away. Marie handed them over. "Keep an eye on mine? They are my academy cuffs."

"You still have your academy cuffs?" He nodded and gave me the stink eye before leaving.

Marie noticed and frowned in my direction. "Did you laugh at him?"

"I thought he was joking."

"You're a jerk."

"How was I supposed to know?"

"Who in their right mind would do that as a joke with someone they didn't know?"

"I thought it was funny."

"Of course you did. How's he doing?" She nodded in the patient's direction, and I gave her the rundown.

"How are the others? I didn't hear anything before I jumped in the ambulance."

"Dead."

I wasn't surprised, but the confirmation stung. I didn't know them besides, you know, the attempted murder, but couldn't help feeling for them. They were like Denise. Manipulated, used, then disposed of.

"More than dead, really."

"What is more than dead?" My mind drifted back to Officer Cuillo's Zombie show.

"They blew up."

"Come again?"

Marie made the international sign for an explosion with both hands while mouthing 'boom.'

"How did they blow up?"

"You tell me."

"Weren't they searched?"

"Of course we searched them!"

"Well, it looks like you need to update your search techniques because I think they missed something."

"That's not possible."

"The results disagree." I knew I was being an ass but couldn't stop. The meaningless loss of life pissed me off, and I didn't even know why.

"You don't get it," Marie said with a little venom of her own.

"Obviously."

"Because with the size of the explosion, we couldn't have missed it. Two cops were caught…"

Marie's voice trembled and she fell silent. Her eyes shimmered with restrained tears. I got up, walked over, and tried to comfort her with a hand on her shoulder. She batted it away hard enough that I felt the vibration up and down my arm. She took a step away, composed herself before turning again.

"The two went nuts like this guy." She threw an arm in his direction. All signs of tears had been erased. "Sofia entered the cell while Jamal stayed back. The explosion killed Sofia instantly. Jamal is in ICU."

"How is that possible?"

"Again, you tell me."

I thought she was using the expression to say I don't know. It was clear now that she wasn't. "Why would I know?"

"The only one of the three that survived is the one that you were locked in with."

"That means I know why they exploded?"

"I watched the video from holding. His activities mirrored the other two right up to where the video cut out."

"And?"

"How did you stop him from exploding?"

That was a damned good question and one I couldn't answer, even if I wanted to admit my supernatural abilities. I tried to say I didn't, but the words wouldn't form. Instead, I shook my head, then a thought occurred to me.

"Vomit."

"Excuse me?" Marie took a step back, expecting me to make good on my statement.

I shook my head again. "He threw up before he passed out. Is it possible that whatever he had ingested caused the explosion?"

"And how would throwing it up stop that process?"

"I don't know, I'm guessing. How is Jamal?"

"He's in critical condition. The explosion threw him back into the wall. He has a concussion, several broken bones, and severe burns."

"Did I cause that?" Curley asked.

We both looked over at him now sitting up in his hospital bed.

"Did I hurt that officer?"

My first reaction was to say no. I almost got it out, but Marie spoke up first.

"Why do you think you did?"

"I'm seeing snippets of memories over the past few hours. At least I think it's hours. What is today?"

"Tuesday." Marie checked her watch. "February twenty-first."

His face fell and his mouth actually hung open.

Marie saw the reaction as well. "What was the last day you remember?"

He didn't answer, staring out into space. His eyebrows furrowed and relaxed, then furrowed again. I could almost see him grasping at threads, trying to weave logic in what was, for him, a gap in reality.

"Sir," I prompted.

His eyes pulled back from gazing into the universe and met mine. "Alex."

"Alex." Marie pulled his attention back to her. "What was the last day you remember?"

He took a second to answer, his eyes scanning his memory. "The twenty-sixth."

"A month?" I said, shocked.

"Of December," he finished.

"Almost two months," Marie said with little emotion.

I regarded her, wondering how she could be unaffected by such a revelation. Then I understood. She didn't believe it. Her mind was not allowing that train of thought to process. To her this was a play, and at the drop of the curtain the actors take their leave back to freedom. Marie was not about to let that happen. I understood her compulsion to rationalize. Six months ago, I would have been right beside her. That was before I watched Denise... I shook my head, clearing the horrible memory.

How was I going to convince her she was looking at an unwilling puppet and not a drug addict trying to get out of the crimes he'd committed? It was time to play a hunch.

"Alex, how long have you been taking drugs?"

He looked more shocked than when he heard he lost two months of his life. "I do not take drugs of any kind."

"Not even alcohol?"

His back arched, so that he was looking at us literally down his nose. "Certainly not."

The heat of his words and the shock clear on his face caused Marie to pause.

"Let me get this straight. You never take any kind of drug?" I had planted the seed, she took it from there.

"Other than what a doctor prescribes, no."

"Then what were you doing the day you disappeared?"

"I was volunteering at a charity function." Alex's brow furrowed. "We were setting up when I suddenly developed a splitting headache. A pleasant woman saw that I was in pain and offered me an aspirin." His voice trailed off, and he stared out into nothingness as though stuck in that moment, reviewing it over and over. Then he looked up at me. "That was the last thing I remember from that day."

"Can you describe the woman?"

He was about to answer, then stopped. "No, I'm sorry. It's strange. I feel like I should be able to remember her, but when I try, it slips away."

"Is there anything you can remember?" I asked.

"Immaculate."

"What the hell does that mean?" Marie asked.

"I'm sorry, but I have no idea. I just know that it was important. Even now, I feel like I should be doing something for it."

"Doing what?" Marie's frustration was showing.

Alex shook his head. She looked at me. I shrugged.

Chapter Thirteen

MARIE WAS GOING FOR the land speed record on her way to the elevator. I was doing my best to keep up without kicking in my gift.

"Marie," I called after her.

She kept walking.

"Ma-rie!"

"No."

"No, what?"

"No, we are not letting him go."

"I wasn't going to ask that."

"Good, then we agree."

"I was thinking more like helping him with a special circumstances defense."

"That's not my job."

"It's not mine either, but someone has to do something."

She finally stopped, and I almost ran into her as she spun around. My closeness gave her pause. She recovered quickly. "Chris, he killed someone. You witnessed it for God's sake."

"And yet I think he is innocent."

"Okay." She crossed her arms. "Why?"

"He was not in control of his actions."

"Just because he was hopped up on something does not mean he is not culpable."

"This is not a drunk driver, or a drug addict too high to distinguish between duck hunt and shooting his best friend. He was literally being controlled as much as a marionette. He popped one aspirin and…"

A thought popped into my head that scared the hell out of me.

"What?"

"I think we have a big problem."

"Yeah, no kidding."

"No worse than that."

I pulled out my phone, and it was Marie's turn to keep up. If this was what I thought it was, the world was in deep shit.

The ride to the Covenant house was quiet. Since I had ridden with the ambulance, I needed a lift. Marie, sensing that I had information about her case, was not letting me out of her sight. She threatened to arrest me for impeding a federal investigation, and I reminded her of my get out of jail free card. I honestly wasn't sure Ima wouldn't let me rot in there, but, hey she didn't know that. So I hung up the phone and got in her car.

She drove a mint condition red Camaro IROC Z. I didn't know if she restored it herself or bought it that way, or had it handed down to her from her parents. It wouldn't surprise me to discover, besides being a DEA agent, she was also a mechanic and an out of work hairdresser. I nearly made my tongue bleed trying not to ask her the ignition timing, but I already sounded enough like an idiot. She drove fast. Not dangerously, just fast, like her foot was made of lead.

The tires squealed as she slid to a stop. I hopped out to escape the awkward silence that had permeated the gorgeous vehicle the entire ride. Marie being asked to bend to someone else's will, and she was not enjoying it. I walked quickly, my longer strides eating up the pavement. Marie had no problem keeping up despite her smaller stature.

"What is this place?" she asked with acid in her voice. Her curiosity won out over the brooding silence.

"It's a kind of clubhouse for us."

"Who is us?"

"Club members."

"It's a church."

I shrugged. "Haven't you ever seen Twenty-One Jump Street?"

I led her around the church to the attached rectory. Adam and Jelena were waiting for me and started hitting me with a barrage of questions.

"Not now. I need to talk to Ima."

"She's in the middle of something," Adam warned.

"We're in the middle of something alright."

As we walked, I pushed out with my senses and found the Covenant Head's door locked. I manipulated the tumblers with my gift and felt it click. It was the first time I had ever done it at such a distance and was feeling very smug.

"Chris, you don't want to do that," Adam warned.

"Actually, I do."

"No, seriously…"

I grabbed the handle and was blown backwards several feet, landing on my back. I wasn't hurt, other than my pride.

"I tried to tell you."

"What the hell was that?" Marie asked, looking around, gun drawn.

"It was my security system." Ima stood in the now open doorway. In order for her to have been there that fast, she either blurred, or knew I was coming and wanted to see the show. I was betting on the latter. "Please put your weapon away. I hate those vile things."

Marie did so, but with an air that said, I have decided to holster my weapon.

Ima nodded as if that was not the case. "As my locked door indicated, I am very busy. I have time later." She moved to go back in her office.

"The Tainted have found a way to convert people against their will."

Chapter Fourteen

"**T**HAT'S IMPOSSIBLE." IMA STOOD firm but appeared somewhat shaken. Adam looked like someone just slapped him across the face. Jelena and Marie just had confused expressions.

I climbed back to my feet as nonchalantly as possible. Ima's scowl basically told me 'not in front of an unblessed,' but I honestly didn't give a shit. "I just interviewed a man who lost two months of his life. I witnessed him commit cold-blooded murder and attempted murder while under the control of one of the Tainted."

"How do you know he was controlled? Maybe he was making the claim to establish an insane plea."

"He didn't make a claim. He was a vessel, a puppet. She talked through him."

"She?"

"She was pretty clear on that, as well as her disdain for men."

Ima's eyes got enormous, then shifted in many directions as she watched a private movie flash across the big screen of her mind. At least, that's what I imagined she was doing. Finally, she met my gaze. "Come in."

We all filed in, making the decently sized office cramped. Music played from a virtual assistant on the left side of the room, which she commanded into silence. I didn't recognize the song, but it sounded like something you could dance to. It felt at odds with the décor of sin and punishment. One wall held a large screen TV.

Imaculada walked up to her desk and rotated her laptop around to face her. She pulled up the program she wanted, and the large screen came to life with an image of a woman taken from what looked like an extremely old photograph. The variations of browns that made up the grainy picture gave it an unearthly feel. The subject was dressed in a traditional kimono, her dark skin tone looked to be only a shade off from her clothes. Her hair was divided and twisted into five horns.

"Uji no Hashihime. This is the only image in existence. We only have this because cameras weren't that prevalent back then, so she hadn't perfected her avoidance techniques yet."

"You're kidding, right?" I looked from Ima to Adam. "We are going after a dragon lady?"

"No. We are going after *the* dragon lady." She paused and let that sink in. "There were rumors she was in the US, but no one could confirm them. The Tokyo Covenant lost track of her about a decade ago."

"If no one's seen her in seventy years, how do you keep track of her at all?" Jelena asked.

"Body count." Adam was visibly shaken.

Ima narrowed her eyes at him. "Nothing so dramatic. However, she has a certain style, and we have word-of-mouth information. She is most known for her revilement of men. Her teachings suggest men are flawed creatures ruled by their passions and are good for little more than breeding."

"No argument there," Jelena interjected.

Marie cocked her head. "I studied Japanese in college. That doesn't sound like a standard name."

Adam shook his head. "It loosely translates to Demon of Uji Bridge."

"Seriously?" Marie had her arms crossed and was looking at each of us in turn. "Listen, I was going along for the ride just in case you people had some kind of lead. But you are talking about a woman that has to be over a hundred, and a demon. You're chasing a myth."

"She's not really a demon." Adam continued, "just the name she was given back then."

"For what?" Jelena asked.

Adam hesitated for a moment. "The story goes that after being betrayed by her husband she bathed in the Uji-Gawa river for twenty-one days after dying her skin red with vermillion made her hair into five horns and prayed to a deity to turn her into an Oni."

Marie raised an eyebrow. "An evil spirit?"

Adam nodded and went on. "She went on a killing spree starting with her husband, his mistress and a slew of other people, mostly men."

Marie threw her arms up and walked out saying "You people are all nuts."

"Marie…" I called after her.

"You suspect a mole in the DEA," Ima's delivery was matter of fact, but it froze Marie in place, her hand halfway to the doorknob.

She faced Ima again. "How would you know that?"

"Because that is her M.O. She doesn't fight law enforcement, she infiltrates them. Umi plays a very long game. Longer than people have the capacity to see."

"But you do?"

Adam folded his arms behind him. "We have a distinctive viewpoint that allows us to see what most people miss."

Ima gave him a nod.

Marie shifted her weight and put a hand on her hip. "Not that I'm saying I believe you but, do you have a name?"

"One name would do you little good. By now, I would expect that she controls a good portion of your organization."

Marie pulled her head back as though avoiding the pungent odor of a restaurant dumpster sitting out in the sun too long. "Now I know you people are crazy."

I was getting a little peeved myself, since none of this was shared with me. Ima obviously had her suspicions already and was not very forthcoming. Now, things were falling into place and I was connecting the dots myself. "Really? That drug bust where we first met. It looked like you had a lot of resources dedicated to that one warehouse which turned out to be empty."

Marie crossed her arms. "Sometimes tips don't pan out."

"It was more than just a tip. You had a whole breaching team ready. How long had you been planning this?"

"A day. But we had people watching the warehouse as we got

everything lined…" Her eyes widened and I could see her following the path. "Holy shit." She stared out in front of her, but I got the feeling that she wasn't seeing the room anymore.

"Holy shit," she said it three more times before coming back to the present and looking me in the eye. "Chris…" She struggled with the words. "The sheer scope of it."

"I get it."

"No, you don't. There were two teams that watched the warehouse since it exceeded one shift. That's four. No one volunteered to watch the warehouse, they were assigned. So that means my AIC is involved or it would just be a crap shoot, and would not guarantee time to clear the place. Then I started thinking about the amount of drugs that were seized, none of it out of the ordinary. That means someone from the lab has to be involved. More than one because I requested a retest several times and none ever came back different. That work is assigned as well, so once again, the supervisor has to be involved."

"As I said." It was Ima's turn to cross her arms.

Marie looked at each of us then walked out. I moved to follow, but Ima stopped me.

"Let her go. She needs to reset."

"Reset?"

"That is how she deals with change." Ima moved back toward her desk.

"How the hell would you know?"

"We have been keeping tabs on her."

"That's messed up. I don't like this big brother shit."

"Don't be so dramatic. We need to know who we can trust and who we cannot."

"And?"

"We were fairly confident she was on the correct side. Now we are more so."

"Great."

"We have more important things to deal with than your girlfriend's feelings."

"She's not my girlfriend."

"I'm really not interested. What I am concerned about is your claim. How sure are you that this person was converted through a pill?" Her eyes connected with mine as though trying to pull the information directly from my brain.

"Very. One other thing." I pointed at the screen bringing everyone's attention back to the Demon of Uji Bridge. "She was in the warehouse that night."

Ima placed both hands on her desk as though looking for stability. Her eyes danced around as she considered everything that was said, then nodded once. "Take Ada and Marie and whomever else you need. Get it done." She sat down and began reading again.

I looked at her, shocked into silence. My lack of movement drew her eye.

"Is there a problem?"

"Not a problem, but a few questions. You have been dismissing me for the past two weeks, now you want me to take point?"

"That doesn't sound like a question."

"Why?"

Her focus on me was making me a little uncomfortable, and I began to long for the days when she ignored me.

"Two reasons. You have gotten further on this in a week than anyone else has in months, including the DEA. When a fountain suddenly pops up, you don't keep digging the well."

She went back to reading.

"And the other reason?"

This time, she didn't look up. "You were going to do it, anyway. At least this time you're following my direction. Maybe in time you will get used to it."

"What do I tell Marie?"

"As little as possible, but whatever it takes to placate her."

I nodded and headed for the door, Adam and Jelena following in my wake.

"And Chris."

I stopped glancing back to find Ima still reading. She looked up again, her green eyes sparkled with an inner radiance. "Do not make the mistake of underestimating Uji just because she is a woman."

"Are you kidding? That scares me more."

I found Marie outside on a bench, her back to me, facing a small pond surrounded by various plants and flowers. I flipped the keys to Jelena.

"Give me a minute."

She caught them with a mischievous smile. Adam groaned. I realized what I had done and immediately regretted it, but I would have to worry about Jelena's driving later. I walked up to the bench. Marie gave no acknowledgment that she heard me, but I knew she did. She missed little.

"Can I join you?"

She was sitting in the middle of the bench, and as an answer, moved a little to one side. I took the cue and sat down.

"How're you doing?"

"Half my department may be in a drug lord's pocket, so you know, peachy."

"Maybe?"

"If you think I'm taking the word of a religious freak, you're more out of your mind than I thought." She continued to stare into the pond.

"I haven't known her that long, but I would not call her a religious freak."

"She lives in a church. The decorations on her office wall are early inquisition, with a hint of eternal suffering. Creepy."

"She is eccentric, but that is not out of the ordinary for us."

"And about that, who the hell are you people?"

"It's kind of hard to explain."

"NSA, CIA?"

"Harder than that."

Marie finally faced me. "How about you try?"

"Did you ever see Van Helsing?"

Her eyebrows drew together. "The one with Hugh Jackman?"

"Yup, that's the one. So, you saw it?"

"It had Hugh Jackman in it, so… *yeah*."

"Right. Well, that's kind of us."

"The Vatican sent you to vanquish monsters?"

"You're actually closer than you think."

"Okay, I'm out." She got up and started walking away.

I caught up. "Why, because we are religious nuts?"

"I'm not sure about the religious part but you're definitely cuckoo for Cocoa Puffs."

Great, now I was craving chocolate cereal. I took a chance and grabbed her arm. She didn't immediately castrate me, but her eyes told me she was considering it. "And?"

"And what?"

"What are your alternatives? Half your department might be on the take. You don't know who you can trust. You're alone."

"Fine, I prefer it that way."

"Let me help." Something in my voice got her to look me in the eye. I saw anger and betrayal, but below that was fear.

"Why? Why do you want to help? What's your deal?"

"Because I care," I said it more vehemently than I intended and, as a result, I pulled her closer to me. We stood there pressed up against each other, me staring down into her eyes. We were inches apart, separated only by our height differences. My breathing came faster, and I felt my heartbeat speed up. Marie said nothing, just stood there staring up at me.

I got control of myself and released my grip on her biceps. Marie stepped back, but her eyes never left mine.

My tongue started working again. "We have resources, connections. People we know are not Tainted." Doubt crept in as I thought back to Denise again, but I pushed the memory away. "You know these assholes. I have a team that can back you up. We are both after the same thing."

"Are we?" Her eyes were still locked with mine.

"Of course. These drugs need to be pulled off the street before anyone else gets hurt."

She blinked finally and looked away. "Fine, let's go. You drive."

She started walking towards the car.

I followed her, thinking I had played that wrong, but for the life of me, I couldn't figure out how.

We got to the SUV. Marie got in the passenger side back seat and I walked around to the other side where Jelena waited by the driver's door. I thought she was going to hand over the keys. I mean, why else would she be standing out there?

She looked at me with a mixture of pity and anger. "You're an idiot. You know that, right?"

"Why now?"

"Estúpido hombre culo." She got in the driver's seat and slammed the door.

I shook my head and got in the back seat of my own car, again.

After a few minutes, I asked no one in particular, "So, where are we going?"

Jelena flipped a hand up. "No clue. I'm just the overwatch, remember?"

"You still on about that?"

She stuck her nose up in answer.

"I'll take that as a yes."

I got the feeling that Adam was rolling his eyes, but whether at me or at Jelena, I couldn't be sure.

"Does anyone have any suggestions?"

Shoulders shrugged all around. "Marie, you're the detective. Do you have a suggestion?"

"I'm a special agent of the United States Government. I'm not a detective."

I was striking out all over the place. "Right, sorry. But you have the most experience with criminal investigation."

"Oh, so now you want my opinion? No, I get it. You want me to tell you what to do so you can do the opposite?"

I exhaled. Somehow, I pissed off every woman I knew. "Adam?"

"Why ask me? I've only been doing this since I was a teenager.

You are obviously much more qualified according to… Imaculada."

Marie grabbed my arm. "Wait, wasn't that what Alex said?"

"Who?" I asked.

Marie rolled her eyes. I saw it. "Curley."

"Oh yeah, right. Yes, and no. He said 'immaculate'."

"I'm not following," Adam added.

I brought him up to speed including the one piece of information he thought would be helpful.

"Immaculate," Adam tasted the word. "It's familiar."

"Yeah, you said it already, Ima."

"No, that's not it." He looked down and started gnawing on a thumbnail.

"Assholes! Move!" Jelena jerked the car to one side and sped up. "Get that piece of crap in the water and off the streets."

Adam picked his head up in time to see an old boat being towed behind a pickup truck as we flew past them. Jelena stuck her arm out the window, but I don't think she was waving. Adam spun around to look at me. "That's it!"

I looked over at Marie, who shrugged, then back at him, waiting for further clarification.

"Holland's boat. The magazine headline was Immaculate Restoration."

I looked back at Marie.

"It's better than anything I have."

"Jelena?"

"I'm just the…"

"I'm sorry. Your insight is important to me. I didn't just hire a trigger finger."

"That's all I wanted to hear." I could see her smile from the back-seat. "I trust Adam. We should follow his lead."

"I'm not sure we can trust going through official channels," Marie said.

I pulled out my phone and hit the speed dial. "Got it covered." The person picked up. "I need your help."

Chapter Fifteen

"THE IMMACULATA? REALLY?" JELENA looked at me like I named the boat.

"I told you that when I got off the phone."

"I thought you were trying to be funny again."

"I don't have to try to be funny, I just am."

"Let me know when that happens next time. I keep missing it."

Marie stepped in. "Can you two stop?"

"Good luck with that," Adam said.

The Immaculata was a good sized sailboat about fifty feet long and thirteen feet wide. I know that's not the way to describe a boat, but I'm not a boat person. It looked to be all wood, mostly painted white, with the trim keeping its natural look. The marina smelled of money. The composite decking used on the floating dock was light colored to reduce heat absorption, the transition plates and cleats were all painted a bright white, and even the pylons had pretty white cones on them to keep seagulls off. The sunset was reflecting over the water and provided a spectacular view that I would have preferred to be enjoying somewhere with a beer. I huffed as we approached the boat. "Okay, let's get this over with."

"I thought you were a Navy Seal," Adam said.

"Hell no. Army Ranger. Parks, forests, countrysides. Throw me out of a plane, but don't put me in the water."

"Seriously, you are afraid of the water?" Marie prodded.

"I'm not afraid of the water. I'm a decent swimmer, but I have a healthy respect for anything that can kill me as many ways as the ocean can."

"Have you ever been on a boat?"

"Yes. The Staten Island Ferry."

"How do you live on an island and not go in the ocean?"

"The same way that if I lived in Egypt, I wouldn't wander into the middle of the Sahara Desert."

Adam snickered, and Jelena swatted him into silence. Being right up next to the boat made me feel a little better. It was lower than I expected, making it less intimidating.

Marie stepped up, grabbed the mooring lines, and pulled the boat closer to the dock. It bumped with a dull thunk that reverberated through the wooden planks beneath our feet. She stepped one foot on the boat so she was straddling the two points. The movements looked to be practiced.

"Climb aboard." Marie flourished one arm.

"I didn't take you for a sailor."

"What, in the extensive time we have known each other?"

I searched for a witty reply, but she continued before I could come up with anything.

"I grew up around boats. We used to go out on it almost every weekend during the summer."

"Huh." I don't know why it didn't fit into the image I had of her, but it didn't. Then a thought occurred to me that did. "No lecture on illegal searches?"

"The only one here who that rule applies to is me. For you, it's just criminal trespass and burglary. Which is why I am staying out here as a lookout. Plus, we're not trying to prosecute this guy. He's already in the morgue."

"What about fruit of the poisonous tree?"

I saw Marie's eyes narrow through the waning light.

"What? I read."

"Law books?"

"I need something to help me get to sleep."

"Do you also decode two soldiers speaking Mandarin Chinese over a static filled, triple scrambled, microwave transmission with a Drogan's decoder wheel?"

Her words tickled something in my memory but I couldn't put my finger on it. I just looked at her while scrunching my eyebrows.

Marie shook her head. "Forget it. But that's why I'm staying on the dock. You bring me the evidence and provide a corroborating witness statement."

Jelena pushed past and stepped lightly onto the boat. "If you two are done with the foreplay…" The rest of her sentence was in Spanish, so you will have to use your imagination.

I looked at my feet, partially so I wouldn't have to meet Marie's eyes, but mostly so I didn't fall in the water. Maybe it was the Manhattanite in me, but I kept thinking there should be a watch the gap sign. I got across without embarrassing myself too much. Adam bounded over with little effort. Showoff.

"Here. Step here on the gunwale." Marie pointed to the top of the edge of the boat. It didn't look like a gun or a whale, but I was showing my ignorance enough, so I didn't point it out. She held out her hand to help me and I took it, stepping where Adam had. I expected the boat to dip down, but it barely shifted under my weight. I wobbled a little before stepping down, disappointed at having to let Marie's hand go.

I looked around, trying to get accustomed to my environment. The steering wheel was mounted on a pedestal towards the back. Aft, I guess, based on my limited nautical knowledge from Star Trek. It was covered with dials and a large compass mounted on top. On either side of the domed compass were two built in drink holders. Maybe I should rethink this whole boating thing. Behind the steering wheel was a small, raised deck, where two cushions acted as seating options and, I assumed, flotation devices. A metal railing surrounded the back — sorry, aft — deck where two horseshoe shaped life preservers were attached on either side. The main mast, I knew at least that much, towered above me and was barely visible in the dimming light. I stepped behind the wheel and took my place as captain.

From my position, I could still see clearly over the rest of the boat. There were multiple hatches visible on top of the cabin. I had to admit; it was pretty cool looking. I turned to Marie. "You have the con number one."

"Aye, Captain."

I almost tripped at her response, and she gave me a little smile.

The door to the main cabin was locked, of course.

I was about to pick it, then asked Adam. "Did you want practice?"

I think he actually growled at me. A quick holy manipulation and the door opened. For a brief second, I considered the irony of a power supposedly provided by God, being used for breaking and entering. Putting the debate to the back of my mind, I opened the door.

For me, the outside of the boat looked fairly typical. It had a place to steer, places to sit and enjoy the water—if you liked that kind of thing. The inside, however, was anything but. As we filed in, I felt like I was walking into a cigar lounge. The only difference was, instead of deep plush chairs, there were well padded bench seats. A door just to my right opened into a bathroom. Not the kind you would find in an airplane. This one was fully appointed. Granted, it was a little cramped, but it had a full-sized toilet, sink and a small shower. Further in was the kitchen. Again, small, but with everything you needed, including a small oven and stove combo, microwave, and even a cappuccino machine.

"You've got to be kidding me," I blurted out.

"Right?" Jelena agreed. "This is nicer than my house."

"And bigger than my apartment."

"This reminds me of the tent in Harry Potter. Looks bigger inside," Adam said. Both Jelena and I looked at him and he blushed. Then he pushed past us and started searching. She and I shared a small chuckle and joined him in the effort. The boat had little nooks and crannies all over the place for storage, but most was the typical inventory you would find in a camper. Even the stove held pasta and other dry goods. I guess he did little baking in here. But no drug stash.

"I'm going to check the bedroom." I moved towards the back of the boat. The master suite sported a queen-sized bed, a small built-in dresser and a closet. After searching everywhere I could imagine, but coming up empty, I sat on the bed to think. This was not my area of expertise.

I pulled my phone out and video called Marie. After a few rings, she picked up.

"Did you get stuck in the head?"

"The what?"

"The bathroom."

"Oh, funny. No, I was looking for advice on stash places. I've run out of ideas."

"Check the V-berth."

"Can you speak English, please?"

Marie huffed. "The bedroom."

"That's where I am."

"Look in the hull… walls."

"The walls?"

"Yeah, there is usually space between the outer wall and the inner wall of the hull. Start pushing and pulling on the walls. Sometimes they're secured with Velcro. Fancy boats may have push release latches."

After a few minutes of pushing and pulling on anything I could find, a section of the wall clicked and swung outward. Inside was a small bag filled with pills and a 9mm Beretta.

"Got it!"

"Good. Get out here. I think there are people coming. This is a small dock and everyone probably knows everyone else's business."

"On our way."

I walked out of the V-Berth, which sounded very pornographic to me, and back into the main area.

"Found it," I said to no one. Then Jelena poked her head from behind the table laying prone on the bench. She quickly stood, Adam, following from his supine position.

"Nope, you were right. Nothing under there," Jelena said. "Oh good, you found it. Let's go." She stepped around the table and exited the boat.

I offered Adam a hand, and he took it. He was lighter than I expected as I hauled him up from the strange position he was in.

"Where did she think it was hiding? Under the table?"

"Uh, yeah." He followed Jelena outside.

I shrugged, following them, thinking it would have been easier to look from the other side of the table as I locked and pulled the cabin door shut. Pocketing the drug bag, I took Marie's hand as I prepared myself to hop back onto the dock. The group of people that she had mentioned was walking towards us. An image flashed through my head and I reacted immediately.

"Gun!"

I still had hold of Marie's hand, which I yanked as I dropped back down onto the boat deck, pulling her after me. Shots rang out, the muzzle flash lighting up the area briefly. Bullets tore through the hull, but we were covered by the raised aft deck. I hoped Adam was as quick to react, but I had a feeling he was better off than I was.

"We need to get off this boat. We're sitting ducks." Marie got up, pulled her service weapon, and crouched against the deck.

I followed suit, pushing up next to her and reached out for my gift. The deep shadows of nightfall crept back, allowing me to get a better view. The dock clarified around me and I saw Adam and Jelena on a boat across the way. He must have been doing the same since he looked directly at me and gave a thumbs up. I couldn't see any of our attackers from my position so I expanded my senses to include sounds and smells. I heard several distinct sets of footfalls. Five? No, Six. A picture developed in my mind of the team approaching. Walking down the wooden dock. Walking, not running, not stalking. I got an indifferent feeling from them, as though they were unconcerned with their own wellbeing.

They weren't at the Immaculata yet. I pointed at the side opposite the dock. "Over the side."

"What? We don't know where they are yet. We can't just run in any direction."

"I know where they are. Six people coming in from the west. Now move while we have time."

Marie looked at me, maybe trying to gauge my competence or my sanity. Whatever she decided, she followed my suggestion. She holstered her Glock and slipped quietly over the side, holding on to the rail. I followed her and we started shimmying towards the front of the boat.

I lifted myself up to get a view of our attackers. I could see them approaching, like a bizarre family preparing for a night on the water. Three men, two women, and one… my best description is a villain straight out of From Russia with Love. He towered over the rest of the group even without the leather top hat that sat upon his head. It was decorated by a skull entwined with roses and sitting in a pool of fire. He wore a black leather vest and black jeans, each decorated with a plethora of skulls.

I lowered myself. "The welcome wagon doesn't look very welcoming."

Marie shook her head. "Welcome wagon? What are you, a reject from the fifties? Who talks like that?"

"That was kind of harsh."

"Sorry, I get a little cranky following a group of civilians into an illegal search that turns into a gunfight."

I nodded. "Noted."

"So, what are we doing?"

I did a chin-up and checked on the small group approaching the back of the boat, then lowered myself back down. "I'm thinking."

"Oh, dear God." She let go of the railing with one hand and drew her pistol again.

"No." I said.

"No, what?"

"These people are doing this against their will. I don't want them hurt."

"I don't see anyone holding guns on them while they are shooting at us."

I sighed, then pulled the drug bag out of my pocket and handed it over. "Get this out of here so we can find out what the hell is going on."

She looked first at the bag, then into my eyes. "What are you going to do?"

"Cause a distraction."

"There are six people with guns."

"Yeah, I know. I told you, remember?"

"You are going to get yourself killed."

"Nah, piece of cake."

She looked at me, and for a second I thought she was going to say something. Instead, she took the bag, wrapped it around her pistol, and released her grip on the gunwale. She sank into the water, holding the package up in the air above her head. She gave me one last look. "Don't get killed."

She said it like a scolding, so naturally my response could only be. "Yes, mistress."

Her eyebrows pulled into a frown, but I thought I saw the beginnings of a smile before she focused on getting to the other dock. I wanted to watch her all the way there, but I didn't have the time. Psyching myself up for the attack, I pulled myself up onto the bow in one swift motion, took three small running steps and leaped into the small group of marionettes. In midair, Tub-thumping started playing in my head.

During combat training, your weapon became part of you. It's what keeps you alive, what allows you to do your job defending the nation. It's right there in the name, Armed Forces. You sleep with it, train with it, learn how to strip it down and put it back together blindfolded. What you don't do, ever, is drop it. These people were not trained. When they fell, their instincts said something else. Drop everything and stop your fall.

They were walking two-by-two thanks to the limited space on the dock. I hit the two in the rear, knocking them into the water. They dropped their guns as they tumbled over the side. I grabbed a lamppost before I followed them in and swung around it, centripetal forces redirecting me back onto the dock. I landed just behind the next two. One was attempting to see what just happened. I kicked the back of his knee and the man crumpled, falling backwards, arms flailing. I plucked the gun out of his hand with a little help from my gift, tossing it into the black water before shoving him after it. The woman next to him raised her pistol six inches from my head and pulled the trigger.

My gift kicked in reflexively, though it was almost not fast enough. I felt the bullet graze the side of my head, and a searing pain shot through me. I ignored it, grabbed her wrist and twisted violently before she could fire again, then smacked the pistol out of her hand. The hold I had on her was a painful one. I know because I've had it done to me. When I looked into the woman's eyes, I didn't see any pain. Her eyes were empty, as though she was sleepwalking. I half-heartedly pushed her into the water.

I turned and stared at the remaining two. Both had their weapons pointed at me; one a pistol, the other a sawed-off shotgun. Guess which one the Bond villain held? I was just going to put up my defenses and hope it held when my whole body convulsed with pain. I dropped to my knees, unable to stop the shaking that had overtaken me. Screams echoed in my head, and I unconsciously covered my ears to block out the sound. Pain, loss, misery. Not just for those in the present, but the future generations of descendants that would never be. I'd felt this pain before, but not to this extent. This was twice as strong as my normal reaction and it only happened when I killed…

I struggled to find the source behind me. The last few bubbles were rising from where the attack squad had fallen in. Where I'd pushed them in. I put my head down almost touching the dock panting through the pain. I raised my eyes in time to see the top-hatted character smile and elbow the woman next to him to get her attention. He nodded towards me. Apparently, my time was up. There was no way I could reach my gift through the haze of pain, and the wailing of the faceless multitudes crying out in anguish. They both lifted their guns.

A blur shot out of nowhere and solidified into Adam. He materialized right behind the two attackers, grabbing the back of both shirt collars and hauling them backwards. The woman flailed, falling on her back and dropping the gun, but the mad hatter kept his grip and squeezed off a round. Buckshot peppered the dock beside me, the lamppost, and one boat. Adam released the woman and used both hands to continue yanking the man backwards. The man smiled at me as he was dragged back and pumped another shell into the chamber.

I watched the scene, still unable to move though the agony as drowning victims slowly perished. I couldn't help Adam, nor them. Once again my inadequacy endangered everyone. The woman started getting to her feet as Adam pivoted, whipping the man around, trying to launch him in the other direction. He twisted, using the momentum to run along the back of one boat, defying gravity. Adam lost his grip, and the man landed back on the dock facing him, shotgun leveled. Adam blurred into a dodge as the blast rang out, taking the woman, who had finally regained her footing, full in the chest. She flew backwards onto the dock, dead.

Adam grabbed the shotgun, wrenching it sideways, and tried to pull it away, but the man kept his grip. I could feel Adam's shock as he looked from the gun to the man's smiling face.

"DOWN!"

He dropped, and bullets started flying. One took the attacker in the shoulder. He jerked backwards, grimacing. Adam took the opportunity of being low to sweep his leg out from under him. The big man dropped, then disappeared. Adam looked around for him, but Jelena was rushing over, dropping to my side.

"Chris, what is it? Where are you hurt?"

I shook my head and pointed to the water. "Drowning. Help them."

She didn't question, but moved to dive in.

Adam appeared next to her and put a hand on her shoulder. "I can find them faster."

She nodded. He handed her his gun and jumped into the water. The last woman that entered the water surfaced and Jelena helped to pull her sputtering back onto the dock. As she drew breath, my pain finally backed off a little. After a moment, Adam resurfaced and climbed up, shaking his head. "She was the only survivor."

"I don't understand," Jelena said. "With everything we've seen these people do, they can't swim to the surface."

Adam shook his head and wiped water out of his face. "I don't know. They looked surprised. Like maybe Uji released them and the shock caused them to drown."

Footsteps echoing on the wood planks drew our attention. Marie was running towards us, gun drawn.

I climbed to my feet as Jelena rushed over to help but I waved her away, barking, "I've got it."

The pain was still there, as were the echoes of the mourners. I could function if barely.

"Who was that last guy with all the skulls?" I asked.

Adam had water sluicing out of multiple pockets. His wet clothes clung to him. Through my mental fog, it surprised me how slim he was.

"I don't know but he wasn't your average puppet. I think he was a Converted, and a powerful one."

"Nothing we can do about him now." I said. "Let's go."

"What do we do with her?" Jelena asked, nodding at the dripping woman.

"We can't leave her here."

"Can you determine if she is still compromised?" I asked.

The half-drowned woman was on her hands and knees still coughing and sputtering. Then suddenly she wasn't. She snapped her head towards me, her hair spraying water. "I must admit you surprised me." The woman's lips were moving, but it was Uji's voice. "I didn't expect you to kill with such indifference. Your predecessor didn't have the stomach for it."

Anger swelled in me. "Let her go, Uji. You don't need her anymore."

"Don't be stupid, boy. Once they have dedicated themselves to me, they are mine forever. They live at my whim." Then her face drew into a ghastly smile before she sped off. Taking a few steps, she launched herself onto the Immaculata. Within seconds she was scaling the mast. In almost no time at all she was thirty feet in the air clinging to the top with one hand and one foot. The possessed woman looked down at our stunned party gaping up at her. "Next time Christian you will not be so fortunate," she yelled down. "You have as little effect on me as you do on this one's fate."

Uji launched the woman into the air then immediately fled her body. With my enhanced vision I could see her expression change at the apex. She screamed all the way down until she landed impaling herself on the cone topped pylon.

Chapter Sixteen

WE ARRIVED BACK AT the Covenant house without further incident. Well, unless you count Adam outright refusing to take his suit jacket off even long enough to wring it out. I think he had an MIB thing going.

As we walked back to the main house, I asked Adam, "Do you have a lab to test the drugs?"

"Lab yes. Lab tech, no."

"Then why do you have a lab?"

"We know a person. We call her in when we need her."

"I think it's time to call her in. Marie, do you have the drugs?"

"Yeah?"

I waited a heartbeat, thinking the implication in my question was self-evident. "Can you give it to him?"

"No."

"Why not?" I asked a little more heatedly than I intended. I was still pissed from the deaths at the dock.

"Because it's evidence. We have to maintain a chain of custody or it will not be admissible in court."

"Court? This has nothing to do with court!" Jelena broke in, gesturing wildly. "Why don't you wake up and open your eyes? Does this look like something the court can handle?"

"Jelena." I gave the international sign to ease up.

"And somehow I think these ass hats have enough lawyers to get away with whatever they want."

"Torres!"

She threw a hand up and stepped away, continuing her litany of berating statements.

"I am a special agent of the US government. I don't just go off and do what I want."

Jelena reengaged. "Yeah, the same rules that put me on the front lines. Had me kill who I was told to kill then tossed me away when I was injured with a fraction of the money I needed to support my family. Forcing me to take shady jobs…"

"No one forced you to take those jobs."

"Yeah, you're right. I could have taken a federal desk job and gotten fat like you."

"Enough!" I bellowed the veins distending in my neck.

"That's quite a team you have there," Marie said. "Does anybody follow orders?"

"Follow this," Jelena said and gave her a less than friendly gesture.

I stepped in front of the marine sniper, blocking out the source of her anger. We made eye contact. Her eyes dared me to say the wrong thing, say anything. I wanted to talk her down, but I knew there was nothing I could say that wouldn't set her off. Instead, I silently asked her to stand down. She held my gaze for a few seconds, then lowered her eyes and her face relaxed.

I closed my eyes for a second drawing the calm of the field to ease my mood a fraction then faced Marie. "You're right, it is quite a team, because that's the way we work. I don't ask them to follow my orders without question."

"But you're asking me to, as well as betray my sworn oath."

"No, I'm not. I'm asking you to look at the facts."

"Your facts?"

"Not mine. You connected the dots when you realized the lab had to be compromised at multiple levels. Is that who you want to trust with the one puzzle piece that might show us what is killing people?"

It was Marie's turn to hold my gaze. She pulled out the drugs, and I held out my hand. She didn't hand it over. Out of another pocket, she pulled out another Ziplock bag and transferred half into it. She resealed both and handed me the fresh one.

"Half for your lab. Half I will hold as evidence once we cut out the rot that's infecting the department."

I nodded and handed the bag to Adam.

"Call your lab tech. I hope he's good."

"She is." Adam's voice held an unmistakable sense of awe.

"Really." Jelena rolled her eyes and walked away.

Adam shook his head and walked away, pulling out his phone.

"What was that about?" I asked, turning to look at Marie, but not really expecting an answer.

Marie examined my aura intently. "You really are clueless."

"What? Jelena doesn't do lab work. Does she?"

"I'm going to put these in my car's evidence locker." She sighed walking away, leaving me alone.

It was my turn to shake my head. "Batman didn't have these problems."

The lab was very much what I expected based on all the navy crime shows and spin-offs I had recently become addicted to. The lab tech was another story. I'm not sure what I was expecting. Maybe someone out of Revenge of the Nerds, or a tall goth girl with pigtails and a sunny disposition. She was short, thin but not frail, and looked like she came off a retirement cruise ship, complete with the oversized bag.

"Who's the pretty boy?" She pointed at me with a slight nod.

Adam made the introductions to Mrs. Dorothy Summers.

I flashed a smile and extended my hand. "Nice to meet you."

"Doubt it, and I'm sorry I can't say the same."

"Excuse me?" I was so put off, her words didn't register.

"I'm also not a circus act, so how about you beat it so I can work?" She stepped away and started switching machines on.

"Dorothy, I…"

"Dr. Summers."

"Sorry, Dr. Summers."

"What are you sorry for? How about you run along and fetch me some tea?" She walked over to her bag and started rifling through it.

I was determined to win her over, and so wasn't dissuaded. She was all business, so I tried that approach. "Dr. Summers, we are looking to figure out—"

"I was told. Find the strange element in the drugs that is making people go berserk." She took my hand and placed a tea bag in it. I stared blankly at her, trying to understand where I went wrong.

Dorothy looked to Adam. "Is he always this dense?" To me she said, "you take it and dip it in boiling water. It will make pretty colors then bring me the water." She resumed getting the lab ready. "Drugs." She called out without looking up.

Adam tossed the bag to her, and I moved to intercept before it hit the side of her head. Her arm snaked out and snagged the bag out of the air.

"Hey, pretty boy, I know I didn't explain that you had to go boil the water first, but I assumed you could work that out by yourself."

I looked over at Adam, who was still standing in the doorway as though not daring to cross the threshold, smiling from ear to ear and even chuckling a little. As I passed, he said, "Isn't she awesome?"

"Oh yeah, like if Don Rickles and Rosanne Barr had a ninety-year-old love child."

"She's my Godmother."

"Of course she is."

I banged the full teapot onto the stove. I wrenched the knob too hard, passing the lighting stage and filling my nostrils with the smell of natural gas. Taking a deep, foul-smelling breath, I twisted the knob back until I heard the distinctive click, click, click. The flame whooshed to life, and I stretched trying to work out the pain that was radiating through my body since the car chase. I grabbed a mug from the cabinet and placed the tea bag in it, wrapping the string around the handle.

"I wouldn't have pegged you as a tea drinker."

Ima breezed in, her standard voluminous outfit fluttering around her.

"I'm not. This is for the ray of sunshine testing the drugs."

"Ah. I see you met Dotty. She takes some getting used to. I was referring, however, to the trick with the string." She went to the refrigerator and selected a peach yogurt, then grabbed a spoon and sat down at the long wooden table that looked like it came out of an old farmhouse.

I sat down across from her. "I had many elderly clients with my business. Most of them wanted a little company, so I would sit with them and have tea. I learned the trick from one firecracker of a woman who had an affinity for tea and teapots. She must have had over fifty decorating her apartment." I smiled at the memory. "We had some great discussions, her and I. She had a very distinctive view about many things. She told me once that she couldn't stand Newt Gingrich. I don't remember the specifics of why, but I do recall that whenever she wandered around bookstores, she would find his autobiography and turn them all around on the shelf so you couldn't read the title." I shook my head. "It was her own personal protest."

"She sounds nice," Ima said between spoonfuls.

"She was."

"Was?"

The pot started whistling. I got up and shut off the burner, then picked up the kettle, which let out a higher-pitched squeal as the water sloshed against the sides. I filled the cup as I thought back.

"She passed away suddenly a few years ago." I felt myself welling up and cleared my throat as I replaced the kettle. "Her daughter gave me one teapot from her collection. Told me she used to talk about me all the time. It's now in storage, along with everything else I own."

"I'm sorry. She sounds very special."

I nodded, not trusting my voice at that point. I'm not sure why recalling my old friend was affecting me now. Maybe it was the ritual combined with the memory. I looked up and found Ima studying me. She covered it by finishing her snack and cleaning up after herself.

"I was talking to Mr. Hager this morning."

"Oh yeah, about what?"

"All the Covenant heads keep in touch regularly. He asked if I was ready to kick you out yet."

"And?" I dunked the tea bag a few times to help the steeping process.

"I said almost."

I huffed in response.

"He said I could expect a revelation from you anytime now. Apparently, you shine right about the time people get fed up with you."

"Good to know." I said then rubbed the back of my neck trying to work out the stress that had taken up residence there.

"Is there something bothering you?"

Hell yes. The body count surrounding this so-called mission was climbing, all innocent bystanders. I may have connected with my gift, but I might as well have been fishing with dynamite. I didn't know shit about running an investigation; I was just trying to connect one guess with another. To top it all off every part of my body ached from the damage I supposedly never took or had already healed from. Whatever I thought I'd accomplished back in New York was obviously just a fluke. To put it in one sentence, I didn't think I could do this job.

"No, everything is wonderful." I got up and went to the cabinet.

"Are you limping?"

I silently cursed the healed bullet wound in my calf given to me by the now dead soccer mom getaway driver. "Old war wound. Sometimes it gives me trouble."

I searched the cabinets and found a small Pyrex dish.

"What is that for?"

"Some people feel that being handed tea with a tea bag still in it is an insult, others would rather leave the bag in there while they drink. Based on Mrs. Summers' responses to normal conversation, I don't want to take a chance on choosing poorly."

"Good plan."

"Maybe. We'll see."

If it goes like everything else has been going, probably not.

Chapter Seventeen

"You could have told me she was a grandma."
Jelena was on the attack again as I passed her and Adam coming back from the lab. I'm not sure if my tea bag theory was any good. Dorothy was focused on her task at hand and didn't look up when she told me to drop it and get out. Guess I have more work to do to win her over. Challenge accepted.

"Why?" Adam didn't sound as confused as he was playing.

"What do you mean, why? So I didn't make an ass of myself."

"You think that would've helped?"

Her eyes looked like they could have shot lasers, and after a moment or two of trying to melt his brain, she stalked off.

"What is with you two?"

Adam shrugged but could not hide his devious smile. "What's the plan?"

"Plan? I honestly don't know what to do at this point. I'm just hoping that Dr. Summers can find something."

"Like what?"

"Something that points to where they are manufacturing it."

"Where's Marie?"

"She went home to get some sleep, shower and change. I need to work off some adrenaline. Where's your gym?"

"You know that dilapidated building on the far side of the complex?"

"Seriously?"

"Okay, let me get changed and I'll meet you there. You up for a little sparring?"

The grin returned. "I could use a workout. Meet me at the back of the church."

It was the first time I had seen Adam in something other than a suit, and it was a little disconcerting. He'd chosen a loose-fitting martial arts Gi, presumably to keep his movements unrestricted. I thought he was going to bring me through the back door, but instead led me downstairs into the basement. In the corner was a rickety old cabinet marked 'Danger, Flammable'. Adam opened it. Inside were several gallons of leftover paint, as well as spray cans, and thinners.

"Are we doing some tagging first?" I asked only semi sarcastically.

He smiled and pushed one shelf. The entire inside of the cabinet opened backwards and slid to the side out of the way. Behind was a lit tunnel.

"A little low tech, no?"

"You're chipped, right?"

It has been a while since being in an environment where the chip embedded in my forearm was needed. So, it took me a second to realize what Adam was referring to. "Yeah."

"If you weren't, the shelves wouldn't have budged unless I overrode the system."

"Eve?" I asked, assuming it was the same virtual assistant that the New York Covenant used.

"Marianismo."

"How can I help, Adalina?" The disembodied voice asked.

I looked at Adam. He had closed his eyes and gave a small sigh. Based on my limited experience, it was the equivalent of Jelena going on a tirade. "Who is Adalina?"

"Me. My mother wanted a girl." He regained control of his facial muscles and motioned to the tunnel. I felt there was more to it, but let it go. In the very slim chance that he wanted to discuss it further, I would let him introduce the conversation.

Instead, I focused on a different question. "Why the stealth way into the building?"

"Abandoned buildings are a draw for urban explorers. We needed to make sure no one could get in from the outside."

"And usable buildings get inspected."

"Exactly."

The underground tunnel continued on for about fifty feet, then curved sharply, ending in a door. This was the type I expected, more akin to a vault with a biometric lock. Adam unlocked it and the thunking sound of metal retracting rang out and the door swung open. The first few rooms on either side of the hallway were the typical changing rooms, showers, latrines. The double doors at the end didn't open on a stadium like in New York, more like a large gymnasium. An empty gym.

"Uh, did you get robbed?"

Adam smiled. "Marianismo, obstacle course level three."

The response was immediate. Partition walls rose out of the floor, creating rooms and corridors with multiple levels.

"Nice." I didn't need to fake my enthusiasm.

"We don't have the space that you guys have up north, though I can't figure out how you managed that."

I held up my hands. "It was there before I got there."

I walked up admiring the technology. I rubbed my hands over the walls. They weren't solid but were instead made from 4x4 metal pylons. The entire floor was a grid of squares. I walked into the first room, which was lit by a soft glow coming from various points. I looked up.

"How did it make the ceiling?" I answered my own question with some more analysis. Half inch metal sides of the pillars had been lifted via piston and interconnected to form a mesh like floor for the second level. "Very cool."

"The system can simulate almost any kind of structure." Adam sounded proud, as though he had designed it. "Ready to try it out?"

"Hell, yeah."

"Mari, set timer." Adam pointed at the base of the doorway. "Laser sensors will register when you enter. The exit has a similar setup that will pick the completion of the course. The time between them will be your course time. Questions?"

"Nope."

With a flourish and a grin, he said, "Whenever you're ready."

I got the feeling there was something he wasn't telling me. I ignored the feeling and set myself to run the course. I reached out for my gift, let it fill me, felt the tingling sensation over my skin almost like when sensation returns to the body after a lack of circulation, but without the accompanying pain. It was the difference between hearing a scratchy early recording of music and sitting in a concert hall listening to a philharmonic orchestra. I sank down into high running stance. I bobbed up and down a few times, warming up my muscles and working through the residual pain, then shot forward through the door, just a touch of Soul Glow added to the movement. I kind of liked that phrase.

I knew where the other door was from my initial review of the surroundings. At least I thought I did. The doorway had moved, Adam trying to trip me up. Apparently, that's what the grin was for. Apparently, he underestimated my prowess as a Bishop. I adjusted quickly and aimed myself at the door, adding a little more speed. The next room had varying obstacles, requiring me to either duck or leap. Each room provided a unique challenge. One even had swinging bags the origin of which I couldn't fathom. The last door appeared in front of me, and I put on more speed. Two feet from the finish line, something hit me from the side with enough force to send me flying. I picked myself up and made it through the exit.

Adam was on the other side, his smile wider than before. "A few surprises in there?"

I grunted. "A few."

"Again?"

I nodded. The second time through, I managed better even though the course was different; including when the surprise heavy bag came out. My time improved.

"What level is this again?"

"Three."

"Out of how many?"

"Twenty."

"Damn."

"Spar?"

I nodded. "Let's do it."

"Would you like to spar?" Mari's voice asked.

"Yes," Adam replied.

The obstacle course withdrew back into the floor and was replaced by a fifteen-by-fifteen mat, also made up of small squares. We removed our shoes and entered the ring. We faced each other, bowed, then slid into a fighting stance.

Mari said, "Begin."

Adam immediately began moving. Not towards me, just moving, I would almost call it dancing. As I tried to figure out what he was doing, he spun around, his hands brushing the floor, and he kicked me in the face. I went down hard.

"I'm sorry. Were you not ready?"

In answer, I sprung back to my feet then dropped to the floor, trying to sweep his legs. Adam hopped over my leg before going back into his dance. I anticipated his next spinning kick and evaded it. He followed it up with another, and another, and another. I narrowly avoided each one. But just as I was going to counter what I assumed was going to be a fifth kick, he changed tactics. His fists were just as fast as his feet, and I felt myself on the defensive again. An opening finally came, and I took it, driving in with my own attacks, punching and kicking. We went back and forth like that a few times, then I took advantage of a gap in his defense and scored a palm strike to the chest. Adam staggered back a pace or two, smiled, then came back in for more.

Twenty minutes later, we were dripping with sweat and panting. We had each scored about an equal number of hits, though neither of us was keeping score. This wasn't about who was better, it was about getting out of our heads and killing time. There is nothing that will distract you more than someone trying to beat the crap out of you. It leaves no room for worry, concern, or second guessing. You focus on the task at hand or you get hit. My pain had waned somewhat. It was still there but not as acute.

"I could watch you beat the crap out of each other all day, but Dorothy finished her tests." Jelena stood just inside the doorway, leaning back against the wall. I didn't know how long she had been standing there.

"Okay," I managed between gulps of air. I held my hand out to Adam, whose turn it was to lie flat on the mat. He took it and I helped him up, not that he really needed it.

"How did you find us?"

"Adam showed me this place before."

Jelena was the only person ever to be chipped who was not a Bishop.

"Let's go find out what's going on," Adam said.

"Not so fast." Jelena held up a hand. "When Dorothy heard what you two were doing, she made me promise to get you to shower first."

"We don't have time for that," I said.

"She said, and I quote 'Only way I want to smell a sweaty man is if I was the one that made him that way.' So I guess you can either shower or…" Jelena left the rest unsaid.

"Okay then. Shower it is."

"It's about time." Dorothy was as pleasant as ever. I was the last to arrive at the lab. We were all in attendance, except Marie, who was still back at her apartment. Even Ima showed up. "You're not that big. What took so long? Never mind, I don't want to know."

I closed my mouth. For what might be the first time in my life, I thought keeping quiet was my best option.

"Be nice, Dorothy," Ima's voice made me think this was something she said often.

"I was. What I wanted to say was—"

"Okay, we get it."

"I wanted to hear the diss," Jelena said.

Dorothy looked like she was going to let loose, but a look from Ima silenced her. "Fine."

"What did you find?" Adam pulled us back.

She started packing away her things. "Blood."

"I'm sorry what?" I asked. "And what, no preamble? No description of how you got there?"

"You want useless dialog explaining scientific principles, watch any crime scene investigation show. If forty years of this work has taught me anything, it's get to the point."

"Anything else special about it?" Adam pressed.

"Nope. It's Ecstasy, pure and simple. Not even a large dose." She thought some more. "I take that back. One other thing was strange." We all looked at her, waiting for the other shoe to drop, waiting for all this to make sense. "It wasn't every pill. In fact, it was only about a quarter based on the sample I took."

"Is it possible the chemist cut themselves while making the product?" I asked.

Dorothy shrugged, picking up her bag and heading for the door. "That's your job to find out. I'm just telling you what I found. I ran a DNA sequencing, so if you find a suspect, I can try to match her."

"Her?" Adam asked.

Dorothy picked up her bag, stopped in front of him and patted him on the cheek. "Yup." She headed for the door.

"Anything else you can tell us?"

"I'm not friggin Ancestry," she called back.

Chapter Eighteen

W E SAT IN THE conference room adjacent to Ima's office hashing out possibilities. The pills sat in the middle of the table. We weren't getting very far.

"Blood in a quarter of the pills, I said again. It had become like a mantra hoping that one time it would make more sense. "That seems like too much for a person cutting themselves."

"Agreed." Ima leaned on the table while standing. "Plus, odds are whoever was pressing the pills would be wearing gloves."

I nodded. "That makes sense."

Jelena was balancing her chair on the back two legs. "So not an accident. They were putting blood in the pills on purpose? That's disgusting."

I rubbed my cheek stubble like Indiana Jones. "But not in all of them. Why not in all of them?"

"To give them good product to test?" Jelena offered.

"Yeah. I like that." It started to click. "Now they are not having to falsify documents which could get noticed by other lab techs. They just need to make sure they test the right pills."

"How would they do that?" Adam asked.

"Oh, dear Lord."

We all turned to look at Ima who had gone ashen.

"What is it?" Adam asked.

Ima didn't speak. Instead, she left the conference room, and went into her office. She returned moments later with a device in her hand.

Adam practically recoiled from it. "Oh shit."

"What?" Jelena and I said in unison.

Ima pulled the bag of pills close to her, slipped a pair of blue tinted glasses on and held the device over them. Nothing seemed to happen.

"Well?" Adam's voice was tense.

Ima removed the glasses slowly and nodded.

Adam kicked a chair and it slid across the room. I had never seen him react like that.

"Can someone clue me in?" I asked.

Ima handed over the glasses. I put them on. Light streamed out from whatever Ima was holding. It bathed the bag of pills in an eerie glow causing several of them to take on an iridescent sheen.

"Great. You figured out how they identified the pills." I took off the glasses and passed them out to Jelena.

"Not great," Adam was still fuming.

"Weird," Jelena said. "What kind of light is that thing giving off?"

"A very specific variation of ultraviolet light. We created it to help identify the blood of a Bishop."

Both Jelena and I stared dumbfounded at Ima. I dropped into a chair and spun around putting my head in my hands. This was getting crazy fast. Scrubbing my face I looked up again. I was facing opposite the table looking out into the hall. On the opposite wall sat the wall of fallen Bishops. Without Jelena blocking it I could see the most recent picture. It was a woman. The name below said "Kristina Kipling."

The voice echoed in my head from the night in the warehouse. If you move again without my permission, I will feed you to Krissi.

I dragged Adam out of the conference room and back down the halls to the dormitories. Jelena followed, slinging alternating questions and insults.

"Is her room still here?" If this was anything like the New York Covenant, they had more than enough rooms to support the small number of Bishops actually in residence.

"Whose?"

"Krissi's."

"Yes. Why?" Adam stumbled. I let go and faced him.

"I have a theory, but I need more data."

"So, you need to see her room for that?"

"It will sound a little crazy without backup. You'll just have to trust me." He searched my face for a hint of what I was thinking. Or maybe he read my mind. His eyes widened, and he took off, grabbing my arm this time.

We came up to a door and Adam stopped short. I wanted to reach for it, but I knew this was something he had to do. He came back from wherever he was and looked over at me. "I need to tell you something before we go in."

I was in a rush but I could tell this was important, so I took a breath. "Okay."

Adam didn't speak right away and seemed to be struggling for words. Jelena stepped up and took his hand. He looked at her and smiled which solved another mystery. If this was what he was going to tell me, it could wait. I was about to say so when he finally got it out.

"I was assigned female at birth."

My mouth hung open. I closed it with effort.

"I wasn't consulted on that decision, but about a year ago I stopped identifying with it."

I struggled for what to say but nothing was coming to mind. In the silence Adam opened the door and walked in.

The decor was spaghetti western meets the Care Bears. There were movie posters featuring John Wayne, Gary Cooper, and Sharon Stone. The last was an ad for The Quick and the Dead and hung prominently above her bed. Splayed across her comforter were several stuffed animals including a Laugh-a-Lot bear. On a table to one side sat a pitcher and basin like you would find in the late eighteen hundreds. A peg over it held a holster and gun. I examined it, a real Colt 45 Peacemaker.

On the table next to the pitcher was a photo. I picked it up and recognized Kristina from her memorial. She was standing arm in arm with a woman who had long, black, curly hair. She looked familiar. Then I realized it was Adam. I replaced the photo now understanding why he chose that time to confide in me. Around the room were numerous other pictures showing how often the two of them were together. They looked to be inseparable.

Jelena walked in behind us and looked around like she was inside a shrine. She gazed about with reverence, reaching out a hand once in a while but not touching anything. Her hand went to her mouth several times, and her eyes shimmered with tears. She was seeing what I was: losing someone from your life that was more than just a friend or family member. There is sadness and pain in those losses, to be sure. But losing a person so close to you leaves a hole that can never be filled. It's a constant ache that may wane to a twinge or surge to a pulsing torrent, but never dissipates. Allowing us into this room was a poignant act of trust.

Adam looked around shell shocked, shoulders hunched, as though the weight of memories around him were too much to bear. He didn't look at any of the pictures but stared at the poster over the bed.

"I used to call her Ellen, Sharon Stone's character. Especially when she did something particularly badass." A tear slid down his cheek and he brushed it away violently. "She used to say that Ellen wished she were as cool as her."

He walked into the bathroom and came out with a round hairbrush wrapped with hair and thrust it out to me.

I took it carefully by the handle, not for fear of somehow damaging it, but afraid of doing anything that would push Adam over into the abyss of grief. "Call your Godmother."

I hovered outside the door to the lab. I had suggested Adam and Jelena go spend some time with Enric to get their mind off of things. Dorothy shuffled from station to station focused on her task. I was hoping she wouldn't notice me.

"Are you going to linger in the doorway, pretty boy, or are you coming in?"

"Is that allowed?"

"Didn't I just say so?"

I moved in slowly expecting a trap.

"My Godson thinks highly of you."

"How did you determine that? He barely speaks."

"That's how. He may not be a chatty Cathy, but he is only that quiet when he is around someone he is trying to impress."

"I think that may be Jelena."

"No, he's impressing her in other ways."

"You figured that out already? I've been with them for several days and I just put the pieces together about an hour ago."

"I'm not surprised. You don't seem too swift when it comes to personal interaction."

I shook my head and sat on one of the stools.

"I'm very fond of Adam. Try not to get him killed."

"Me?"

She looked up from her work. "There is a dangerous feel about you."

"Trust me. I'm not dangerous."

"That's not what I said." Her eyes narrowed and I got a chill. "Occasionally a non-firstborn direct Bishop descendant develops a hint of something supernatural."

"A hint?"

Dorothy nodded. "It's where psychics come from–the real ones that is. And there are other practitioners. Reikis, yogis, wicken."

"Seriously?"

"Do I look like a comedian to you?"

"Sorry. It's just that no one has ever mentioned this before."

"Based on what Imaculada tells me, you barely understand more than the typical third year acolyte. Why would anyone cover this?"

"Fine. What's your point."

"I feel auras."

"Okay."

"Listen kid. I have been around this," she waved a hand, "for a long time. I have met more of your kind than I can count. You all have a power emanating from you. Some more than others. But I have never felt one as portent as yours. It's like you are being followed by a lightning storm." She looked back down to her work. "Just make sure you don't get anyone caught up in it. Especially Adam."

I thought about what she said. Thought back to everything that has happened over the past few months and the people I was pulling into my orbit. "Great. Something else to worry about."

"Sorry, pretty boy. I call them like I see them. I'm not here to blow sunshine up your ass."

"No shit."

"Well, here's something else to brighten your day." The printer whirred and Dorothy grabbed the paper and pushed it in front of me. "It's a match."

Chapter Nineteen

IMA DIDN'T BALK. DIDN'T ask for clarification. She crossed her arms and looked deep in thought. "Then it's true."

"You knew?" Adam looked shocked.

She looked up at him. "I suspected."

"And you didn't tell me?"

"And let you go off half-cocked and start tearing buildings down?"

"What made you believe she was not dead?" I interjected, trying to keep everyone on task.

"I felt her."

My eyebrows knitted into one.

"It's one of my gifts."

"I thought you could only feel someone if they were close to you. Like in the same building," Adam's voice held anger, and hurt.

"You can understand my confusion when I started feeling whispers of her all over the city."

"We need to find her," Adam sounded desperate, Jelena put a comforting hand on his tricep.

"We will. Now that we have evidence that she is alive, and it's not just my sanity in question, but Adam, you understand what this means."

Adam nodded. Jelena looked from him to his mother. Neither looked inclined to elaborate, so she looked at me. I sighed deeply, not wanting to put it into words. "Well?"

I met her gaze. "It means she's been turned."

"What the hell does that mean? She's a vampire now?"

I shook my head. "You've heard me talk about the Converted?"

"Yeah?" She said it like 'get to the point.'

"They get their enhancements from drinking the blood of a person who has betrayed their vows."

"What vows?"

"Any vows." Ima jumped in. "The stronger the vow, the more power obtained."

"If you cheat on your taxes a little," I continued, "they may get a more refined pallet. But if you get someone who has cheated on their spouse, or betrayed the vows against God…" I let the thought hang there.

"And the more recent the betrayal, the more power can be gained," Adam concluded.

"What?" Jelena put her fists on her hips, "if I want superpowers I just drink the blood of a pendejo?"

"No," Ima's voice was grim. "First, you must give yourself over to the Tainted. We don't know exactly what that involves."

"How do you know anything?" Jelena asked.

Ima paused. "We were able to reclaim some who were converted." Ima's tone held a level of emotion it usually lacked. "They didn't remember much, and what they did they… found difficult to discuss."

The silence that followed filled the room like the stench of death. It didn't take long before I needed to break it. "What happened to Kristina?"

It took a moment for Adam to answer, "She died."

"Apparently not." It was hard to keep the sarcasm out of my voice.

"No," Adam insisted. "I watched her die."

"We watched her die," Ima corrected.

I looked from one to the other, then to Jelena, who shrugged. "How is that possible?"

The two shook their heads. It was Adam that finally spoke, "She fell through a rift."

My eyes narrowed. "A what?"

"A rift."

"What the hell is a rift?"

"You know a tear."

I waited, but they thought that was explanation enough. "A tear in what? The space-time continuum? Should I stay away from aquatic themed dances?"

"The veil."

I nodded. "Okay, not DeLoreans, more leprechauns and banshees."

"There are no such things as fairies." Adam waved a hand as though pushing the thought aside.

"Are you sure? Six months ago, I didn't believe in demons, and I had never even heard of the Tainted."

"We are fairly certain." Ima didn't sound as convincing as she might have once been. I got the feeling that her truths were being shaken as of late.

"What veil? Then the veil between what and what?" Jelena asked.

"The Seraphic veil between the mortal realm and the Divine," Adam answered.

"That doesn't sound so bad." I mean how bad can the Divine be, right?

"Let me ask you, Chris, what is the key difference between anyone on this side of the veil and those on the other?"

I considered for a moment. "Life."

Adam nodded.

"You said Divine. Wouldn't that be Heaven? If so, wouldn't she be protected from the Tainted?"

Ima shook her head. "You are buying into the idea that Heaven and Hell are two different planes."

"They're not?"

"Well, we cannot be sure, of course, but no. We believe they are two sides of the same plane."

"How is that possible? Wouldn't they cancel each other out?"

"The way fire and ice do?" Ima offered. Her voice told me she was about to make her point.

"Yeah, exactly."

"They both coexist on this plane, along with good and evil."

I thought about that and didn't like what I was coming up with. "Tearing through the veil, you couldn't know if you were walking into Heaven or Hell." As I talked it out, I made other connections.

"Maybe they're influenced by what is on this side. Not physical location." I rubbed the stubble just under my bottom lip. "Possibly the people. The group emotions, values, and focus of large numbers of people."

I asked Ima. "What do the tomes say?"

"About the veil? Very little, as far as I know."

"As far as you know?"

"I haven't read every book."

"You must have researched it after she disappeared into the rift. Right?"

Ima's eyes became hard. "She didn't disappear, she died."

"Apparently not."

"No mortal being can live on the other side of the veil."

"How do you know?"

"The same way I know no mortal can live underwater. It is a place not meant for us."

"Wrong."

Ima blinked at me, shock plain on her face.

"Your knowledge of what happens when a person tries to breathe water comes from countless generations witnessing what happens when a person drowns. You are making an assumption based on worthless information. Like when people believed the world was flat." I was getting a lot of mileage from this argument.

"Some people still believe the world is flat," Adam added.

I nodded. "Throughout history there have been those who ignored facts because of fear. Fear of what the truth might mean to their way of life, fear of change, or just fear their views may no longer be relevant. It becomes dangerous when those people are the ones in power."

"Are you calling me a Flat-Earther?" Ima looked down her nose at me.

"No, I'm saying that you allowed your personal biases to color your view."

"Now I'm biased?"

"Those things we believe absolute in life will direct the conclusions we come up with. Your understanding of the world said people can't live on the other side of the veil, but now we have empirical evidence to the contrary."

"What evidence?"

"Krissi's not dead."

Chapter Twenty

I WAS BACK WHERE I was most at home, the library. Well, it may be a tie with Citi Field. This didn't have the same feel as the multi-level version in the New York Covenant. But not being locked into a small island, things stretched out instead of up. The few comfortable armchairs up north were replaced with long rectangular tables surrounded by seats covered in light colored fabric. This setup was more conducive for me, anyway. I sat in the middle seat, surrounded by piles of books. Some were open, some stacked to one side, discarded due to lack of information.

The process was frustrating. The filing system was a database of all the indexes of every book they had. I searched on 'rift', 'veil', 'portal', 'fissure', 'gateway' and any other synonyms that thesaurus dot com could come up with. The resulting mountain of books all had tangential references to the veil between us and the angelic world. A few mentioned rifts that occurred naturally or were opened on the other side. None even considered the possibility of one being opened from this side.

I slammed another book closed and it echoed through the open area before being swallowed by the rows of books. "Why the hell wasn't all of this digitized?" I rolled my shoulders and stretched my back. The pain from all my injuries had returned.

"We don't have a librarian," Adam said from across the table, while quietly turning the page. He read for another moment or two, then flipped the page back, a quizzical look on his face. He shook his head and closed the book, setting it in the discard pile. "We have many jobs that need to be done with very few people. We take turns helping keep the library up, but I'm afraid there is not enough time to dedicate to digitizing all of this." He made a dramatic sweep with his hand pointing out the many rows of shelves and the hundreds if not thousands of books.

"What about hiring someone not affiliated with the Covenant?" Even as the words escaped my lips, I knew the impossibility of the task. A librarian or a curator would have to have extensive knowledge of the subject. How else could they hope to be of any help? In doing so, they would be given access to all the knowledge and secrets the Bishops have collected since, if the texts are to be believed, the beginning of recorded history. "Never mind."

Adam nodded. Whether he was acknowledging my grasp of the issue, or agreeing as to the stupidity of the question, I wasn't sure.

I tilted my head towards him. "I guess you haven't found anything either."

"No. Though I have to be honest, I'm not sure what we are looking for."

I had been a little vague in my explanation, to keep him from discounting information based on my restrictions.

"I'm trying to understand the whole concept of the veil."

Adam closed the book he had just opened. "The veil is not a concept."

"Sure it is. There is no scientific proof of its existence. Or pick any other description. Theory, hypothesis, supposition, abstraction."

Adam looked at me askance. "Chris, the point is, it can't be proven. It is an element of faith."

"How does that help us?"

"Any element of faith is available to all. You need only believe." Adam spoke it like an axiom.

"That's great, but it doesn't answer any of my questions. What is the veil made of? How does a rift come into existence? Are they naturally occurring, or can they be manipulated? How do we even know about them? Has anyone encountered them? If so, where, when? And what was occurring during that time?"

Adam quirked his head. "For a person who derives his gifts through his connection with a higher power, you focus a lot on the scientific method."

"Hey, something works for me, I stick with it."

I was still at the beginning of my journey into faith. I had gotten over the hurdle of connecting with it and as a byproduct with my powers. But acknowledging the existence of something and giving yourself over are two different things. Picking up the next book on the pile, I checked my reference pages and flipped to the section.

I followed the Tainted at a discrete distance, keeping to the rooftops knowing if he led me to his lair, we may get a better idea of his plan. He continued west on East 32nd street crossing 3rd Avenue. In the distance loomed the monolithic structure being constructed in the middle of the city. It had been eight months since they had broken ground and already it towered over the surrounding buildings. The sight always drew my interest, and I nearly missed my quarry turning into a side alley.

I found a spot out of view of pedestrians and dropped into the street. Quickly making my way to where I had lost sight of him, I entered the alley. I let my senses guide me so as not to stumble into a situation I was ill prepared for. I have no delusions of my prowess. A face-to-face encounter with one such as the Jackal would mean my demise.

When I opened myself to my surroundings, I felt almost physically struck with the level of power emanating from up ahead. I expected to see a bright glow, as though from something acutely radioactive. Never in all my years have I ever felt such raw power. I approached with obvious caution, creeping like a cat burglar around the detritus strewn about the alley.

Finally, I caught sight of the source. The Jackal

stood in front of a rip in reality. That is the only way I can describe what I saw. It wasn't a door with squared off sides, nor was it a portal rounded or ovoid. The sides looked frayed, and it appeared to be pried open by some invisible force. The tear fought against the restraints, reverberating as though trying to contract and heal itself.

A faint red glow emanated from the other side of the tear. I felt a foreboding though from where it derived, I know not. But it filled me with such dread I was fearful I might soil my britches.

The Tainted walked through the rip and disappeared into the other realm. I steeled my resolve and forced my legs to pursue him. Creeping towards the rift in the fabric of reality, I expected to smell brimstone and sulfur, but neither were present. Intermixed with the red glow was a darkness that I struggle to describe. Even now, hours after the encounter, I sit at my desk sweating; my hands shaking so as to make it hard to hold my pen. A fight to write legibly enough for others' eyes. That darkness writhed and churned. I could feel it trying to escape the boundaries of the realm that contained it.

I moved in closer, trying to discern what lay beyond. Without warning, the bonds holding open the tear released, and the hole wove itself back together. The view into the other realm was gone, as was the tear itself. With my naked eyes, I saw only the bricks and mortar of the seedy building. With my enhanced senses, I could see the outline of the tear. It looked like a wound. If I could touch it, I would have sworn it would feel warm, as though infected. I examined the area for several hours after trying to glean what I could, which was very little with my current knowledge. I must research this phenomenon further.

Looking up from my reading, I said, "I think I found something. It's not much, but it does more than just reference the idea. This one actually describes it."

"Which book?"

I closed it, my finger holding my place and rotated the spine to Adam.

"It's a copy."

"A what?"

"It's from another Covenant. When someone finds something of note, they make an extra effort to distribute the finding to other Covens."

"It looks like this might be the start of a larger endeavor." I tilted my head slightly as one does when speaking to a disembodied voice. "Marianismo, are there any other books by—" I checked the spine. "—Alrick Williams?"

"*The only book by that author is the one you are currently reading.*"

"Any additional volumes are probably back at his Covenant. If resources were light, the chances are copies were never sent out."

I considered that for a moment. "How do I find out where it's from?"

"Check the author page in the beginning."

It read:

Alrick Williams
1930
Manhattan, New York

"Now that is a stroke of luck." I pulled out my phone and double tapped the back to bring up the virtual assistant. "Call Bossman."

As it rang, Adam asked, "Luck or Divine intervention?"

I rolled my eyes and the line connected.

"What mess have you gotten yourself into now, Mr. Bateleur?"

Chapter Twenty-One

I APPROACHED MARIE'S DOOR, lifted my fist to knock, and it hovered there. I didn't know what was stopping me. Well, maybe it was the fact that I was not invited. She told me where her apartment was when she left but she didn't say 'hey, stop over anytime.'

I took two steps before I halted again. Stop being stupid. You're not dropping by for a booty call. No, but will she see that as my intention? For the past hour, I've been... what? Worried? Uneasy? Maybe it's my Bishop's sense tingling.

"Yeah, that's a thing."

I spun around but didn't move towards the door. "What can she say? How about 'Get away from me, you freak!' Why would she say that? Well, you are a freak. But at least I'm not talking to myself."

I wanted to move, but my feet were stuck. This is ridiculous. It's just a door. I made the few steps, lifted my fist again and almost did it. I cursed and went to turn around again when the door opened.

Marie stood in the doorway. "I was going to wait for you to knock, but I couldn't watch the show anymore."

"You were watching?"

She lifted her phone, which showed a profile shot of her with me in the peripheral. With her other hand she tapped what I thought was the peephole, but was apparently a camera.

"Well, luckily, this isn't awkward or anything."

Marie hooked a thumb backward. "Are you going to come in or were you trying to get in your steps for the day?"

"Um, sure." *I sounded like an idiot.*

She walked back inside, holding the door open for me to follow.

I caught sight of the door camera as I entered. *And I must have looked like one too.*

Her apartment wasn't large, but it was well furnished. A small section off to one side was made into a dining area by a multi-use table with a bench on one side and chairs on all others. The couch with matching chairs looked welcoming and I imagined them to be comfortable. Hanging on the wall in front of the red couch was a fifty-five-inch TV framed by shelving units stocked full with DVD's and Blu Rays. The genres ranged from chick flicks, to sci-fi, to old black and white movies.

I walked up to the display like I was approaching an altar. "Whoa." I said the awe clear in my voice.

"You like?"

I could only nod in response, and I think my mouth was hanging open. "How many do you have?"

"Two hundred forty-six total."

The number immediately connected with me, and my head snapped in her direction. Her smile said everything.

"Are you sure?"

She nodded once. "Eighty-two, eighty-two, eighty-two. Two hundred forty-six total."

I stared at her dumbfounded. She presented it straight on. Here it is, you will either get it or not. My heartbeat sped up.

"I don't have the heart to buy anymore. Now, any I want I purchase digitally."

I almost asked her to marry me right there.

"So, What's up?" Marie asked.

"Up?"

"You stopped by for a reason I assume."

What did bring me here? Throughout my whole internal debate in the hallway, I hadn't even come up with an excuse to be here. "We've got a break in the case."

She scrunched her face. "Okay, Crockett, what did you find out?"

"Blood."

"Blood? What the hell does that mean?"

Yeah idiot, what can you tell her that won't give away everything?

"It's the bloody pills."

"Why are you talking in an English accent? And a bad one at that."

"What are you talking about? It's good."

"Sure, if you were trying to imitate Dick Van Dyke."

I gasped dramatically. "Take that back."

"Will you get to the point? What did you find?"

"Fine, I will tell you, but you will need some background first."

"Like?"

"I'm a superhero."

"I would give you points for originality, but you've basically stolen from any number of comic books."

"I'm not making this up. Wait, you read comic books?"

"Enough to know when I'm being bullshitted."

"I'm serious."

"Okay, go get me coffee before the banana hits the floor."

"First, I'm not the Flash."

"No, just a watered-down version."

"Okay then, how do you explain what happened in Josh's apartment?"

Marie crossed her arms. "Vest."

"The car chase?"

"Stupidity and dumb luck."

"The interrogation room?"

"Now that guy had superpowers, but they were drug induced." Her phone chimed. She looked at it and shook her head. "Great, probably Jehovah's Witnesses." She plopped the phone on the coffee table and walked towards the door. The doorbell app was still open and I could see the small group of people who were approaching the door. They walked almost trance-like towards the door with blank expressions.

"Stop!" I yelled as her hand touched the doorknob. I slipped into a blur, grabbed her, and pulled her to the floor just as the shotgun blast tore through the door. The barrage of bullets ripped the door and wall to pieces. I reinforced my skin and picked up Marie, shielding her while we dove behind the couch.

I was on top of her again. She stared at me, shock clear on her face. "You good?"

She nodded, then pulled a pistol from a hidden compartment in a small side table.

"No, these people are not in control of their actions." I ducked reflexively as bullets made stuffing and feathers fly as they pummeled the cushions.

"I really don't give a shit. It took me months to decide on this couch. For that alone, they deserve to be shot."

As the shooting died down, I leapt over the couch and crashed through the bullet ridden door like a battering ram. The force ripped it from its hinges, plowing into one of the three attackers. That should have caused enough of a surprise to allow me to disarm them. But puppets don't get surprised. They staggered back from the impact, but quickly aimed their weapons. Bullets pounded me, pain flaring up with each strike. The only thing working to my advantage was that my stampede had taken out the woman with the shotgun.

"Chris, get down!"

I didn't. Marie would take them out without hesitation. I covered my face with one arm. Having never been shot in the face before, I wasn't eager to test my defenses in that area. I put on some extra speed and dipped down into a spinning leg sweep, taking them both down. Three moves later, they were both unconscious. Marie came running up behind me.

"Are you hurt?"

I stretched, trying to work out the pain from the bullets. "Nope, all good."

She spun me to face her and lifted my shirt up, exposing my bare chest.

"Hey!"

"How is that possible? They were shooting you point blank." She ran her hand over my abdomen and my breath caught in my throat.

I forced myself to ignore her touch. "I already told you."

She gaped at me. "You were serious." Her attention went to the three people on the floor. "Chris, who are they? No one knows where I live. Special agents' residences are kept strictly confidential."

"Your department knew."

"No, I refuse to believe that." She turned away.

"Let's debate it later. Right now, we are getting out of here."

"You think there are more coming?"

"Would you send just one squad?"

Marie met my gaze for a moment, then headed back into the apartment. I thought she was going for the fire escape, figuring, as I was, both the stairs and elevator would be covered until she turned towards the bedroom.

"What are you doing?"

"I need a few things."

"I can buy you new stuff."

"Thanks, but no thanks."

I followed her as she grabbed a backpack and threw into it a laptop, pistol, knife, a few clothes, and undergarments. I tried not to look at the last. She slung it onto her back and headed to the fire escape in the living room. On the way, she picked her cell phone up off the floor. I was about to tell her to leave it when she shoved it in the still-open compartment that had held her alternate weapon and closed it.

Marie went to the window, threw it open and put one foot on the sill. We heard the distinct sound of the elevator. We both looked backwards, then at each other.

"Go, go, go."

She scrambled out the window.

"Not down, up."

"Are you nuts? We'll be trapped."

"Trust me."

She gave me a dubious look, then headed up the ladder. I followed, closing the window.

We climbed quickly, the metallic clang of our footfalls echoing much louder than I would have liked. If it were possible to deaden sound with my gift, I had no idea how. My leg screamed with every step, the rest of me was just blanketed with pain. We reached the roof and hopped down. It was a small area that someone had tried to make cozy but didn't look like an official gathering area.

"Okay genius, where to now?" She did a Vanna White impression, presenting the space with no visible exit.

Without preamble, I boosted my strength and scooped her up. Her arms flailed. "You are not going to like the next part."

"Chris, what the hell? Put me down!"

I took off running towards the other side of the small area, picking up speed. She realized immediately what I was planning. "No! Don't be stupid, you'll never make it. Chris stop! STOP!"

Marie punched me again. It was the sixth time she had done so, but it had been several minutes since the last blow. The surprise almost made me steer the car into a lamppost.

"I said I was sorry."

She put an elbow on the passenger door and rested her head on her fist. "Not good enough."

"Giving me a dead arm will fix it?"

She glanced at me sidelong. "No, but it makes me feel better."

I took one hand off the wheel to rub my shoulder.

"Aw, did I hurt the poor superhero?" Marie cooed as though talking to a toddler.

"I have feelings, you know."

"Me too. And they didn't enjoy sailing over rooftops." She punctuated her sentence with another blow that she put her whole body into.

"Ow. Quit it. You're going to make us crash."

She settled down into a brooding silence that made me wish for her punches again. I rolled my shoulder without trying to make it obvious. Damn, she hit hard.

"Where are we going?" she said eventually.

"The Covenant house."

"Sounds like a bad charity name."

"No argument here. We have empty rooms where you can stay for now."

She was silent for a bit.

"Chris?"

I took my eyes off the road.

"Thanks." She indicated backwards with her head.

I nodded, then forced myself to look back at the road. Then she changed my music.

Chapter Twenty-Two

"So, when I said tell Marie as little as possible, you assumed I meant tell her everything and ask her to move in." Ima folded her arms in front of her as we talked in the hallway.

"What should I have told her?"

"Anything but the truth."

"That's a very convenient non-answer."

"Secrecy is key to our existence. The more people that know about us the more likely the Tainted will find us as well."

"And you already have a contact in the DEA, so another one is superfluous."

"What makes you say that?"

"You got me released when I was detained, eventually."

"You're welcome."

"Marie was also strong-armed into working with us. The first, you could have accomplished with a high enough up politician, but the other would take someone actually in the DEA."

Ima was finally silent.

"That's what I thought. I don't mind being rebuked when I do something legitimately wrong, but how about you save me the lecture when I'm breaking a rule you already broke?" I walked away.

I found Marie in her temporary apartment conveniently located next to mine.

"Settling in?"

"No. The bed feels like a medieval torture device and the sheets might as well be sandpaper. There is no TV, so I have no idea how I'm going to get to sleep, and the decorative motif is early Quaker."

"But other than that, it's nice right?"

She rolled her eyes and sat on the bed.

"Chris, what is going on? I mean really. Read me in. I'm not going to just go happily along for the ride."

I told her everything. Or at least as much as I was told or had read on my own. She asked questions incessantly, diving deep into areas that she didn't fully understand. The whole time, she fingered the crucifix that dangled on a thin gold chain. The conversation shifted to my parents, and that I got my powers from my mother. That she was the head of the New York Covenant and had left me a stack of letters.

"You haven't read them all?"

I shook my head. "Only a couple."

"Why not?"

I shrugged.

"That's bullshit."

"Hey are you hungry?"

"I'm past the point."

I check my watch. "Do you like empanadas?"

"Chris!"

"Hey Norma."

"Where have you been?"

"Busy. The place you suggested was perfect."

"I can see that." Norma crossed her arms and scrutinized Marie as I introduced them. "You like empanadas?"

"No. I love them. I used to eat them all the time back home. There was a little place on 68th street. Ba Ba's."

Norma's face lit up. "That is my sister's place! You grew up in Brooklyn?"

Marie nodded, smiling, and I swiveled so quickly I nearly snapped my neck.

"You have a sister?" I asked.

Norma nodded.

"What's her name? Barbara?" I asked.

"No, Grace."

"Of course it is."

"Sit, sit! I will show you why she has the second-best empanadas."

We sat and she hurried into the back, yelling at the kitchen staff in her combination of languages.

"Brooklyn?"

"You didn't know?"

I shook my head.

"I had you pegged from day one. Why are all the cute ones so dense?"

I tried to think of a suitable response, but Rudolph the Red-Nosed Reindeer was screaming in my head. I'm cute, I'm cute! She thinks I'm cute!

We pulled into the Covenant Compound, got out and made our way to the dormitory.

"Feel like a nightcap?" Marie asked.

I looked over at her, but she didn't look back. Almost like she was shy about asking, but I knew that couldn't be the case.

"Sure. How about we take them into the back by the pond?"

She hesitated for a fraction of a second. Or maybe I imagined it. "Okay."

We went to the kitchen, and I fixed orange-tinis for both of us instead of my usual scotch. Seemed like the thing to do, but that was just me guessing. I went all out, even pre-chilling the martini glasses with ice. I poured the extra that didn't fit into an insulated container in case either of us needed a top off, put it all on a tray, and we made our way outside.

We walked in silence to the bench overlooking the pond. Sitting, I handed her the drink and put the tray aside. We clinked glasses and each took a sip. They were pretty good. I was heavy on the vodka and light on the triple sec, which made for a potent mix. It had the right amount of bite with a smooth citrus finish. I might get to like this.

We sat quietly for a few minutes looking out over the pond. The crickets were calling out to each other, creating a nice background score for the view.

"Thanks for dinner."

"Thanks for coming. With me. Thanks for going with me." Wow, could I play the bumbling idiot or what?

"Norma is something else."

"And a half. She was the first person who made me feel welcome here. Went out of her way to do so."

"You bring that out of people."

"Yeah, right."

"You really don't see it, do you?"

I looked over at her to find her staring at me as if trying to divulge some secret.

"What?"

"People are drawn to you. They follow you almost without even realizing they're doing it."

I looked back out over the lake, making a sound like a horse. I took another sip.

"I have never met someone so influential and so oblivious."

"Well, you have it half right." I said after I swallowed.

Out of my periphery, I saw her return her gaze to the lake and take a sip. "How long have you been doing this?"

"About four months."

Marie laughed. "No, seriously."

When she met my glance, I raised my eyebrows.

She sat up straighter. "Wait really?"

I nodded.

"How is that possible?"

I gave her the highlights of my experiences from the beginning of the holiday season.

"Holy shit!"

"Quite literally."

"No wonder you are out of your depth. At the beginning, I thought this Maxwell Smart vibe was an act."

I put on my best nasal infused accent. "Would you believe he is my father?"

"No."

"Uncle?"

She shook her head.

"How about a reclusive neighbor that spent too much time with my mother?"

"Oh Max," she said in the breathy, scolding way that ninety-nine always used.

We both stared at each other until we fell into a fit of laughter, nearly spilling our drinks. It lasted long enough that my stomach muscles hurt, and we had to struggle for air. Her laugh did something to me, like what I expect to feel looking out over the Grand Canyon or down at the earth from space. It gave me peace and got my heart racing at the same time. It was a sound I felt I could listen to forever without it ever getting old.

Marie amazed me, confounded me, made me doubt everything and somehow feel like I had all the answers. She was strong in every sense of the word and wore a confident air like a cloak. So sure of herself, but still able to open the door to the possibility of what the Bishops represented. I found myself staring at her without realizing it. I don't know how long I sat entranced. When I finally realized what I was doing, my smile faded. I became self-conscious and pulled back, feeling like I had overstepped.

"Oh no you don't."

Marie grabbed the back of my head and pulled me towards her. We kissed. I didn't realize that's what we were doing until already engaged. At first, it was forceful, as though neither of us wanted to let up for fear of breaking the connection. Then our lips softened, melting into one another. Our arms encircled each other. The drinks fell forgotten to the grass. We held each other as though clinging to life itself.

Our kisses became more passionate, hands entwining into hair and exploring further. My one hand was at her waist and slipped up just under her shirt, touching the skin of her back. A soft moan escaped her lips and I pulled back.

"Is this okay?" I asked, no longer sure of myself. Maybe I had gone too far.

She looked me in the eye and nodded with a smile that held passion and promise. Then she pulled my ear close to her mouth and whispered. "Speak again and I will shoot you."

Then she bit my ear.

"You really need to get new sheets." Marie's head was on my shoulder, and she traced a short fingernail around my chest.

"What is wrong with these?"

"Are you kidding? They are scratchy, old, and pilly."

"Pilly?"

"You know, when the fabric forms little lint balls."

"You're a princess."

"What?"

"You know, the princess and the pea."

Marie smacked me in the stomach, and I grunted and laughed. Her hand hovered around my side. "What is this?"

I craned my neck to see what she was talking about. "Oh that. I got shot."

Marie propped herself up on an elbow and looked down at me with her interrogation face.

"When was this?"

"While I was in the army."

"Does it hurt?"

"It did at the time."

"I mean now, you idiot."

"No. It was just a flesh wound. I got lucky. Mostly I forget it's there."

"It's a nice scar. I can't see how you would forget it's there. Can you tell me how it happened, or is it classified?"

"Ha. You make me sound way more interesting than I am. Yeah, I can tell you. We were on patrol in Kandahar…"

"Are you building suspense?"

I didn't reply. My brain had kicked into high gear based on

something Marie said. What was it? What was it connecting to?

"Chris?"

I went back through what she said in my mind, found it again, and sat bolt upright.

"What is it?" Marie's voice held an edge of concern.

"That's it!" I kissed her, then jumped out of bed. "Come on."

I started grabbing my clothes, then looked back at her, still lying there.

"Are you coming or what?"

"Just taking a minute to enjoy the view."

Chapter Twenty-Three

I GOT OUT OF the car and stretched. I could still feel every phantom injury. The pain seemed to ebb and flow at odd times. Maybe if I had the time and energy to focus on it, I might figure it out. I just didn't see that happening anytime soon. Adam was staring up at the top of the building where Kristina died. I envisioned him seeing the past. Which version was the real question. I had a feeling it was the version where he blamed himself. We are all Monday morning quarterbacks of our own lives. Imagining what we should have said to the rude guy in the store. Kicking ourselves for not pulling over and helping the victim of an accident that you barely avoided. Or maybe it's just me and everyone else is content with everything they have ever said and done.

"Hindsight is twenty-twenty," I offered as consolation.

Adam looked at me over the roof of the car. "What?"

"You know… hindsight." I nodded up at the building.

"I was just trying to decide what side we should scale."

"Uh, right. How about we use the elevator?"

"Are you sure you're a Bishop?"

"Confucius said never climb a mountain if stairs are available."

"No, he didn't, and that is insensitive towards Chinese heritage."

"But it's okay to make fun of the Mets."

"The Mets are not a religion."

I took on a shocked look. "Heresy!"

"What did you do to piss off Marie?"

I looked back at him, concerned I missed something again.

"I ask because she's not here," he clarified.

I sighed, visibly relieved. "She has a contact further up the chain in the DEA that she wanted to vet."

"She trusts him?"

I nodded. "Old friend of the family. She is looking for a way to clean house when this is all over."

"You think that's possible?"

I shrugged. "Either way, I will not be the one to tell her otherwise."

"There may be hope for you yet."

I gave him a dubious look.

"If you two hens are done gossiping, I'm in place." Jelena said through the earbud.

Adam shook his head and started towards the building. It was nothing out of the ordinary, a typical twelve-story office building. Getting past security and into the elevator was a non-issue thanks to Adam's Jedi powers, of which I was still extremely jealous. The rooftop was adorned with shrubbery and a few plants, someone's inadequate attempt to make this urban setting more in tune with nature. Several seating areas, as well as metal, circular tables with attached benches, were staggered around bolted to the rooftop.

"Are they afraid someone will steal the benches from on top of the roof?" I joked.

"I would assume it is more an attempt to keep them from becoming missiles in the next tropical storm."

"Well, that makes more sense, but it's not as funny."

"This way."

Adam guided me around the corner to a gated area. It was padlocked, but easy enough for me to get around. It was Adam's turn to be jealous. He pointed to an area at the edge of the rooftop facing a taller building across an alley. The corner of the other building was painted with an ad for a furniture store a few doors down. We walked to the three-foot wall at the edge of the roof.

"This is it."

"Here? Are you sure?"

"Trust me. You never forget where your best friend sacrifices herself to save you."

I watched Adam for a few seconds. He looked hard, harder than I had seen him before. I could tell when a person was steeling themselves for an emotional difficulty, having been there enough times myself to recognize the signs. I left him to it and stepped up to the wall, gazing out over the alley into the nothingness where Krissi had supposedly disappeared into another realm.

"Can you tell me now why we're here?"

"I was shot."

"And?"

"It left a scar."

"I figured that out by myself, but what does it have to do with the rift?"

"It reminded me of the way Alrick described the rift that he saw. He called them a wound to the natural world. I figured that if there was once a wound, then it may leave a scar."

"Great, so how do we see the scar?"

I shrugged. "Faith?"

Adam looked at me askance. "Saying that as a question defeats the whole concept."

I nodded. He was right, of course. I had a few tricks down, but my faith was nebulous at best. I made a connection while battling the two demons back in New York, tapping into my well of power. It had been more instinct than conscious effort. If I was going to find the scar I believed existed on top of this roof, I would need to be able to through deliberate action.

I closed my eyes and found the calm meadow beside the lake. Although it was the first step in every use of my gift, it was not something I usually had to think about. However, whenever I tried something new, this was the place to start. I found the place in my head. Felt the breeze on my face, heard the rustle of the grass as it swayed, saw the ripples on the glassy, still surface of the lake. The phantom pain pushed itself to the forefront and I struggled to focus my thoughts on my objective. To see what is hidden, to unmask reality and reveal what is underneath.

With the scene etched in my brain and my directive clear, I opened my eyes and saw... nothing. Nothing had changed. I faced the same brick building as before. I sighed and looked at Adam, but it wasn't Adam. The visage of a wiry man was replaced by one that looked more like Adonis. His aura had a faint glow, as though he were backlit. The sudden change startled me and I took a step back. The Greek godlike image cocked his head slightly in confusion the way Adam did.

"You good?" The voice was definitely Adam's.

I was about to answer when the rest of my surroundings came to my attention. The rest of the building looked to be a scene from a post-apocalyptic movie. Everything was in the same place, but it looked like we had flashed forward a few decades. I unconsciously checked my watch, which told me I was still in the present. The rest of the building looked also decayed. No, more than decayed, diseased. The tan brick I had seen was a dark gray, the surface cracked and crumbling in places. It leaned precariously, casting deep shadows that gave me a feeling of hidden lurking creatures awaiting their prey to wander too close. Eerily absent was any plant life, as if nothing could live attached to the rotted surface.

I looked past what was right in front of me towards other buildings. Many had changed, some for the worse, like the building where I stood. Others shone as though the sun reflected on their polished surfaces. Plants blossomed and life buzzed around the latter. Most fell somewhere in the middle, sections of a single building having both dark and light areas. It was a dizzying view of the city. Whether from its extreme dichotomy or just the fact that I stood on the worst site in view, my stomach lurched.

I closed my eyes, shaking my head to try to clear it, and leaned on my knees.

"Chris, everything alright?" Adam stepped up and put a hand on my shoulder. The contact grounded me and everything settled.

"Yeah, thanks." I opened my eyes again. The visions were gone.

"What happened?"

I explained what I had seen. He stood in silence long enough that I looked over at him to see if he was still there. "What?" I probed.

"What you're describing sounds eerily like the descriptions I've read about true sight. It's very rare, only a handful of Bishops in history had the power."

"Great."

"Of them, the most famous is—"

"Please don't say it."

"Why?"

"Sore subject."

Adam shrugged.

"I'm gonna try again. Keep an eye out if I look like I'm going to lose my balance. I don't feel like tumbling over the side of the building."

I took a few deep breaths and closed my eyes again. My gift came quicker this time. I thought about what I had done last time and its results. Although I had unlocked something, it would be a while before I could master it so it was not overwhelming. I needed a different approach.

When I hit a dead end, I start from the beginning again rather than trying to navigate around the obstacle in my way. I was trying to find a portal that had been ripped into the world. No, that wasn't right. I was trying to find the scar that was once a wound. Maybe instead of trying to see what wasn't there, I could use the same method I used when trying to heal.

I focused on making the world my patient, but connection wasn't forming. When I had healed someone, I had a direct connection with the person. I went down to my knees and immediately felt Adam's hand on my shoulder. I gave him a thumbs up, not wanting to break my concentration with words. Laying my hands on the roof, I tried to ignore the visions of what this place looked like through true sight. The concrete felt rough. The individual components of sand and granite were clearly visible to my senses. I delved deeper, pushing through to the street and expanding outwards. A sense of the area was forming, the good and the bad. Trees, wildlife burrowing into it, both insect and mammal, biped and quadruped alike, and the pollution they all left behind.

I pulled back again. While interesting, this was not helping me. Start again. A wound, a scar on the world. No, not the world. Well, not the physical one, anyway. The scar was on the veil. The separation between planes of existence. I refocused on that image in my head, pictured a shimmering wall like that of an aquarium tank. A separation of two realms. A curtain between the players and the audience. I held my hand up to engage with it and felt its gossamer touch. As though made from a combination of finely spun webs, dandelion spores, and goose down. Delicate as the first layer of ice over a pond, but hard as diamonds.

I opened my eyes. It was almost as disorientating as true sight. Replacing the myriad of images was a fine mist blurring what was around me. It shifted, becoming denser in places and thinner in others. After a few moments, my eyes finally focused. What I'd imagined as mist was really an infinite number of translucent, shimmering curtains surrounding me in all directions.

I twisted my body around, careful not to make myself dizzy again by going too fast. They danced around me. I could see them all at once, some running parallel to me, some perpendicular even bisecting me. Vast numbers aligning to every degree on the compass. More since they began at every point and radiated out in every direction.

"You still good?" Adam's voice echoed through the layers of veils surrounding me, coming from everywhere at once. It was as if my vision was affecting sound in our plane. I looked to where I expected him to be and focused. Veils dissipated in that direction, and he materialized out of nothing.

"Yeah. I think I'm tuned to the right channel now."

"Right channel?"

"Yeah. It's almost like a TV. The channel you're on defines what you see."

"What do you see now?"

"I'm surrounded by a multitude of veils. It's kind of like looking at one of those 3D art pieces with the hidden picture in it."

"Sounds dizzying."

I nodded then wished I hadn't. Thinking more about the idiom of the 3D art gave me an idea. I focused on the place where the portal was supposed to be. I tried to focus on that particular veil, the thin line between realities at the exact spot Adam had pointed out. It ran parallel to the exterior wall. This was like finding a single piece of paper in a three-foot stack. I didn't know what specifically I was looking for but thought I would recognize it when I saw it.

Figuring I would need to go one at a time, I focused on the thin ribbon separating dimensions and examined it. I felt a hum; a vibration that carried a tone so subtle I might not have noticed it. I went to the next veil and the tone changed in frequency almost imperceptibly. Finding nothing, tried the next. Again, and again, and again. A new tone accompanied each veil and I set into a rhythm, like when I was prepping plumbing pieces to use for a job. I went faster as I became more comfortable with the process; quickly progressing from one at a time to speeding through them like an animated flip book. The hum sounded like a harp being strummed. I came on my target so fast I would have passed it if not for the translucent quality of each layer.

"I see it."

"Seriously?" It was obvious that although Adam had come along for the ride, he hadn't expected this branch of the investigation to bear fruit.

I peeled back each layer carefully, not sure how I would tell the actual one from its cousins. It was like looking at a drawing through several sheets of tracing paper. When I finally reached it, there was no doubt in my mind that I had found what I was looking for.

"Got it!" Alrick had described it as a wound, and I didn't disagree. The scar was there, though not like I had imagined.

"What does it look like?"

"Picture the Mona Lisa being ripped from top to bottom and fixed with spiderwebs."

Adam made a sound that matched my disgust. "Okay, so now what?"

That was a damn good question. I reached out to touch it, but it was as ephemeral as a ghost. Okay, the usual stuff isn't working.

"I can see it, but I can't touch it."

"Of course not. Your physical body cannot affect the astral plane."

"Thanks, captain obvious. How about helping with a suggestion?"

"I thought I did."

I considered his words. "You want me to touch it with my

astral form?"

"It is the most logical next step."

"And how would I go about doing that?"

"You haven't astral projected?"

"I must have been absent that day. Alright, I guess we'll pack it in until I have time to figure that out."

"Seriously?"

"You keep using that word."

Adam sighed. It sounded too much like Hager. "What I mean is, you just discovered that you have true sight, which is a wonder in itself. Then you bumbled your way into not only seeing the actual veil between worlds, but navigating it. And what has you flummoxed is the ability that every new Bishop learns in his first year?"

"Did you just use flummoxed in a sentence? What's next? Will you tell me I will rue the day?"

"I can help you if you're done deflecting your sense of inadequacy with humor."

I thought about repeating his sentence back to him in a mocking tone but thought better of it. Instead I said, "Thank you. I would appreciate your help." It was a lie. I enjoy learning, but I don't like being taught. Most teachers in my experience go way too slow and I lose interest. I would much rather read a book or watch a YouTube video at high speed. However, I had just tunneled through the core of the earth to reach a pond I couldn't cross because I hadn't learned to swim. I could walk all the way back and read a book or suck it up and learn from the swimming teacher right next to me.

"When you are in your personal oasis, do you picture yourself there?"

I thought about it. "Sometimes it's like I'm playing Gears of War, while others it feels like Call of Duty."

"I don't know what's worse; your examples, or that I understand them. Fine. The times when you can see yourself, the third person view as if you are a camera behind yourself, that is your astral form."

"Cool."

"Very. Although it's easier to project yourself in your oasis, it is not a far leap to projecting into the real world. It's a matter of layering your oasis over the here and now."

I tried that, focusing on the field and the pond and slipped back there, losing the veil completely. A wave of panic washed over me, thinking I lost the other channel and would have to go through all the searching again. But I found having reached there once it wasn't as difficult to go back. So, I tried to overlap the field with the view in front of me.

"I just keep jumping back and forth."

"Think of it as an augmented reality."

That was something I could connect with. I went back to the veil, then projected my image in front of me.

"Got it."

"Great."

"Now, how do I control it? I don't have a joystick."

"It's not an it. It's you. How do you control yourself?"

I moved my arm. My avatar moved his arm. "Oh, I get it. Hey, you're an excellent teacher."

"Thanks. Good teaching is not about the teacher or the student. It is about how the teacher relates to the student and communicates information in the language they can relate to."

"Weird."

"What's that?"

"Mansplaining is the last thing I expected from you."

"You're an ass."

Smiling, I refocused on my projection kneeling in front of me. Tuning back to the veil channel, I was finally facing the poorly healed wound. I stood, or he stood, or we both stood. I wasn't sure how to separate my astral self from my physical self. I had a clear image of toppling over into the alley below.

"Adam, despite me being an ass, you won't let me walk off the edge, right?"

Silence.

"Adam?"

Still silence.

"Adam!"

"Payback is a bitch, isn't it?"

"You're killing me."

"The fall isn't so bad, it's the sudden stop——"

"Can you just——"

"You're fine. If you are seeing your astral self, then any movement you make will be his alone."

"Okay, thanks."

"Although sleep walking syndrome has been known——"

"Dude, seriously."

"Sorry, couldn't help it."

I approached the tear. It hovered, its bottom level with the short wall and about a foot into the open air of the alley. I reached out my hand and brushed my fingers over the stitching—for lack of a better word—that sealed the opening. My hand sensed that it was hastily woven and lacked integrity. I pushed and it gave way, like trying to grab a cloud.

"I can feel it, but it moves when I try to grab it. It's like trying to grab a thread off a sheet hanging on a clothesline while wearing welding gloves."

"Don't use your form. Use your gift."

"How?"

"The same way you pick a lock."

I nodded, then realized Adam may not be able to see it. "Okay. Can you see me? My astral me?"

"Now I can. I had to engage my astral sense. I can see you, but not the veil. Right now you look like a mime."

"Great." I focused on the webbing, pulling at different parts as if I was finding a loose string in a knot. When that didn't work, I went harder, hoping to rip the stitches. "This is frustrating. It looks frail, but it's strong."

"What are you using?"

"What do you mean? I'm using my gift like you told me."

"Your gift isn't a single tool. It's a toolbox."

"What the hell does that mean?"

"How can I put this so you will understand? Oh, I've got it. Think Green Lantern. Shape your gift into the tool you need to do the job."

"We can do that?"

"Not to the extent you are probably thinking. But it will allow you to rip instead of pluck."

I grunted and considered Adam's suggestion. My gift didn't have a visible form. There was no green glowing shape that I could manipulate, just what my mind constructed. I didn't knowingly create tools to pick a lock. I felt through the lock and identified the parts that needed to be pushed. This would form an invisible force into a hook or a knife.

I focused again, creating the image in my mind of a hook. It formed for a second, then dissipated. It solidified a few times to a point where I could almost see it but disappeared when I tried to use it. The constant hum of the veil's harmonic resonance became like the emergency broadcast warning tone. The old annoying one, not the new one. After many bumbling attempts, I created a hook, looped it around one thread, and pulled. I felt rather than heard the satisfying snapping. I panted from the effort of getting it done.

"How's it going?"

"Slowly. One thread down, about a thousand to go. Trying to imagine a floating hook picking at the webbing is more than my attention span can handle."

"Why is it floating?"

"What do you mean?"

"Do you normally use floating tools while putting in a heating unit?"

"Well, no."

"Then why are you trying to do it now? The closer you mimic something familiar, the easier it will be. Picture the tool in your hand."

"Ooookay."

I held up my hand, or my avatar's hand. It was getting difficult to separate the two, and I hoped that was a good thing. Whatever, I'd deal with that later. Again, I created the form of the hook, which appeared much more easily. I reached out, wrapped the image around a few of the threads, and yanked. I felt resistance before the webbing snapped in half. The two sides separated where the stitching was cut and darkness showed through.

"Good God almighty. You did it. I can see a hole in the air." The awe was clear in Adam's voice.

"Yeah, that tool in the hand advice worked great. Let me get the rest."

"Before you do that, maybe you should make sure you can close it again. Now that I see it, I'm not sure if it's a good idea to leave a tear in the veil of reality just hanging there."

"Didn't Alrick say that it snapped shut by itself?"

"Is that something you want to test?"

"Good point. Any thoughts on how to do that?"

"Uh no."

"Great. Okay, let's think about this. If it looks like a wound, maybe it can be healed."

"Too bad we can only heal ourselves, not others."

I kept quiet, not wanting to start a conversation about something I could do that no one else could. Well, almost no one. Instead, I put my hand over the hole and let my gift flow in. The hole sealed itself.

"It's gone."

Gone was right. The small part I closed wasn't done so with another spidery patchwork of threads. The fabric of the veil wove itself back together as though it had never been cut.

"Huh."

"What?"

"Nothing."

"So, how did you do it?"

"I'll tell you later."

Adam appeared to want to argue, but let it go.

I sighed. "Okay, let's see where this hole goes." Instead of a hook, I formed a utility knife in my hand. A tool that was much more familiar and useful in this situation. It appeared quickly taking the form of the one that was back in my toolbox in New York, scuffs and all. In one swift move, I sliced through all the remaining threads and the hole opened.

"Holy shit!"

I stared through the portal into the realm of the Divine.

"That is an accurate description."

Chapter Twenty-Four

"**G**UYS, WHAT THE FUCK is that?" Jelena asked over the coms.

"Not much, just your typical inter-dimensional portal."

She continued to curse, but this time in Spanish. "For once, I'm glad I'm not with you."

There was no bright light, no shining city. No harps were playing and cherubs wrapped in white togas didn't flit around on tiny wings. There were no pits of fire either. No slithering, goo dripping, half man, half snake like visages. It did not perpetually rain ash among a gray landscape, and no one dragged around chains or was strapped to a torture rack.

This was another plane of existence where my eyes didn't function correctly. It was like trying to see underwater or through thin fabric. I got impressions of dark colors moving around, but I couldn't tell if they were beings or objects, and nothing seemed to notice me or the portal into my world.

But the feelings that poured forth from it were undeniable. If you've ever sat in a dark room as a child, staring out into the creepy void of the night, you can understand how I felt. The point of time where reality and fantasy mix. The logical part of your brain that says monsters don't exist shuts off, and you would swear with all your sanity that something out there was watching you. Deciding whether it was hungry enough and if your soul was tasty. You could almost hear it breathing, smell its rancid breath as it contemplated which part of you would be the best place to start its feast. That feeling was hammered into me now.

The hair on the back of my neck stood and I had to take a deep breath in order to not run screaming. This was Hell, and it wasn't a place. That scared me more than anything else. Because if Hell wasn't a place, then there was nothing to stop it from raining down on me.

I took a step away and looked back at Adam. He was standing next to my body, which was still kneeling on the rooftop. It caused me to feel light-headed and then things shifted.

"Woh, head rush."

"Don't look at your body."

I glanced away again. "Why not?" I had a hunch as my head cleared.

"If you're not experienced with astral projection, seeing yourself will throw off your whole equilibrium. The result is not pleasant and can last for a while."

"Yeah, I'm getting a little of that now and I only got a glimpse."

"That's nothing. Looking yourself in the eyes can cause you to vomit for hours."

"Got it."

Adam walked over to the rift, shivering when he got close, then peered in. "I can't believe you did it." He stared at the opening as one might at a hole in the universe. "I was half convinced that what I saw was placed in my head. But here it is, the same hole that swallowed Krissi."

I stuck my astral hand inside the portal. Well, more like a finger, then a hand. I was getting vibes akin to when Willie stuck her hand in the bug infested hole in the Temple of Doom. Like something was waiting on the other side to yank me into its world. I didn't know what the loss of an astral form would do to my physical self, but I wasn't in the mood to find out.

"Here goes nothing," I said as I stuck my astral head through the opening. My expectations ran from looking into the jaws of the demonic presence, to my head exploding like I was putting it in a microwave. Luckily, none of that happened. I wasn't imbued with any clarity either. What I got was a sense of disorientation. If you have ever hung out a window a few floors up and looked towards the sky instead of the ground, it was kind of like that. The awkwardness of your stance, along with staring into the vastness of the sky above, creates a vertigo like state.

"What are you doing?"

"Sticking my nose where it doesn't belong, as usual."

"Be careful. We know little about inter-dimensional gateways."

"So juggling chain saws is not recommended?"

"You know you're not funny, right?"

"You just don't get my humor."

"No one gets it."

I huffed in response, then tried to make sense of what I was seeing.

"I'm looking into the realm of the Divine." The awe in Adam's voice was pronounced.

"That's not all."

"What?"

"There's another one."

"Another what?"

"Another rift."

"What do you mean, another rift?"

"Really? That needs additional explanation? I can see a faint outline of a similar scar."

I opened myself up to seeing more veils. When the infinite layers appeared, the stain that showed a repaired rip in the veil became more refined. I started peeling them back as I had done before and found this one much faster.

"Like there's another one next to it?"

"No, like there's another one inside the first."

"How is that even possible?"

"I'm not even sure how the first one was possible."

"Where do you think it goes?"

"Only one way to find out." I flicked open my astral knife, wondering if it would disappear inside the other dimension, like a projector blocked by a guy in a tall hat.

"Is that a good idea?"

"Probably not." I reached into the Divine. The knife remained solid—well, as much as a thought projection can be—and with a flick of my wrist the second portal was open.

"Is that what I think it is?"

I took in my surroundings. "I don't know. Are you seeing a bathroom, too?" One side held a row of stalls, the other a row of sinks.

"I don't get it. Why the hell would there be another portal there?"

I thought about it. The gap between the two was minimal, maybe three feet. They were exactly aligned. "What if they were both open when Kristina went through?"

Adam looked from the portal to me, then back. "That's how she survived."

I nodded. "This was planned from the start."

"Not a plan to kill a Bishop at all."

"It was a kidnapping." All the pieces finally made sense. Though whether this super drug was really the end game or just a byproduct was still unclear.

"And that's where she is." Adam looked like he wanted to throw himself through the rift. I understood the feeling.

"Or at least, that's where she ended up." I corrected. Her final destination was still in question.

"I'm going." Adam stepped up onto the wall and prepared himself to leap through the portal. I reached out to grab him, but my lack of solidity was causing a problem.

"Adam, stop!"

"Forget it Chris. I failed her once. I won't do it a second time."

"Good, then start using your brain."

He didn't turn around, but neither did he jump into the abyss, so at least I had his attention.

"If Kristina is there, it's not some random public latrine. This is a building occupied possibly by one of the Tainted, some Converted, and a whole slew of henchmen. If you go barreling in there, you may reach her, but the chances of getting her out are almost nonexistent."

Adam cocked his head as he considered my words.

"We need to figure out where this is without letting on that we figured it out. Then we can make a recovery plan with a chance to succeed."

He still looked poised to leap to his death.

"While you're ruminating on my logic, consider also that it is only a matter of time before someone requires the facilities and notices a guy staring through a hole in the wall from an impossible location."

Adam dropped to the roof. "a slew of Henchmen?"

"It got my point across."

"Fine, what's the plan?"

"I do some reconnaissance with this form."

"Forget it. I'll take my chances with the henchmen."

"Why?"

"Because you have exactly five minutes' experience. Because most Bishops are limited to traveling little more than the room they're in. And finally, because I can almost guarantee that no one has tried to cast their projection through a rift, much less two."

"You are very negative."

I faced the portal again.

"Adam." Jelena's voice came over the coms. "Trust him."

He looked towards the general direction of where he knew her to be. "I can't. I can't lose this chance to find her."

"Listen, I've only worked with Chris a short time. But he is more capable than anyone I've ever met. The things he does seem stupid, but they work anyway. If he says he can do it, it's not misplaced ego. Maybe there is someone watching over him protecting him from his stupidity. Either way, the result is the same. His words become Gospel."

Her last words felt like a slap to me. Adam looked almost as gobsmacked. But apparently Jelena convinced him. "What do you need from me?"

"Watch the door and don't let anything through. Jelena watch his six."

She made the psht sound. "No shit."

Adam nodded, resigning himself. "How do you think you're going to manage this?"

I looked back at him. "By not thinking too much."
I dove through.

The journey through the looking glass had not been difficult. My quick passing may have minimized any ill effects that the Divine realm would have on my mental projection. I felt a moment of pressure as I passed through, like going through the keyhole to get past a locked door.

I found myself face down on the bathroom tiles, both disgusted and relieved that this was not my actual body. Although the phantom pain still had a hold on me.

"Can you still hear me?"

"Yeah, I've got you." This was something I was hoping for. Since Adam was really standing next to my physical body and my ghost like visage was tied to it, I theorized I could still hear him. So far, so good.

"You are not instilling me with a significant amount of confidence."

"Yeah, yeah, yeah."

"Did he fall on his face again?"

"Oh, yeah."

"Damn, I wish I could have seen that."

"Can you two cut the crap, please?"

"Cutting the crap, boss." Jelena's sarcasm came through clearly enough.

I stood up and dusted myself off. Actual dust puffed away as if I had been rolling around on a dry dirt floor. The unconscious self-actualization was an interesting discovery. I briefly wondered if little birds would flit around my head if I hit it. I checked my surroundings quickly to get my bearings and looked for the way out. "You're kidding right?"

"What?" Adam asked.

"The portal is in a mirror. I can see my reflection in the corners."

"So?"

"It's just a little cliché."

"Maybe there is a reason for that."

"Huh. I never thought of it that way."

"I thought we were in a rush," Jelena said. Apparently, she only joked with Adam.

"I'm going."

The mirror containing the portal hung on an outside corner adjacent to the small corridor that led to the exit. So, the portal was not immediately noticeable when someone walked in, but they had to walk past it to leave. I made my way to the door, attempted to grab the handle, and was met with as much success as one might think.

"How do I get out?"

"What is stopping you?" I forgot Adam couldn't see me anymore.

"A door."

"Just walk through it."

"I just face planted because of my inability to fly. Why would I be able to walk through walls?"

"Theoretically, you should be able to float through the ceiling, sink into the floor, and walk through anything or anyone. Unfortunately, with your lack of experience, you are limited to whatever your mind will allow you to do."

"Don't make a liar out of me," Jelena jibed.

I rubbed my hands together then reached out my hand to touch the metal of the door. It passed through it like a cheap visual effect. I took a few steps back and ran at the door. I flew through it, as well as through a woman in a lab coat on the other side, causing her to stumble as though she'd tripped over a ripple in the commercial carpeting. She frowned at the ground behind her before continuing on her way.

She was bespectacled, carried a folder and wore her hair in a bun. Under the unbuttoned lab coat, she wore a black skirt and light pink blouse. Her shoes were black with a small heel. Cute, but sensible. I decided that the fastest way to find out what was going on in this building was to follow her.

She walked with purpose, muttering slightly to herself. I followed. As I got further away from my body, the connection to my projected self deteriorated like on a road trip, when the radio station it took ten minutes to find fades. I relayed my feelings to Adam.

"As you get further out, your view will become clouded. It will become more difficult for you to see. It is important that you identify where you are before then. We can do additional reconnaissance when we know where to go."

"But if I find out if she is here, it will save time."

"If you reach your limit before figuring out where this place is, it will be a colossal waste of time. You don't even know if the woman you are following is part of this. She could be an accountant."

"You're very pessimistic. Plus, I haven't done my taxes yet and I'm going to need help with the whole Bishop thing."

"Chris."

"It's complex when you think about it. Am I an employee of the Covenant, or an independent contractor?"

"Chris."

"Can I claim my new Walther under business expenses? What about all the sneakers I'm going through, blurring all over the place?"

"Chris," Adam's voice was becoming more agitated.

"Oh, wait!"

"What? Did you find something?"

"As a religious organization, do we have a tax-exempt status?"

"Can you take this seriously?"

"Okay, sorry. But seriously though, are we tax exempt?"

"Where are you now?" The exasperation was obvious in his voice now. Hey, I had to get him back for the face plant B.S.

"We are getting in an elevator."

"You are what?"

I realized my mistake.

"Oh, shit," I said as I watched the doors close.

"Get out," Adam warned.

"I can't. It's too late." I felt my signal fading quickly. The cloudiness that Adam warned me of started creeping in, obscuring my view.

"You're a projection, a ghost. Just jump!"

The reality of the situation fought against the instincts my psyche had developed since birth. Don't touch a hot stove. Don't drive on the railroad tracks. Oh yeah, and don't jump off a moving elevator.

My vision was dwindling to nothing. I steeled myself for the pain and
leaped at the closed doors.

Chapter Twenty-Five

I DON'T KNOW HOW many floors I fell or even what kept me from falling through the floor. I came to a sudden stop on my hands and knees. A sharp pain pulsated through me though I'm not sure from where it was radiating. Probably just another connection of my mind assigned to expected situational reactions. Pain, after all, is something that is interpreted by the brain. This pain, luckily, didn't linger like the phantom injury pain.

I stood up and looked around. The other floor bustled with activity: people talking on phones, copy machines whirring, coffee machines grinding beans and squeezing out brews that only tangentially resembled its namesake. This floor was dead quiet, the lighting muted. I walked along the hallway feeling like it was the middle of the night instead of afternoon. I expected to see the cleaning crew round the corner.

"Chris, can you still hear me?" Adam's voice was distant, fading in and out. It reminded me of the Kobayashi Maru distress signal.

"Yeah, I've got you. Barely."

"Where did you land?"

"A parallel universe where no one exists but me."

"I'm sorry?"

"Forget it."

"Dammit."

"What?"

"Someone just walked into the bathroom."

"Did he notice the rift?"

"Not yet. He walked right into a stall. Looked to have been in a rush."

"Understood." I was running out of time. I picked up the pace and double-timed it to where I had seen windows on the previous floor. If there were any, they were covered with sheetrock. I reached out my hand again, feeling my way through the wall. I wasn't sure what I was looking for since I couldn't feel anything, including air temperature. Steeling myself, I took a deep breath and got as close to the wall as possible, closed my eyes, and bent forward.

I opened my eyes to the worst case of vertigo I'd ever experienced as I stared down the side of the building from about twenty floors up. Tiny cars zipped by on the street below, and even smaller people wandered around. I fought to keep my balance, fearing to fall from my little perch, unsure if I would be ripped from this state before reaching the ground. A bird flew past only inches from my face, nearly making me lose my footing. I turned to curse at it, then noticed a familiar sight. LoanDepot Stadium. Instead, I yelled, "Thank you!"

"For what?"

"Not you."

"You realize you are one flush away from discovery."

"I know where the building is."

"Good, get back here."

"Coming." I pulled myself back fully into the building, shivering at the entire experience. I almost leaped out of my skin as two men in black suits appeared almost on top of me. They passed by without a glance, you know, because I was invisible, for which I silently gave thanks. I yelled, "They have a security patrol on this floor." I was about to go back the way I had come when something tugged at my mind. "Hold up."

"Whatever you're considering, you don't have time."

"Something is off."

"What does that mean?"

"I'm not sure. I just feel—"

"Don't you dare mention the force," Jelena added.

"I wasn't." Only because I didn't think about it, but now it was hard not to.

"I have to check something out."

"Chris,"

"I know, hurry."

I headed in the direction that felt wrong. Whatever it was increased as I moved toward it until I came to a door. It almost hummed with energy. I walked through and found a windowed security booth alongside a thick steel vault like door. Another security guard, dressed in a black suit and white shirt with no tie manned the booth. The bulge in his jacket told me he was armed. He sat on a chair, feet up on the desk, reading a woodworking magazine. It was addressed to Douglas, but the rest of the label was covered by his huge hand. Behind him, within easy reach, was a shotgun, an AR15 assault rifle, a taser and several pairs of handcuffs. Whatever he was guarding, they weren't taking any chances on it getting out. The monitor on the desk showed a camera view of another room. I assumed it was the one on the opposite side of the big, intimidating door.

It looked to be a lab filled with various medical and scientific equipment, and one large metal table looking more like an altar than an exam table. One other thing caught my attention: there was someone lying atop it.

I faced the door not sure if the thick metal would cut off my connection completely, but knowing that I needed to get a closer look.

"Chris, what's going on?"

In silent answer, I walked through the door.

Stopping just inside, I tried to get my bearings. I entered the room near the foot of the table, and could now see the heavy metal chains securing the person. I'd seen chains like that used in body building. It was overkill for the frail figure lying there. The walls and ceiling were covered with a thick gauge sheet metal. Just past the table was another door not visible from the camera's view.

I could still hear both Adam and Jelena, though they sounded more like the adults from a Peanuts cartoon. The only other occupant breathed raggedly, the grating, labored breaths of the terminally ill. I crept closer as though my ghost like movements would disturb the tenuous grasp she had on slumber. It was a she or had been at one time. Right now, she didn't resemble any part of humanity. The toenails of her bare feet were long, curled, and blackened.

She wore a single garment that resembled a loose fitting, threadbare housedress. It had become discolored from constant wear and bodily fluids so that it looked like old canvas. It came down to her calves, though I got the impression that it had originally been longer. Walking along her metal bed, I longed to reach out and touch her, provide comfort that she was not alone, not forgotten. I could see the bones of her hand clearly outlined through the pale skin. Her fingernails were like those of her toes, but these had broken off to jagged ends.

The trepidation I felt had me buzzing with the urge to flee. Conflicted, I wanted to believe I had found our lost member but was afraid of what it would mean if this was indeed her. Approaching the head of the surgical table by her bony shoulder, I looked into her face. I honestly could not tell who this person was. I called to mind the photos I had seen of her, but there was barely a resemblance to that smiling woman.

Something jarred her awake, her eyes shot open, and I knew it was her. Nothing could diminish those sparkling blue eyes. I had never met her, but those eyes connected me to her as though to a long-lost relative. A flood of hope filled me and I whispered, "Krissi."

Her head jerked towards me, and she stared me right in the eyes. There was no doubt in my mind that she saw me, though I could not fathom how. A tear slid slowly down the side of her face into the matted black hair. My spectral breath caught.

Somewhere in the back of my mind, the sounds of my teammates became frantic. Krissi cocked her head as though hearing them too, then looked back to me. She gathered up what breath she could, snapped her head toward me, and screamed.

The sound echoed off the walls, glass jars and tubes shook rolling off tables and smashing to the tiled floor. The wave hit me like a firehose. My astral form dissolved, and everything went black.

I came to with Adam yelling at me in one ear and Jelena in the other through the com. Adam looked close to shaking me but was restraining himself. I found out afterward that it was not a good idea to touch someone in my current state.

I shook myself to clear my head. "What?"

"We are about to be discovered! You need to close the rifts."

I looked through both rifts to see a man at the sinks shaking off his hands. The paper towel dispenser was on the wall opposite my view, but after that... I reset myself and jumped into my lakeside plain, rushing through the steps I had taken the first time. Shrugging into my astral form, I lunged forward, reaching through the rift hovering over the building edge to the tear leading to the men's room. I reached down and pushed my gift into the breach. The edges sealed like a zipper as I drew my hand up the gap. With about a foot left, the man turned from throwing his towel in the trash. He looked up, his eyes going wide, then the hole was closed.

I breathed a simulated sigh of relief. The chances that the man understood what he saw and was comfortable reporting it to someone without sounding crazy were slim to none. My relief was short-lived.

A shot echoed against the buildings. Adam was engaged with four people. The fifth was on the ground bleeding out, an assault rifle lying next to him.

"How about you hurry with the closing? I don't think these are the only assholes pissed that we're here." Jelena's voice sounded more stressed than usual. I moved back to the rip in the air and reached up and hesitated for a second, then healed the rip like I did with the first one.

Okay, now what? I wasn't sure how to get back into my body. I rarely gave it much thought. When I was done, I was just done. "I see the hole is gone. How about you finish your nap and help Adam?"

"I'm trying."

"Try harder. I'm gonna have to shoot more people, and I know how much you hate that."

This was really frustrating. I could talk through my body, but I couldn't reconnect with it. It was like running down a flight of stairs. If I didn't think about it, my feet just tapped their way down, barely touching each step. Put too much thought into it though, and I would trip over my own feet.

"Unplug." Adam's voice was strained as he dodged one blow, then pulled his attacker into the path of another opponent's punch.

I looked around. "Where's the plug?"

"Not physically!" He didn't say 'dumb ass,' but I'm pretty sure it was implied. It was enough. I mentally went through the steps to turn off my gaming system and my avatar disappeared.

"Shit, one got through." Adam grunted as the other three kept him busy.

"I've got him."

"Hold your fire."

"But he's right on you with a knife."

"Hold!" I pulled myself back in time to see the knife streaking towards my throat. My hand snaked up and stopped the thrust. It had been so close I believed I could feel the cold metal on my skin. I twisted my head to the offending goon and felt the tip of the blade scratch across my throat, telling me it was not my imagination. I met his shocked gaze as he struggled against my iron grip. He hadn't yet connected to the idea that his other hand was still free, fixated on the one that was trapped.

I blurred into a standing position, disarmed him and planted a phoenix eye strike to his temple. He collapsed unconscious. Too much force with that hit would have killed him. As it is, he would have a monstrous headache.

Three more guards banged through the metal door leading to the roof. Word was spreading of our presence, and we were going to be overwhelmed soon. With a well-placed kick, Adam took another goon out of commission. I didn't think he would have a hard time dispatching the other two, so I focused on the newcomers. I blurred to a stop inches from the lead guy, then planted myself, reinforcing my body with my gift. They collided into me as though a tree had just sprouted up in their path, looking like a scene out of the three stooges.

"Anything you can do about that door?" Jelena asked over the coms.

"I've got it covered. You need to bug out. Meet back at the rendezvous."

"Copy."

I did a quick check on Adam, who was finishing up the last one on his feet. The stooges were extricating themselves from the pile they had ended up in. The door was just past them, a small brick out cropping with the sole purpose of holding the door. Next to me was one of those round metal tables bolted to the roof. I grabbed it and twisted like I was turning the steering wheel of a bus. The welds holding the top to the base gave way with a screech. I threw it like a frisbee, putting some extra gift behind it. It crashed into the bricks next to the metal door frame, getting wedged between them and bending it into an unusable mangle of metal.

"Nice throw." Adam's voice was tinged with awe.

I smiled in answer, then nodded at the remaining attackers. "Help me out with my light work?"

Chapter Twenty-Six

"You did what?" Ima wasn't her usual happy-go-lucky self as we sat around the conference table back at the Covenant house.

"We found the rift," Adam explained.

"The rift was closed over a year ago."

I waggled my hand. "I would say sealed is more the proper term."

Ima's scrutiny moved to me. "Care to elaborate."

I thought for a second. "Like, if you cut yourself but didn't care for it properly, causing it to become infected. The wound is closed, but it is apparent there's something there."

Her eyes narrowed. "How did you see it? I examined that spot for months."

"I thought you didn't think she could be alive."

Her eyes became slits, and I held up my hands in acquiescence. Then I explained the process I had gone through to find it. Adam's suggestion to use the mental projection of a knife. The identification of where the building was and finally finding Krissi. She stayed quiet the whole time, listening intently.

Ima sighed deeply. "My failures are piling up."

"What failures?" I asked.

She shook her head and looked to be grinding her teeth. "I allowed Kristina to be captured, I wasn't able to find the rift, I failed to deduce the meaning of Krissi's echo's all around me, I pulled you off the case when were actually on the right trail, and——." She made a vague motion towards Adam.

"Me, I'm your failure. Right?" Adams voice was thick with emotion.

She shook her head. "You didn't fail me, I failed you. As a teacher because I could not see who you truly were. I failed as your mother for not supporting you in your self-discovery. And I failed as a person for not allowing you to feel confident being your true self with me. My image of Adalina blinded me to the reality of Adam. For that, my son, I am truly sorry."

"How could you see me if I could not see myself. You've always accepted and supported me, even if you didn't fully understand me. That's all I could have asked for."

The lump in my throat got ten times worse and I thought I was going to start bawling. I covered it by clearing my throat. "Kristina's alive, and we know where she is. That big ugly building near the stadium."

Adam pulled up the satellite photos and schematics of the building. "Thanks to Chris's reconnaissance we know that she is being held around the middle of the fifteenth floor. Basically, dead center of the thirty-story building."

I jumped in. "I called Soon-Li on the way back and she checked out the building. Besides Uji there are approximately twenty other legitimate businesses in there, many of them running twenty-four, seven. They take up the majority of both the upper and lower floors."

Ima frowned. "She built herself a human shield."

I nodded. "Fighting our way in or out creates the possibility for a large degree of collateral damage."

Ima smiled. "Luckily we have a new advantage."

"How do you mean?" I asked.

"The portals. We can slip in, extract her and slip back out."

"Well, not really."

Ima's head tilted, and her eyebrows knitted together. "What do you mean, not really?" She looked at Adam and he looked at the floor.

"I closed them."

"Yes, but you found them before, you can do it again."

"No, I didn't seal them. I closed them. Healed them, if you will."

"You can't find them again?"

"No."

"There's no way to figure out where they were? Make an educated guess?"

"That's just it. It would not be educated. I would be a child bowling off a ramp."

"What?"

"Did you ever go bowling?"

She squinted her eyes at me, making me want to make an eye exam appointment for her.

"When a small child bowls, they use a ramp that they set up in front of the lane. No need to lift and throw the heavy ball. Whoever is with them places the ball on the ramp and the child just pushes it down. The chances of getting a strike are extremely low, but it happens, mostly by accident.

"This would be the same. Except instead of rolling a plastic ball at wooden pins, I would be cutting into the fabric of reality, hoping what was on the other side would lead me to a specific place."

"Polyester."

Ima and I looked at Adam.

"The house balls are usually made from polyester. More expensive ones are made from urethane or resin with a powdered metal oxide core mixed with resin." Adam looked from me to Ima. "What? I enjoy bowling."

"Apparently," Ima said.

"I think I'm more shocked than anything else."

"Oh, shut up."

Ima brought us back to the issue at hand. "So, there is no way to make an attempt?"

"Based on what I've divined so far, there is a harmonic resonance on both sides. You need to know the right frequency to get from the Divine to a specific place in our realm. From all the time I spent analyzing the rooftop, I might be able to figure out how to get to it from somewhere. I would have no idea how to get into the building where they're keeping Kristina."

Ima sat quiet for a long while, her eyes darting as I assumed she was negotiating the options. Her expression tightened more and more.

"If we come at it from the ground, they will see us coming. If we can somehow gain entry from the roof and get to her before being detected, breaking her out will set off alarms all over the place and we will be boxed in."

"It feels like we are giving up." Adam's voice was strained.

"Adam." I faced him. "That's it!"

"What?"

"We give up."

Though each had their own version, the general consensus was that I had lost my mind. They weren't following, but I was already working out step five, and I didn't want to divert my attention to explain step one. "The problem is timing. I have a vague idea what floor she's on, but we will need to search surrounding levels to be sure. Splitting up would take the least amount of time but with one of the Tainted possibly on site as well an unknown number of enhanced Converts supporting the normal security, doing this with three Bishops will be near impossible."

"Who said there are only three of you, Mr. Bateleur?"

The deep melodious voice that made my formal name sound somewhere between a curse and a complaint was unmistakable. The short time I had with him had etched him into my memory forever. I turned.

"I didn't think I would ever say this, but perfect timing, Hager."

Chapter Twenty-Seven

THE RELIEF I FELT was physical at Hager and John's appearance. A tightening in my chest that I didn't know existed till the moment it loosened. My shoulders eased down from the position they had taken up guarding my ears. Even my hair settled back down.

Amram Hager looked the same as the day he introduced himself on the streets of New York. Over six feet tall, long white beard and payots hanging down each side of his face. He dressed in the classic black suit and hat that many Hasidic Jews favored.

Next to him, John McCaw looked short, though I doubt anyone would dare call him that. Maybe less than average height, he was in every other way a Greek God with dark skin and shoulder length dreadlocks.

"What took you so long?" Jelena asked.

"I told you we needed to wrap things up. Baldemar may have left, but he was never the only threat, just the most pressing."

I looked at her confused at the exchange. "Wait, you called him?"

Jelena clicked her tongue and huffed. "Of course I called him. You were acting crazy and you are all about that rushing in where angels don't go near."

"You thought I was going to get you killed?" The thought that she felt me so reckless made me sick to my stomach.

She stepped up to me and smacked my forehead with her open hand. "Not us. Yourself."

I was confused again, and it must have shown on my face.

"You would have led us into an impossible situation to save Krissi, and you would have sacrificed yourself to ensure everyone else got out alive. You are very careful with other people's safety, yours not so much."

"Apparently, we need to have the chain of command talk again," I said, smiling.

"If you think it'll help."

"It won't," John added with his hint of a southern drawl.

I looked around at my team. All of them, again except Jelena, were Bishops long before I knew what that even meant. All had fought the Tainted time and time again, some for decades, yet all were looking to me for a plan. They would follow me headlong into the serpent pit without question, putting their lives in my hands.

The question haunting me was whether their faith was misplaced. Was I able to implement a rescue plan in a building full of enhanced demonites? My plan was risky, but I thought it could work.

"To set everyone's expectations." Hager stepped into the growing silence. "You can expect Chisti… Chris's plan may appear to be the most ludicrous idea imaginable. I can also guarantee that it will work."

I met each of their eyes, divined from them their strengths, how best they worked together, and where they would excel alone. As the details of my plan fell into place, I started grinning.

"Oh, my." Hager's face fell.

Ima looked up. "What?"

"I think it's worse than I imagined."

I sat alone at the desk in my quarters, a shoebox open on the desk. It was filled with envelopes. They contained the letters from my mother, left in Hager's care. Most of them were opened. I had read through them once things settled down after the New York incident. I left a few of the later ones still sealed. Once I opened them, there would be no further communication with her. I would have heard everything she had to say. After spending so many years feeling denied because of how young I was when she passed, having the ability to hear her voice through her writing was not a gift I was looking to squander.

I picked out one I had previously read that I thought may provide insight.

Happy 13th Birthday Christian!

It's official, you are a teenager! I hope you had a great day today and got everything you wanted. I am so sorry I cannot be there to share it with you. But always remember no matter what, I am with you in spirit. Whenever you need me, I will be there like the sunshine on your face.

I visited a school the other day. We do that as often as possible to ensure there aren't any Tainted pushing their influence. Corruption of the young is one of their oldest tricks. In one art class there was an angry, frustrated girl sitting in a corner. I sat by her and tried to find out why she was so upset. The girl finally confided in me that she was unhappy with her drawing. After much convincing she showed it to me.

Christian, to say the picture was beautiful would have been a drastic understatement. It was a magnificent representation of the vase of flowers sitting on the table. When I told her so, she didn't believe me and pointed out all the parts she was unhappy with. She wasn't allowing herself to see the beauty by focusing only on the flaws.

We are our own worst critics as we alone see all our faults. Our lives comprise a compilation of both good and bad. If we allow ourselves to focus too much on the bad, it can blind us to all the good things we have, and have accomplished.

I tell you this now so you will always remember. All people, without exception, have evil thoughts. Everyone will occasionally take the wrong path, choose the easy road, make the decision that seems right at the time, or that will lead them to what they desire. We are all flawed, we will all fail at some point. Try not to judge yourself or others based on their failures. If we were to look only at our missteps, we would look as evil as the Tainted themselves. Jesus said it best, "Let him who is without sin among you be the first to cast a stone...."

To walk the path of righteousness doesn't mean you will never stumble or stray from it. It means when you do; you pick yourself up and get back on it. You cannot change what was, you can only strive to do better today.

Give your father a hug for me and make sure Father Murphy goes easy on the scotch.

Love,

Mom.

I folded the letter again. "Great. Basically, if at first you don't succeed, try, try again. Thanks Mom."

Chapter Twenty-Eight

"**I**'M NOT SEEING ANYTHING," I said.

Soon-Li clicked her tongue loud enough to be heard over the speakerphone in the surveillance van. I was still puzzled that this highly equipped mobile unit was just sitting in the garage. "Chris, did you know you're an impatient pain in the ass?"

"Well, the last part I've definitely heard."

"I don't doubt it."

I tapped on the screen.

"Did you just tap the monitor?"

"No." My voice climbed as though I was insulted by the thought. "But I can if you think it will help."

"Touch it again and I will smack you."

"From New York?"

"Do you doubt me?"

I thought about that for a minute. "No."

"See, I knew you were a smart guy."

"I like her," Marie said from the chair next to me.

Somehow Soon-Li had discovered the developing relationship between us and had found several opportunities to have a talk with her while I wasn't around. Before I could respond, the screen came to life. Several more followed suit, showing multiple views of the lobby.

"We're up."

"You have an incredible grasp of the blatantly obvious." Marie smiled and pushed her hair behind her ear.

"I like her." I could hear Soon-Li's smile clearly over the speaker.

"Is this really my life now?"

"You should be so lucky," Soon-Li said.

I tried to ignore the fact that I was being ganged up on. "Hager, are you in place?"

"Affirmative."

I nodded to myself. "John?"

"Ready."

Another mental tick mark. I looked at Marie. Her beauty slapped me in the face like it had on that first day. The fine curve of her jawline, the way her ear lifted slightly when she smiled, the quirky thing her eyebrows did when she thought I was being stupid and her wavy hair that absolutely refused to be restrained in a ponytail.

"What?" she said as my glance passed beyond the casual. I couldn't tell her what I was thinking. That she was perfect for me. That I would gladly trade all this new power and responsibility over to someone else and spend the rest of my life dancing at different night clubs, traveling all over the world, dining at every place ever mentioned in Triple D, or just sitting next to her on the couch eating Chinese food while watching old movies, and making love. I just kept thinking about Dr. Dorothy Summers' words. It's like you are being followed by a lightning storm. Just make sure you don't get anyone caught up in it.

"Nothing. I thought you had something in your hair, but it was a trick of the light. You ready?"

"Ready, but I still think it's a stupid idea."

"Everyone usually does."

I took off my headset and Marie grabbed my arm before I could get up fully. I plopped back onto my chair which spun to face her. She pulled me to her and kissed me. It was short but passionate. She pulled back and looked at me, concern etched in her face.

"Just," she started.

"I know, don't get killed."

"No. Make sure you come back with everything in working order. Sting ops always leave me with pent up energy."

"Sir, yes sir."

We took another second to stare into each other's eyes. Then, I got up and exited the van. Outside I rolled my shoulders, stretched my back and rocked on and off my toes to stretch out my calf. I still wasn't sure what made the pain recede, so I was trying anything. It had escalated over the past few hours. I felt like all my muscles were rebelling against me. It didn't make a difference though. We had a Bishop to rescue, drugs to get off the street and I had a job to do. I just had no idea how. My leg cramped again, and I dug my thumb into it while growling out a curse.

The building was a gray skyscraper in the middle of a cluster of off-white buildings. It was like Spring Garden stuck up their diseased middle finger at downtown Miami. It had been erected about six years prior on the site of what used to be a Winn-Dixie, where North-West Twelfth Avenue met Route 836 along the Miami river. As soon as I had stuck my astral head out the window and saw the stadium, I knew exactly where I was. Where else would an evil villain make their home? Heaven forbid they set up camp in Disney World.

I pushed through the rotating door leading to the building's lobby, then walked up to the security desk. "I don't have an appointment, but I'd like to speak with Uji no Hashihime."

The person on duty, of course, had no idea who I was talking about, which was fine because I wasn't really talking to him. I stared at the camera mounted on the wall, smiled, and waved. It didn't take long for the woman I had met less than a week ago, though it felt a lifetime, to walk out with four of the Men in Black I had seen during my spectral stroll.

"Mr. Bateleur. Please come with me." The staccato rhythm was familiar, even though I had only heard it once before when this whole thing started. I bowed my head formally and did as she asked. The four goons made a square around me. I followed her to an elevator where we all got in. She used an electronic key card, then selected floor 16, and we all watched the floors tick by.

I looked around. "Before we get started, does anyone want to get out?" Only one guy reacted by tensing up, but it was worth it. We reached the right floor, the doors opened, and that same guy exhaled audibly. We stepped out onto one of the floors on which they were possibly holding Kristina and they escorted me into an interrogation room. They probably would have called it a meeting room, but with a chair on one side of a small table and two on the other, it spoke for itself. Before being asked, I chose one of the two chairs, spun it around and straddled it. I was uncomfortable, but I looked cool. No one else sat.

"What can we do for you, Mr. Bateleur?"

"I thought you could get me tickets to the next Marlins game. Big business like this, so close to the stadium, I figure someone here must have season tickets."

"Why are you here?"

"Is that a no?"

"If you would please, we are very busy."

"Are you, though? It seemed like you were just waiting around for me to walk in."

"See Mr. Bateleur out."

"Okay fine. I've come to make a deal."

"To do that, you would need to have something to bargain with."

"What makes you think I don't?"

We both stared each other down.

"Well?" she asked.

"What? It was your turn to talk."

She sighed. "Watch him closely. I'll be back." She eyed me for a few more seconds, presumably trying to figure out my angle, then left.

I looked around at the four security guards still staring at me. "You guys can entertain yourselves, right? I need to do some soul searching." I got no response, which I took for a yes. It took me less time to project my avatar than in the past, and a fleeting thought had me wondering if I could change my clothes or hairstyle. An Indiana Jones fedora immediately came to mind, and I fought to regain my focus. I walked up to the two-way mirror, flicked my wrist, and my trusty utility knife appeared. Calling up the veil channel, I flipped through the frequencies until it matched the harmonic resonance that I couldn't get out of my head. I had the veil in sight and took a deep breath. This was going to be the hard part.

I had chosen my seat strategically, not just out of a rebellious air. I wanted everyone faced away from the two-way mirror where I would tear a hole in reality. Random portals opening into alternate dimensions have a tendency to get people's attention. I had to open this one, then find the right frequency in Hell—theologically speaking — then cut another portal in it hoping it would bring me where I wanted to go. This was the stupid part of my plan.

Like I had told Ima, from the outside trying to get in would be a crap shoot. Harmonic resonance aside, I couldn't guarantee that I wouldn't be opening up a hole into someone's dining room one building over. This wasn't an exact science. Hell, it wasn't a science at all yet. I felt like Madame Curie experimenting with highly radioactive material, not realizing all the while I was poisoning myself, ensuring a slow, painful death. I needed to stop thinking so much.

I made the cut, then immediately started the search again. I found it. Or rather, I thought I found it. Now that I was a swipe away, I doubted my abilities. Was I going to open a portal at the bottom of the sea and flood the building? Or one in space where we would all be sucked out? How could I, someone who couldn't carry a tune to save my life, identify one specific vibration frequency? The tone for this veil sounded the same but how could I be sure. Maybe I should have brought a tuning fork. Or better yet, an autotuner. That would tell me exactly which frequency this was emitting.

I stared at the veil that only I could see. It shimmered in front of me billowing against unknown forces. Who was I to cut into this perfectly unmarred surface. I may as well slice open the Mona Lisa hoping to find a treasure map. This was insane. I had done this once while following the path of whomever came before which left me the equivalent of a big red 'X' marking the spot. The variations I was dealing with were literally endless. How could I possibly think I had the knowledge and experience to mess with forces of this magnitude?

"What the fuck is that?" one guard yelled.

Debate over, I cut the veil.

A view of the rooftop opened, and daylight flooded in as though opening curtains on a sunny day. The rift was in a completely different spot from the original, but other than that, it was the same general location. I let go of the breath I didn't know I was holding.

"There!" Adam yelled, pointing from the other side of the rift. He immediately started towards the opening and leaped through. The guards in the room were all trying to make sense of what they were seeing when he tore into them like a hurricane. He raced towards the back of the room where my body sat and disarmed the two guards closest to me. Hager, John, and Ima jumped through shortly afterwards and, between them, they restrained those remaining before they had time to react. I sealed both rifts and the light returned to the muted glow of the florescent bulbs. It took me a moment to reset myself, then I blinked as I once again looked through my body's eyes.

Ima looked down at me. "You good?"

I nodded.

"Where are we?" Hager asked.

"Sixteenth floor."

He nodded and relayed the message to Marie while Adam handed me my coms unit.

I plugged the com into my ear just in time to hear her. "Is he okay?"

"I'm fine."

"Alright. I'm having the team move in."

"Good. The DEA raid should be a suitable cover for us to slip out into the chaos. I don't want to take the chance of opening another rift. We got lucky this time, but there are too many variables to chance it again."

"I wish I could have seen it."

"I'll make sure you have a front-row seat next time I tear a hole in the fabric of reality."

"To be honest, I wasn't sure I completely believed the theory until I saw it for myself," Ima said.

Adam crossed his arms. "Did you think we were making it up?"

Hager stepped up and placed a hand on Adam's shoulder. "My boy, knowing something based on faith does not diminish the splendor of seeing it with your own eyes."

I had to smile at Hager's wisdom, being pointed at someone other than me. Bending down, I unclipped the key card from a guard's belt, then looked at the rest of the team.

"Let's find Krissi."

We opened the door and stepped into the hallway. Guards were approaching from both directions.

Hager said, "Mr. McCaw and I will take these. You three go on."

We jumped into the nearby stairway as they blurred into action. As the door closed behind us, I looked at Ima. "I'm pretty sure she's on an upper floor."

She closed her eyes for a second, then nodded, and we all started climbing. We didn't bother kicking into high gear since we needed Ima to tell us when we were at the right level. At eighteen she paused for a moment, held a hand out telling us to stay where we were, then continued more slowly. She got just up to the next landing, closed her eyes again for a few heartbeats, nodded, then came back down. "She's on this floor."

I touched the key card to the electronic lock and it responded with a negative sounding buzzer. I tried again but received the same unhelpful results, so I tossed the key over my shoulder.

"Why are you even using that?"

I used my gift to pop the mechanism and pulled the door open. Sirens wailed up and down the hallway and stairwells. I gave him a pointed look. "That's why."

We rushed into the corridor. Two more guards were almost on top of us. Ima moved, catlike, into action, hand springing onto one guard's shoulders. Her flowing layers of fabric completely obscured his view, and her momentum threw him backwards to the floor. She landed on her feet, still partially on top of the first guard. Whipping her leg around, she swept the second guard's legs out from under him. As guard one tried to sit up, he was met with an elbow to the face, knocking him out. Then she wrapped her legs around the second guard's neck, choking him until he too lost consciousness.

It was all done so fast that Adam and I just sat there and watched, me with my mouth open, and Adam smiling. Ima got to her feet and dusted herself off.

I looked her up and down with a whole new level of respect. Her figure may be slight, but it was made of iron. She caught my expression and her eyes squinted. "Something to say?"

"No ma'am."

She smirked and nodded towards the unconscious men. "We were fortunate these were only mercenaries and not Converted. I doubt that will last long. You and Adam take it from here. I will keep our egress clear."

"Copy that." I led Adam to where I remembered the door to be. As soon as it clicked open, I started talking in a loud voice.

"You are out of your mind. There is no way, I'm telling you, no way."

The guard looked up.

"Doug!" I pointed at him dramatically while approaching the safety glass separating the small security booth from the outer room. "Doug will back me up on this." I stuck a thumb back towards Adam. "My man here is telling me you can hit the alarm before I can drag you through that window." Doug looked between us, trying to figure out the joke and where he knew us from. While he was busy taxing his brain, I reinforced my fist and drove it through the safety glass. Grabbing him by the shirt I pulled him back ramming him against the inside of the booth, knocking him out. I looked at Adam again. "Told you."

"You didn't drag him through the window."

I rolled my eyes and reached in through the shattered window and hit the big red lock button. The huge door to the lab opened.

"You ready to get Kristina?" I asked him.

"I've been waiting a year, so yeah."

Chapter Twenty-Nine

SOMETHING HAD CHANGED SINCE I had been here last. Kristina was still gaunt, her eyes sunken back into her skull, pale and dirty. I could smell her rancid body odor that I was spared from in my other form. But now there was a raw power that emanated off of her. She still looked thin, but someone had juiced her up before we got here. Also, this time, she was strapped to the wall by her wrists, elbows, ankles, and neck. Had she wanted to escape, she would have had no leverage to do so. She was awake, watching us. Her fingers flexed, claw like nails dancing dangerously. She was obviously wary of our presence, a tiger sizing up a threat, or dinner.

Adam took a step and I grabbed his arm.

"What are you doing? Let me go. We need to get her loose."

"I think that would be an exceptionally bad idea."

"What are you talking about? It's Kristina."

"Is it?"

Her eyes were shifting between us as we spoke. She didn't seem to be comprehending, but each word agitated her a little more. The version I had seen when last here hadn't had this air of malice. Our plan centered on the idea that she would recognize and want to go with us; that although she'd been turned, she would still have something of her old self in her.

"Of course it is." The delay in Adam's response belied the statement.

"We need to think this through. If this was any normal person held in captivity for this long, their sanity would be in question."

"She is not normal."

"No, she is superhuman."

"We need to take this step by step. She has the power of a Bishop combined with that of a Converted at the highest level. We need to get through to her before we release her or she will tear this place to the ground, starting with us."

Red lights flashed and a deafening high-pitched squeal reverberated through the room. Another sound drew my attention. I turned to watch the huge, metal door slam shut. There was no handle on our side. No way to open it, no other way out.

"How nice. What a sweet reunion," Uji's voice came from a speaker somewhere.

"It's over," I said like I was in an eighties cop show. Did I really have to be this cliche? "We have your distribution ring, and we have all your product."

"You have neither, but even if you did, I have enough of this one's blood to start over. Along with something of which you have very little. Time."

She was right, of course. Her immortality meant she could just lie low for a few decades again and ramp back up in another location. But that was apparently not what she meant.

A loud clicking sound echoed throughout the small, reinforced room. We looked in time to see the last of the straps fall away from Kristina. She closed her eyes and flexed her muscles one at a time, from her toes to her neck. When she opened them again, they screamed of danger, and the promise of death.

"Aw shit," I said.

"Don't hurt her."

"Somehow, I don't think that's going to be a problem. Circle right, keep her between us."

I went left, my muscles sluggish from the deep ache. No part of her moved except for her eyes which darted between us. We approached her from either side so slowly we barely disturbed the surrounding air. Still, she didn't even twitch.

"I need to touch her," I kept my voice low, instead of a whisper that would sound like I was hiding my intentions.

"What are you going to do?" Adam tried to match my tone.

"Give her what she needs. Or at least I hope so." Although not a Bishop long, I had gained experience in this a few months ago on Sixth Avenue when facing two demons. I had reached one of them, deep down through layers of pain, guilt, and suffering. I felt Kristina would be the same. She just needed a hand; someone to lift her out of the pit. That was the theory, at least.

"It's okay," Adam sounded like he was calming a skittish horse. "No one wants to hurt you. We're here to help." Kristina focused on him ever so slightly.

That's it. I mentally coached him. Keep her focused on you. I'm almost there... I reached out my hand towards her shoulder. But an inch away, and my hand became stuck. It took me a moment to understand why. She was holding my arm. She had moved so fast I could not even call it a blur, the rest of her body remaining stock still. She looked at me, casually. Then she showed her first emotion since we entered the room. She smiled. My bladder almost let go.

Again, I didn't see any movement. My first sign of a problem was the pain in my chest as I flew backwards across the room. My gift kicked in, hardening my body for the impact with the wall where I left a large dent in the metal. I looked over at Kristina, who stood with her leg still extended where she had kicked me. I had to admit; it looked impressive. The pain radiated from my back and chest. Underneath, I felt the bones reassembling themselves from the shattered mess her foot had made of them.

Adam's face registered shock. Her leg still raised as though forgotten, she struck out at his shoulder with enough force to spin him around. Then she grabbed his hair and pulled him backwards, off balance. He was in one of those ballroom dancer positions, bent at the knees with all of his weight held aloft by his head in Kristina's grip. She lowered her head over his, eye to eye. She searched for something, smelling the air. Slowly, she lowered her leg and grabbed Adam around the jaw with her other hand.

She was intent on him, so focused that all else was ignored. At least, that's what I was hoping for. I took my shot, going into a blur, not bothering to pick myself up from the floor first. I wanted nothing to pull her attention back to me. Kristina was fast, but I was faster. I had proven I could move faster than any Bishop. I put everything into the blur, poured every ounce of my gift into it. All of my focus, all of my intent to get to her before she could react. My body screamed with the waves of pain every motion seemed to bring.

I moved fast, faster than I think I had ever had shy of that record-breaking moment. Then I slammed into something. I didn't know what, since it hit me in the throat. My vision went black around the edges, telling me I was nearing unconsciousness. I struggled back to realize what I had run into was Kristina's hand. The force had crushed my larynx. I struggled for breath as I felt it slowly pushing back in shape. She still held me casually. I noted somewhat angrily that she had switched hands before grabbing me out of the air like a pesky fly. I don't know why that bothered me out of everything else.

I hung there, grabbing at her iron hand. I could breathe again, throat made whole. Kristina wasn't bothering to strangle me, just left me dangling. I felt helpless and I hated that feeling. What the hell was going on? I fought two demons. My brain finally kicked in as I realized my intention hadn't been to beat her, simply to reach her. I looked down at her hand as well as I could from my position and acknowledged the obvious. Her arms were much shorter than mine.

I let go of her hand and reached out, grabbing both sides of her head. She finally turned to stare at me. The malice in her eyes was terrifying to behold, so I tried to ignore it and focus on her aura. I don't know how I did it last time, and trying to force it this time was proving to be problematic. She squeezed my throat, her expression mimicked mine when I had caught a fly that still buzzed annoyingly in my hand. My air passage closed again. I let go of trying to force the process, closed my eyes and just tried to feel. Her image formed in my mind and the black aura around her felt viscous. I ignored my struggle to breathe and pushed my mind into hers. The pressure around my throat stopped and I fell into the depths of her soul.

Chapter Thirty

WHAT THE HELL DID I do now?

I was falling. There was no wind in my face, but the feeling in the pit of my stomach was undeniable. This was not what I experienced with the demons. Then it was more of a surface scan. Like looking at their life on a highlights reel playing at high speed. I looked around as I plummeted into blackness. There was nothing surface level about this, but what the hell was it? I wasn't in the dark since I could see my hand in front of my face without issue.

Below and off to one side, a glowing light appeared. It approached fast, coalescing into a cloud-like shape. It was massive. From my perspective, it looked to be the size of a large house. As I drifted by, I could see colors swirling in its misty interior. More of them soared up randomly around me, or I should say, I fell past them. They became more plentiful the further I descended, one coming so close I felt I could reach out and touch it. I heard voices coming from it, and the colors I saw in more distant orbs now looked more like a scene viewed through a frosted window on a cold winter day.

I was just forming an opinion of what these little round clouds were when I noticed one coming up rapidly right below me. My training officer's words echoed in my head from my first solo jump out of a perfectly good airplane. 'It's not the fall you have to worry about, it's the sudden stop.'

She walked into the vet's office, fighting back tears. The weight of the pet carrier swinging gently in her left hand was both impossibly heavy and heart breakingly light. Pulling open the door to the Hilton Animal Hospital, she stepped up to the front desk and checked in. She sat down in a chair that afforded the least possibility for someone to strike up a conversation and ruminated on the name again.

What pet parent wouldn't want to take their little darlings to the Hilton for their regular checkup? 'No, no Sassy, we are just going to the Hilton for a little mini vacation.' It's what she used to say, but Salsa knew. He always knew and would fight going into the carrier. If it were a cardboard box, there wouldn't have been a fight. He loved cardboard boxes of any size and thought he could fit in them all. She imagined they were like a warm blanket on a wintry day to him. He didn't fight her today.

There was no fight left in him. A shell of what he once was. The proud Calico now skulked in corners, a constant flow of drool, a by-product of the mouth tumor, coating his chin, throat, legs, and the floor around him.

Four months ago, the doctor had prescribed medication that she now suspected was more for her benefit than Salsa's. She had forced it into him three times a day for a few weeks and he improved. She could see a little of the kitten she had adopted fifteen years ago. He was so small at the time he could fit in one hand. She had made a little box for him and put it on the floor next to her bed. He meowed incessantly in the barely audible cry that all kittens possess.

Every couple of minutes, she would reach her hand down and stroke his tiny body. He would quiet down while getting attention but would return to mewing as soon as she withdrew back under the covers. She finally brought him into the bed with her, despite her intense fear of rolling over and crushing him in the night, yet thrilled at cuddling in with the little fur ball. He settled down immediately and started purring, and that's where he slept every night after that.

The carrier shifted as Salsa tried to get comfortable, pulling her back into the present. She tried to say comforting words but couldn't get them past the enormous lump in her throat. She searched the room for something to focus on, but the cheery posters and little joke cartoons only mocked her. Especially the slogan painted on the wall.

Hilton Animal Hospital, we will pamper your pet more than you do. All she could think of was the Raid Roach Motel catchphrase: They check in…

"Salsa?" The receptionist called.

She picked up the carrier and followed the smiling woman, wanting nothing more than to beat that cheerful face off of her. Of course, none of this was her fault. The woman in cartoon printed scrubs was just trying to keep the mood light. Being happy was the last thing she wanted right now. This was a dark day, and she was in a dark mood. She took a deep shivering breath and followed her into a small room.

"The doctor will be right with you."

Famous last words, she thought as the receptionist exited. At least she was alone here. Alone with her best friend who she was walking to the executioner's block. It was dramatic, she knew, but it was the way she felt. The process was all logical. Salsa was in pain. Constant pain. His meow had transitioned to a full-time low growl. Where at onc time he would push his way under her elbow for attention, he now preferred solitude. What was worse, was the feeling of relief at his distance.

This was no longer the Salsa that she would snuggle with. The companion that would hop up on her lap, unperturbed by the computer currently taking up residence there. She couldn't remember the last time she could pet him without him striking out, or her hand coming away covered in slimy saliva.

Was she doing the right thing? Her friends all believed so; assured her that Salsa was in pain, and it was torture to let him keep going like this. Doing anything else would simply be selfish. It made sense, but it was not how she was feeling. She felt guilty and considered her actions a betrayal. She couldn't even look in the carrier, expecting to see him looking back, judging her.

The vet entered the room. "So, what are we doing today?"

Oh God, don't make me say it. Don't make me put it into words. She opened her mouth, her throat closed, and tears started pouring down her cheeks.

"What the fuck was that!?" I gasped as I fell free of the ball of light. I was falling again, but that was no longer my issue. My throat felt like I had swallowed an apple whole, and my face was streaked with tears. I was panting like I had just sprinted the length of a football field. I looked up at the quickly receding sphere but couldn't see the vet's office anymore. That was the most disturbing thing I had ever experienced. I felt everything as if it were me. My heart ached, as it hadn't for decades. Memories of my mother's death flooded in, called upon by the common thread of grief.

I scrubbed at my face, attacking the tears as if they were ants crawling across my skin. Grabbed at my hair, trying to clear my mind of the conflicting images. Standing next to my mother's closed casket, trying to get some sleep, but worried about crushing my new kitten. I screamed, squeezing my eyes shut, pulling my hair until it caused more tears to flow.

After a few moments, I finally separated the two of us. My breathing slowed and I took a deep breath that only shuttered slightly. I slowly opened my eyes.

I plunged into another sphere. I didn't even have time to curse.

She stared out the window into the night; her nose so close that her breath fogged the glass, partially obscuring her view. She didn't care. She wasn't looking at anything in particular, just gazing at the stars and trying to imagine herself anywhere but here. She didn't want to be in this room at this moment in time. Star gazing, however, had a dual effect. It was her father who had first introduced her to the night sky. The two of them would lie in the backyard grass, staring straight up into space. He would point out the constellations, name them for her, then tell her the stories of how they earned their place among the stars.

"Like Hercules?" she had asked, having seen the Disney movie recently.

"Yes, just like Hercules."

They would sit there for what felt like hours until her mother would call them back in. She would put on her ritual pout about having to go inside until her Mom brought out the hot chocolate.

BEEP… BEEP… BEEP.

Her vision blurred and she wiped at the tears. The incessant beeping and whirring kept drawing her out of her escape. She refused to turn around. Refused to be back here again.

"Ms. Kipling?"

"No," she said too softly for anyone to hear. It wasn't meant for him. It was another denial of her reality.

"Have you come to a decision?"

"No," she said, louder this time.

"I understand this is difficult."

"Do you?" The response was almost a growl.

"I can't imagine…"

She turned on him and reality took hold again. All her little memory jumps faded and she was left in the present. She hated him for bringing her back here. Hated him for forcing her to make this impossible choice.

"You're right, you can't imagine," her voice was low, but acidic. "You cannot fathom the loss that I am enduring."

She looked over at him. Her father lay in the hospital bed. His pallor was that of dirty chalk. The noises that plagued her were emanating from the numerous machines to which he was connected that kept him alive. Well, kept him breathing. She knew it was too late. Knew in her heart he was gone. Knew in her brain that this was only the vessel that had carried his spirit. But she also knew that once she made this decision, it was over. No more Sunday dinners. No more political debates. No more watching Dancing With the Stars and taking bets on who was hooking up. And he would never walk her down the aisle. A tear fell down her cheek and she slapped it away.

"I'm sorry." The ass of a doctor was smart enough to back his way out of the room.

Her eyes burned a hole in him and the door as it closed. Then she took a deep breath, looked over at her father. She had asked the nurse a lot of questions about how it would go at the end, so she knew what switch needed to be thrown. She padded over to him, lowered the guard rail and slipped into bed next to him. There was barely enough room and she balanced partially over the edge, clinging to him for support one last time. She breathed him in, memorizing his scent, the feel of being cradled in his protection. Shifting over onto her back and balancing with half of her body hanging off, she stared up at the ceiling. It wasn't tiles she was seeing, nor the fluorescent light fixtures. She was seeing stars. Tears flowed unrestrained, drawing trails back across her head and pooling in her ear. She focused on the planetarium projected from her memory, found Cassiopeia, stayed in that moment as long as she could bear. When she felt it was burned into her memory for all time, she reached over and switched off the machine.

The scream ripped from me, a demon needing to be expelled. Pain, grief, and guilt battled in my head for dominance. My emotions were a raging sea, conflicting waves crashing, then ebbing. I flailed around trying to punch something, turn the grief into anger, but it was useless. There was no floor to plant my feet, no way to engage my body, put force behind it and drive the feelings out of me. My breathing never had time to slow as I approached the next dome of light. I could see shapes moving around in this one, flashes of lights and small shadows zipping around. I could taste the blood in my throat as I yelled from my already hoarse vocal cords.

"Look out!" a woman yelled.

Krissi ducked back behind the low wall that surrounded the dock's warehouse just as a fifty-five-gallon drum sailed over her head. It careened wildly, clipping the wall where her head had just been. She looked over at Adalina, who had warned her, and waved in thanks. The heavy metal drum wouldn't have killed her, but it would have hurt like hell until her gift healed her. It would also drain more of her waning reserves.

There had been six of the Converted guarding the warehouse full of drugs. Four of whom she and Adalina had contained. The two left, a man and a woman, were the most powerful, and both she and Adalina were nearly depleted. This was going to take finesse, but luckily, that was her biggest strength.

Krissi stroked the pistol at her side. It was a Colt single action revolver with an ivory handle. The same one Calamity Jane had used. She carried it the same way, high on her right hip facing out so she could draw with her left hand. She thought it made her look like a badass. She carried the revolver because of her passion for westerns. If she needed more than six bullets, she wasn't doing her job right. Her daily practice with the pistol included the quick draw. Many saw it as a waste of time or a childish fantasy. Krissi didn't care.

She chanced another look. The last one had nearly caused her a dented skull. They were running for a boat at the end of the dock.

"They're bolting," Krissi said, and took off after them. With her reserves so low, she couldn't chance bottoming out during the actual fight. So, her sprint was only enhanced by the rigorous workouts she put herself through every morning. It was enough.

She was gaining quickly on the two Converted. One, she felt she could disable without inflicting too much damage. She wasn't sure about the other. If the second continued to flee, Adalina could take her. If they both stopped to fight, she might have to be more aggressive.

Luckily, to date, Krissi had never needed to kill, and she wasn't about to break that streak today. The Covenant didn't have any such restrictions. In fact, they frowned upon her hesitation to kill. Especially the boss lady. Almost tripping, Krissi wondered where that expression had come from. She had never referred to Imaculada in that way. It didn't even sound like herself. She shook off the feeling and dug deep, determined to overtake the two before they reached the boat. It would be close and it was looking like one may get away.

Apparently, she wasn't the only one who thought so. Adalina streaked by, burning through the remains of her gift. It was a foolish move, born out of impatience and inexperience. Though she was smart enough to grab the lead person by the collar and spin her into the other. It was a bold move and looked to have worked. The two went down in a jumble and struggled to get up. She was nearly there when Adalina stepped in to detain the Converted.

"No," Krissi yelled, trying to warn her off, but it was too late. As she reached in, the woman grabbed her by the wrist. In a flash, Adalina was on the ground and the converted was lifting a knife to deliver a killing blow.

Instinct kicked in. The Colt Peacemaker on her hip called to her. The hours of practice moved her hand. The pinging sound of the hundreds of metal targets rang in her ears. She moved faster than she ever had before, using the last of her gift to add speed and focus. She squeezed the trigger, the Colt an extension of her hand. The old pistol rang out like cannon fire and the side of the Converted's head exploded as the bullet exited. Shifting, she fanned the hammer back and the Colt exploded again, taking the other in the chest, knocking him off his feet.

She staggered to a stop as time hammered back into place. Adalina lifted her head from her supine position on the dock to stare back, her face covered in her attacker's blood. Krissi stumbled over to the water, gazed at her wavering reflection, and vomited.

Chapter Thirty-One

I OPENED MY EYES and the pain reemerged as I stared across at Krissi, still holding me by the throat. The malice in her expression was gone, replaced by confusion and sadness. Had we both experienced that together? Was she as disconnected from her former self as I was during those experiences? I could still feel the wracking grief, a hole in my chest that could never be filled. I understood her need, felt how lost she had become. Now I needed to heal her. I had done it before during the fight with the two demons. One's heart was black as coal, the other could be redeemed. I had sensed that spark and somehow had used it as the source for cleansing the taint away from the rest.

This entire experience had been vastly different. Then I had only been given a feeling, an outline of what was contained in the person's heart. Fleeting images that built a picture almost like a collage of their life. It was nothing like I had experienced with Krissi. The depth of the experience we shared, based on the look on her face, was an ocean compared to the puddle of insight I had received in the past. Whatever the differences, whatever I needed to sacrifice of myself to bring her back from the edge, I knew I had to try. I lowered my hands from her head and cupped her cheeks. My last fleeting thought was that the last time I had done this, the woman had died.

My touch brought Krissi to focus on me. Her eyes were wide and pleading for release. I met her eyes, tried to connect on a deeper level. "You are forgiven."

Her expression changed, and the animosity crashed back into place. Krissi took a step and hurled me away from her like an Olympian shot putter. I flew across the room, crashing into the far wall and caving in the metal. This left another Chris-sized dent in the wall. I had instinctively protected myself at the last second, saving myself from the crushing injuries. But, as before, the pain rushed in like the ocean into a sunken wreck after its last windows finally gave way to the immense pressure. I fell to my hands and knees.

"That could have gone better." I groaned the words out.

Krissi started flailing wildly, lashing out at anything close to her. Adam ducked, dodged, and dove to avoid the onslaught. I was missing something again. My brain was firing on all cylinders, driving through option after option, searching for a logical plan forward, but that was the problem. It wasn't a logic problem. It didn't have an equation that would solve for 'X'. This was a spiritual problem.

There was something there. A connection was being made in my subconscious that my conscious mind hadn't yet. Spirit. Super Ego. Soul. They all rang true in my head. What was the connection? How were they interrelated? Inter… In. Internal. They were all something that could not be directly affected by the outside world. It was colored by the perspective of the one. Not something someone else could fix. Or forgive.

"Adam."

"A little busy right now." He avoided being crushed by a thrown chair. Krissi was escalating. If she used that well of power for something other than brute force, we were going to have a big problem.

"She needs to forgive herself."

"For what?"

Krissi lashed out again, barely missing Adam and rending four-foot-long gouges in the metal paneling. He looked above his head at the wreck she made of the wall and paled at the sight.

"For everything. She feels guilty for everything she has ever done wrong."

"Welcome to the club."

Another swipe and Adam jumped back so high his hair brushing the ceiling. Landing halfway up the wall behind him he pushed off with his foot, then ran across the side wall, dropping in back of Krissi.

He grabbed her from behind, one arm over her shoulder, the other under her arm. She let out a hideous shriek that sounded as though it would shatter glass.

"Calm down, relax."

Krissi flailed around so violently that Adam's legs lifted perpendicular to the floor.

"When has telling someone to calm down ever worked?"

"How about some useful suggestions?"

"You need to let her know it's you!"

She finally reached back over her shoulder, grabbing Adam by the back of his shirt and tearing him off her. She threw him, crashing against the wall back first and upside down. He slumped down and was fighting to recover as Krissi closed in. Her arm arched back for the death blow.

Adam held out his hands. "ELLEN!" he yelled.

Krissi stopped, her head snapping towards me as though looking for some kind of trick, greasy hair whipping into her face.

I could see the confusion in her eyes. She looked at Adam, who had just righted himself.

"Talk to her," I urged.

"Yes, it's me," Adam's voice was softer as he reached out a hand. "Do you remember me?"

There was no recollection in her expression, but she didn't pummel him into the ground. So that was something, I hoped.

"Do you remember the night Mom caught me with that goth girl? What was her name? Terri? Not the way I wanted to come out to her. I wouldn't give her the satisfaction of crying, so you cried for me. Then we drank until we both threw up."

Krissi blinked, but otherwise kept as still as a statue, her expression blank.

"Keep going."

"How about that raid we did against the Tainted out in Clear River? The two of us ran through that den of locusts like a couple of bosses. Took the whole warren down by ourselves. Man, the Elders were pissed about that one."

Krissi's mouth moved like she was trying to say something, but no sound was coming out; like she was trying to remember how to form words. Her straggly hair partially covered one eye.

I looked over at Adam. "The dock." He glanced at me. "Remind her about the dock."

"How do you know about that?"

I gestured at him to just do it, afraid that too much talking would break the spell.

"Remember the dock, Krissi? When you saved my life."

Her eyes became enormous.

"This is a guilt trigger. Change the perspective."

"Guilt?" Adam's question wasn't for me. "You feel guilty about that?"

Krissi's eyes shimmered. Her elongated fingers alternated between open palms and clenched fists. Adam approached her one step at a time.

"That whole thing was my fault." Step. "I was trying to impress you, show you I was as tough as you are." Step. "I used the rest of my blessing to get there first." Step. "And put you into a situation that forced you to make a choice that you had been avoiding for years."

They were face to face now, inches apart. I thought it was too soon. Krissi was barely hanging on to her humanity. Any second, she would let loose her rage and tear Adam to shreds. I wanted to warn him off but was afraid to break the tenuous connection that Adam had established. I stayed silent, and very still.

"You were so proud of never taking the life of a Converted. In one stupid, self-serving move, I ruined that. I forced you to kill. Forced you to make the choice between my life and that of another. So many nights that scene plays itself out in my dreams. Do you know what makes me wake up screaming? It's not the woman standing over me with a knife, waiting to plunge it into my chest. It's not the blood splattering my face as I watched them die, knowing it was my actions that caused it." Without breaking eye contact, Adam reached down with two fingers and brought Krissi's hand up to chest height between them. "It's when I looked over at you and saw your pale, blank expression; your haunted eyes, and the torment I could already see behind them."

Adam closed his hand around hers in the classic blood brothers' handshake. The same pose I saw in picture after picture. The physical manifestation of their bond. Their connection to each other was beyond friends or family. The silent vow of unconstrained love and support. The acknowledgement that either would willingly lay down their life for the other. A symbol of their oneness. Adam held Krissi's gaze, as intense as a bride and groom during their vows.

"I wake up screaming at the moment that I first failed you."

I held my breath watching the two: so close together, searching behind each other's eyes. Tears flowed freely from Adam's, drenching his face. His hand clenched hers as though it was the only thing keeping him anchored to reality. Her hand was still wide open; fingers extended, practically vibrating from tension. Those menacing looking claws practically brushing his throat.

Krissi stiffened. Her back arched as she took in a violent, rattling breath. Her fingers finally closed over Adam's hand and he put his other on her elbow to lend support as she slid down to the floor. She exhaled, letting her head fall. When she lifted it again, her eyes were clearer. Her eyebrows bunched as she looked at Adam as though for the first time.

"Adalina?" Krissi's voice was akin to someone who had just stumbled out of the Sahara Desert.

It didn't appear that Adam could speak, so he just nodded his head, smiling.

"What the hell did you do to your hair?"

A half-sob, half-laugh erupted from him. He wiped at his face with his free hand. "It's Adam now."

"That's no excuse."

I finally released the breath I was holding, though as quietly as I could, still afraid to cause a relapse. Pulling the flask I had strapped to my belt, I whispered and waggled it. It was filled with the restorative holy water that gave us our powers.

"Adam,"

He looked at me, sniffed back the remnants of his tears, and held his hand out. I debated walking it over, but I thought keeping my distance was more prudent. So I tossed it to him. He caught it without looking.

They were both sitting on the floor facing each other, right hands still clasped at chest height. He opened it without letting go of his friend, then held it up to her.

"You need to drink this."

She grabbed it, obviously parched, then stopped halfway to her lips. "What is it?"

His silence answered her, and Krissi's face fell. She looked at the flask as if it contained drain cleaner.

"Are you trying to kill me?"

"You need to be cleansed."

"Great, I'll take a shower when we get back."

"Be serious."

"I am serious. Do you know what that could do to me?"

"Guaranteed to kill or cure." I wanted the words back as they left my mouth.

Krissi looked over at me. "Who the fuck is this joker?"

"He was the one who found you. The one who risked his life to save yours."

Recognition sparked in her eyes, as well as something deeper. "He's an asshole."

"No argument there." He pushed the bottom of the flask towards her mouth.

She resisted. "I'm afraid."

"I know. But this time I'm not letting go."

"I'm not sure that is such a great plan," I offered, but Adam silenced me with a scowl.

He reengaged their gaze. "Together."

She nodded. "Always."

Krissi took three deep breaths, closed her eyes and downed the whole flask. I was honestly impressed. It took shot gunning to a whole new level. She tossed the empty vessel, gasped and panted for a second. She looked up at Adam and smiled, relief clear in her expression. It didn't last long.

Her eyes went wide and she shot to her feet, stumbling backwards into the wall pulling Adam with her. She tried to shake his grip loose, but he held on like a tick.

"It's okay Krissi, I'm here. I'm not letting go."

Her eyes danced wildly around the room; whether looking for escape or for something to grab onto, I wasn't sure. She grabbed their clasped hands with her free one. Tears streamed down her face. Her bottom lip quivered as though shivering. The atmosphere changed, as though all the air rushed in towards her. There was a heartbeat of complete calm. A silence deeper than anything I had ever felt.

Krissi screamed. It was heart wrenching and torturous to listen to. I involuntarily covered my ears, which did nothing to drown out the sound. More than being audible, it clawed at my soul. It was sorrow, grief, misery, loss, and guilt. Her scream made me swim in the emotions, not just hers but my own. All of my missteps, all of my regrets, all the pain of everyone I had ever lost, compounded into one torrent that made a hurricane seem like a whisper. I fell to my knees, begging for it to stop; debating on ending my life if the torment would end with it.

It ended as quickly as it had started. The silence was a jarring relief. Krissi gasped and I waited for it all to start again, wondering if I could survive another onslaught. Her breath came in gasps. Then she turned and projectile vomited. I had never seen an eruption like this before. It held enough force to hit the ceiling, like a geyser gone wild. It was the same black tar-like substance that had come from Alex back at the police station. But this was laced with blood. The blood of victims, the blood of innocents, the blood of the betrayers.

Krissi finally collapsed into Adam's arms. Her shoulders shook with whimpering sobs. I got to my feet and stumbled over to them, expecting to see the restored aura of a Bishop. But this was not a fairy tale. She looked as could be expected of a person who was held captive and tortured for a year. There was no miracle cure for that. It would take a lifetime of hard work to live with the experience. She needed to build for herself a new normal.

I put a hand on Adam's shoulder, and he looked up at me.

"You need to get her out of here."

He nodded. I moved to help him get Kristina to her feet. She grabbed me before I could move away. Taking a deep breath, she said, "she's here."

"Uji? Yeah, I figured, but we need to get you out."

"The drug."

"You know about that?"

Nodding, still breathing hard, she continued, "She has a lot of it." She stopped often to catch her breath. "I was there for all of it… wasn't really in my right mind… but I remember."

"Do you remember where it all is?"

She shook her head. "Not all… some."

Adam looked up at me. "We need to find the rest. If we don't stop her now, she will move it and we will have an epidemic on our hands. She will drug her way to an army."

I redirected my attention to Krissi. "The mission was you, not her."

"Stupid plan."

"You too?"

She took a few more deep breaths. "Deal with Uji now or you will be up shit's creek…"

She trailed off again.

"I know, without a paddle."

"No… without a boat."

"What are you suggesting? Kill her?"

Adam chuckled. Krissi rolled her eyes.

"The stash locations are all on the server."

She was getting her breath back, but still looked like death warmed over.

"So, is there a control room?"

She looked back at Adam, who was still cradling her. "Does he do anything besides watch movies?"

"Quote movies."

"Right, fine. I'll get it from the server room. Do you know where that is?"

Krissi looked up, her eyes darting back and forth, presumably trying to remember. "Next floor down." She met my eyes. "I'm pretty sure it's right below us."

I nodded, then grabbed her arm and slipped my head under it. Adam took the hint. We lifted her up and moved to the door.

"What's the plan?" Adam asked.

"You are going to take her out of here."

We got to the big, locked door and I keyed my coms.

"Ima, we need help to get out of here."

"Coming."

I was relieved when I heard her voice, not sure if I could get a signal out of this place. I explained what she needed to do to release the door.

"Hager, we have Jackpot. Rendezvous egress point."

"Understood," he replied.

Chapter Thirty-Two

THE NUMBER OF BODIES strewn around the hallway during the walk back to the stairwell was shocking and impressive. We hadn't heard anything in the sealed lab, but it looked as though a small war had raged around us. Most of them were mercenaries, currently zip-tied and moaning. A few were Converted judging by the carnage around them. They were not moving.

There was a brief outpouring of emotions at the sight of Krissi again, and I brought the team up to speed on what she had told me about the drugs.

"Any resistance?" I asked Hager.

"Some."

John frowned at him. "Some?"

"Any issues?"

John shook his head. "None besides Badrick getting away again."

"Who?"

"The guy with all the skulls you ran into at the docks."

"You know him?"

"Old friend."

"I need to hear that story."

John shrugged which told me more than enough.

Marie weaved her way to my side.

"I made it," I said. "All parts present and accounted for."

"Better be. I'll be taking roll call later."

I smiled at her then got back to business. "How is the raid going?"

"As expected. A clear path to the lobby is almost open."

Finally, something going as planned. I addressed the group. "Ima, take Adam, Jelena and Marie. Get Krissi out. Hager, John and I will get the data."

Ima shook her head. "No. This is my responsibility. I will take the risks."

Jelena flipped her hand in the air. "Yeah, what kind of male chauvinistic bullshit is this? All the guys stay and fight while the girls run to safety?"

Adam tilted his head and squinted at Jelena. "Excuse me?"

Jelena made the psht sound she used to discount people without words.

I held my hands up. "There is no time to argue about this."

"Then stop arguing." Ima stood her ground.

"It's okay." John stepped in and took my place supporting Krissi. She actually smiled at him. "Thanks."

"Any time."

Seriously? Was any woman immune to his charm?

"Fine, Ima stays with us."

Marie tapped me on the shoulder. "Where you go, I go."

I didn't bother to start another debate that I was doomed to lose. Instead, I smiled. "Of course."

Jelena stepped up on my other side and scowled at me inches away from my face. "We will talk about this later."

"I have no doubt." I mumbled. To the rest I said, "We are not out yet, let's move."

The six-legged race team tried to double their time, but trying to coordinate that type of rhythm on a staircase was not a simple task. Before they got halfway down, the doors opened on the floor below and a security team burst through. It didn't take long for them to see John, Adam, and Krissi hobbling down. Both Marie and Jelena brought up their guns.

"No!" I pushed Marie's gun down, blurred down to Jelena and did the same. I could hear the curse she was forming as I put one hand on the painted, metal railing. I set both feet and pushed off into a dive that had me soaring over the dizzying view. I hit the first guard as he was raising his assault rifle. My momentum slammed him against the wall, driving all the air from his lungs. I got my feet under me, grabbed him by the shirt, and whipped him around into his two friends. They fell back into the door, slamming it shut. The guard in the back hit his head on the metal door, taking him out of the picture along with the first guy being used as a human bowling ball. I knocked out the last one, who was sandwiched between his compatriots, with a left cross.

"Lefty?" John asked with a tone that sounded like he was saying 'really.'

I did my best Mandy Patinkin impersonation. "If I use my right, it's over too quickly."

"Did he just—" Krissi began.

"Yes, and don't acknowledge it, it will only encourage him," Hager said from above.

John met my eyes and smirked as he helped guide them around the cluster of bodies. Then they continued down the stairs.

"Jelena, come take John's place."

She mumbled a string of curses as she came down but did as I asked.

John transferred Krissi's weight to Jelena. "It would be easier if she could walk on her own. You think you can top her off?"

Ima, tapping her way down the stairs, gave a quizzical look. "What do you mean, top her off?"

I ignored her question, not really wanting to get into it. "Not sure if that's the best idea. She's had a lot of conflicting influences in the past few minutes. Anything I do may render her unconscious."

He nodded and pulled his knife. The charming southern gentleman with dreadlocks took on a dangerous air when holding the menacing weapon with the nine-inch-long darkened blade. It sent shivers up my spine; despite the number of hours we spent drinking and swapping stories since we met—was it only six months ago? I shook my head to pull myself back to the task at hand and put a hand on the arm that held the knife.

"Not all the guards may know what is going on here."

He looked at me and gave a little smirk. "I'll try not to do too much damage."

Krissi whipped her head around, her face tense with barely controlled rage. "Fuck that. Kill them all. None of them are innocent."

She locked eyes with all four of us, daring someone to argue. When she received only silence, she started down the stairs again, practically pulling Adam with her. John nodded at me and held up his fist with the knife in it facing toward him. I gave him a sideways fist bump and he hurried after the other two.

Ima, Hager, and I pulled the unconscious guards up to the railing and zip tied their arms behind them through the bars. "The servers should be on this floor. We ready?"

The two nodded, and I opened the door. Four guards aimed assault rifles at the door, standing behind four more with riot shields. I closed the door.

A torrent of gun fire pummeled the heavy metal from the other side. I looked back at Hager and Ima, my shoulder still pressed against it.

"We have a minor snag in the plan."

I told them what was waiting for us. I was the only one who got a good look.

"Is a hyper human frontal assault not available to us?"

I shook my head at Hager's question. "They left enough distance to put thirty or forty rounds in us between all of them. I don't think any of us can stand that many bullet hits."

Ima put it into words. "They are prepared for Bishops."

I nodded and relayed the information to John and Adam and Jelena, who had already gotten two floors down.

"So much for your stealth operation," Jelena said.

Marie looked over the railing, following their progress and trying to see if anyone was coming from the lower floors yet.

She looked up. "What's the plan?"

A frontal assault may not be available, but that didn't mean I couldn't hit them from the side.

"Hager, can you keep them busy? Keep them there?"

He picked up one of the assault rifles that the guards had dropped, opened the door a crack, and fired a quick barrage right at the riot shields. Then he closed it again. "Indeed."

I grabbed another rifle and tossed it to Marie. "Cover Hager."

"What did I say before?" Marie looked sexy, a Glock in one hand, an AR-15 in the other. I stepped up to her and wrapped my arm around her waist, leaned down and kissed her. Her lips softened and opened to meet mine. It didn't last long, but burned with promise from both sides. I pulled back and looked into her eyes.

"I want you with me too. But what I need to do requires me to move faster than physics usually allows. Please stay here and guard Hager's back."

Marie let out a long slow breath, a euphoric smile splayed across her face. "Okay."

I smiled back, still staring into those beautiful hazel eyes. "Ima, would you accompany me?"

"As long as you don't ask me in the same way."

I peeled my eyes from Marie and addressed her. "Deal." I blurred up to the next floor, followed closely by Ima. We blew through the door and into the hallway, not bothering to check if anyone was waiting. I was betting security had been ordered to defend what we were now after. I was half right. They weren't set up on this floor yet.

Three guards were getting themselves organized in front of the doorway. Two more were coming from the hallways in both directions. Though neither pair could see the other yet they could both see their three compatriots and us. I nodded towards one pair coming from the right and Ima blurred in that direction.

I couldn't spare her further thought as the three in front of me finally realized I was there. All three brought their riot shields up and drew their side arms. There was little time for options and, of the few I had, I chose a dangerous one. I blurred at them as fast as possible in the short space. Then I shifted quickly to harden my body, making myself a human battering ram. I slammed into them, knocking them all to the ground with such force it rendered them all unconscious. Hoping I didn't do any lasting damage, I grabbed one shield and held it up. I used it to block the gunfire that started pouring from the last two guards down the hall.

The force of two automatic weapons being unloaded against a

shield is not insignificant. I physically braced in my position, not wanting to squander any of my gift for what my muscles could already handle. I waited for them to reload so I could blur into a position to take them both out. It didn't take long.

The shooting stopped and I took a quick peek just to make sure they weren't trolling me. Both guards were down and Ima walked casually towards me.

"Oh, hey. Uh yeah, just like I planned. Great job."

Ima sniffed in response. I looked down at the battered shield and tossed it to the side.

"So, about this plan of yours."

I nodded. "Right." I walked over to the exterior wall perpendicular to the stairway door and punched through the drywall. Grabbing the nearest stud, I pulled down a large section of the wall. Light streamed in through the window behind it. Ima smiled as she understood. I stepped up, reinforced my fist again and drew back to take out the window.

"Wait."

I looked over at her. "The team is boxed in and running out of time."

"You are so concerned about protecting life. Are you less concerned about the people on the street?"

I got her point. Punching through the window would send a shower of debris raining down below. "Okay, do you have any suggestions?"

She stepped over the remnants of the partition wall and up to the window. Taking her index finger between her thumb and middle finger, she traced a large circle. A high-pitched screech accompanied the action and a scratch mark trailed where her nail touched. She shifted her position halfway through, then completed the process on the other side. She followed this up by placing both hands lightly within the circle. After a second, she jerked them backwards and the window came loose, still attached to her open hands. She placed it to the side and peeled her hands up and away.

"How did you do that?"

Ima smiled. "Experience has some advantages over raw power."

"You can make your hands sticky? Like Spiderman? You've got to teach me that!"

"You are the oldest adolescent I have ever met."

"But you will teach that to me, right?"

"Can we get Oscar Mike?"

"Right." This was the phonetic radio transmission to get on mission. It had the intended response. I made a mental note of the skilled manipulation while pulling a rope from one of the larger pockets on my leg.

"You carry around rope?"

"There are three things I try to have with me as often as possible: a knife, duct tape, and rope." I unrolled the rope and handed one end to Ima. She nodded and gripped it with both hands. I considered asking Hager to let me know when they were reloading. But alternately, they might be more cautious at that point. Well, no time like the present. I wrapped my end of the rope around my hand, nodded at Ima, and ran at the window.

I added a little something to the jump to get an extra bit of momentum. Hitting the end of my rope, literally, I curled into a ball, steeling myself into a solid mass. I hit the window. Hurtling through, letting go of the rope, I blew right through the wall. The last thought I had was the hope that my calculation of their location was correct.

I rammed the group of guards from the side, taking them all down and scattering them into a dazed jumble. Hager burst through the door and Ima swung down from the floor above. Between the three of us, we made quick work of the security team.

Marie strolled in, her boots crunching on the debris my entry had caused. "Nicely done."

"Thanks. I came in like—"

"You finish that sentence, we're through."

I closed my mouth and gave her a thumbs up, not trusting myself with talking.

"Okay children, where are the servers?" Hager asked.

"Krissi said they were right below us when we were in the lab, so in the middle of the floor."

Ima nodded as she entered from the stairway. "Let's go."

We all double timed it down the hall until we found a door

conveniently labeled Server Room, Authorized Personnel Only.

I pointed at the door. "Why don't we try this one until we find it?"

Hager ignored me and examined the lock. "This one is complicated. It may take a few moments for me to bypass…"

Ima interrupted by stepping up into a wide stance and double palming the door. The hinges popped and it pivoted on the locking bolt, falling inward and off to the side. She looked at me and said, "Raw power has its time and place."

I smiled at her, then rushed into the room and started checking the servers to find the removable hard drives.

I got a bad feeling in the pit of my stomach. "We need to find those files and get out."

I felt a tapping on my shoulder and found Marie standing near but looking past me. I followed her gaze and my heart jumped into my throat. Standing twenty feet from me was Uji.

Chapter Thirty-Three

"**G**OOD OF YOU TO finally show up."

She wore a nearly identical kimono to when I'd seen her in the warehouse. This one was blood red, which was only a few shades darker than her skin color. Even the socks and sandals were the same frightening color. Her hair was arranged in the same five horned crown. From a distance it had been eerie. Close up it was ominous.

I had to work moisture back into my mouth to speak. "You knew we were coming?"

"As I said during our first meeting, you are very easy to read. Once you understand the nature of a person, their values, their motivations, it is easy to anticipate their moves."

"You must be one hell of a poker player. No wait, chess, right?"

"I don't play games. They are a waste of time. A way for inferior minds to distract them from their miserable lives."

"Obviously you have never played Tetris."

I tried signaling for the team to back away, but I didn't get the impression that they were moving. Somehow, I needed to get her out of here before she killed them. But how? We were all in a very contained space, and I couldn't figure a way to get her and I out without everyone else trying to follow. Then I got an idea. I got a dangerous, really stupid idea.

"Well, Amram, I see you are still alive." Apparently, Uji was done with me. So much the better.

"And it is wonderful to see you again as well, Uji."

I turned around to face him. "Really? You are polite to a Tainted."

"I am polite to everyone. It's costs me little but returns much."

This time it gained me the opportunity to mouth instructions to him. 'Get the servers and get them out.'

I closed my eyes, preparing myself. Having only done this twice before, I was hoping the need would drive me. I opened my eyes and addressed the Tainted. "So, what is your game? You planning on creating an army of superhuman drug addicts?"

I sorted through the layers, trying to find the right harmonic resonance faster than I had ever done; while trying to look like I was still having a not so casual conversation. Uji caught my eye movements and misconstrued them. "Looking for a way out? You are free to leave, Mr. Bateleur. I contacted my guards when you first entered." Apparently, she was pissed about the door. "They will be here any second, and you will be forced to flee or die. I am fine with either outcome."

My astral form stepped out of my body. I walked around her and, not being able to resist, I put my thumbs in my ears, waggled my hands at her while sticking out my tongue. Childish and stupid but, if you are going to do something, at least try to have fun while doing it. Especially if it may get you killed.

"Afraid we will best you in combat, so you are giving us an out?" I cut an opening in reality behind her with my astral utility knife.

Uji chuckled. "Sometimes opening a window is easier than killing a fly. But believe me when I tell you that your buzzing about is affecting me as little as that insect."

"Buzzing. An interesting word for the collapse of all that you have built here." Ima stepped in to take up the conversation.

I mentally thanked her as I searched for the matching harmonic resonance that would lead me away from here.

"Is that what you think you did, Imaculada? You are like the child in the backseat of a car with a toy steering wheel, imagining that your actions are actually making the car move. Everything that has happened has done so according to my will. The only reason you feel you have had a hand in anything is because I have allowed you to believe so."

"Your overconfidence is your weakness." I said and Marie rolled her eyes.

Hager joined in. "You planned on our presence? For the DEA raid on your building? To lose your key asset?"

"If you are about to close the door, and the wind blows it shut first, do you curse the wind? As for my key asset, I was done with her. You taking her back saves me the trouble of disposing of her. I have siphoned enough of her blood to stockpile my needs for many years to come. If at some point I run short, I will simply capture another Bishop." She flipped a hand to highlight how inconsequential it was.

I found the right layer. It sang to me like a well-remembered song. Just in time too, as I got the feeling that Uji's monologue was ending. I cut through and looked back into this reality in another location.

"I even know about the gateway that Christian is opening behind me. It is plain on the human's face." I had forgotten this was not something Marie would be prepared for. My astral form noted that her mouth hung wide, and she had gone a ghostly pale. I also caught sight of myself and a massive wave of nausea hit me. I staggered toward my physical body trying to reunite my two halves, and in the process nearly falling onto Uji. It was then that she swiveled her head and looked me straight in my ghostly eyes. "Sometimes when I'm in the mood, I close the window and pick up the fly swatter."

Hager blurred, trying to force Uji back through the rift. She shifted her weight a minuscule amount and redirected his momentum, sending him flying past her. Ima blurred to a stop in front of her, trying to force her back with hand-to-hand combat. She moved like lightning, throwing attack after attack. Punches, elbows and kicks came at a speed that would have made Morpheus envious. Each was blocked with barely even a movement from the Tainted. She held her ground like an oak being attacked by children with sticks. Uji grabbed Ima on the last punch and flipped her onto her back, then drove her foot into her neck while still holding her arm locked in place.

Hager attacked again, this time from behind, and she grabbed his hand as well. She twisted and raised it above her head so that his hand was forced backwards. I didn't think it was possible for such a tall man to be rendered incapacitated by someone a foot shorter. She had two highly trained, powerful Bishops at her mercy. The absolute futility of our efforts struck home. How could we hope to defeat this ancient being? What she knew she had learned over centuries of training.

Marie regained her composure enough to pull her Glock and start firing, her eyes wide with fear. Uji shifted her weight, dodging first one, then another. Somehow, she was still keeping both her captives in place. At the third shot, she did the impossible. Before it rang out, she blurred in place; jumping into a spin, still holding onto Hager and Ima's hands. I heard both arms break. She came out of the blur right before the slug connected and she kicked it back towards its origin. Marie staggered back, crying out.

Something in me snapped. The nausea fled, pushed out by blinding rage. Without thinking, I grabbed Uji from behind with my astral projection. The shock read clear on her face as I looked at her from two perspectives. Still holding on with my astral self, my physical self blurred into her like I did with the guards on the floor above, this time into a tackle that took both versions of myself and Uji through the open rift. My astral-self riding on the back of the spinning quarterback sack, sealing the holes as we passed through.

Chapter Thirty-Four

WE ALL TUMBLED OUT onto the rooftop. 'All' is a strange way to put it, but it was how I felt. I had split myself into two separate beings, both working independently. Yet, somehow, I controlled both. I also felt both as we hit the cement. That part was not so great. The pain I had been carrying around doubled.

Uji regained herself from the shock of being touched by a thought projection. She performed a very Kung Fu theater version of an escape, twisting about six times before landing softly a few yards away. I imagined this was where Ang Lee got his inspiration for Crouching Tiger Hidden Dragon. I stood up casually, as did my alternate self, which leaned over and picked a leaf out of my hair, tossing it aside.

"Impressive trick. Where did you learn it?"

"Oh, it was something I picked up along the way." Like five seconds ago.

"Maybe you have some promise after all. Join me and together we will make a formidable force. No one could stand against us."

"See, this is the advantage of a robust movie background. How else would I know that the only reason you want me to join you, is—'A' you need my help to defeat a more powerful adversary after which you will betray me. Or 'B', you doubt your ability to defeat me."

The ghostly image of me folded one arm across his chest and propped an elbow on it, resting his chin in the crook of his thumb and index finger. "I think you should pick 'B.'"

I looked at myself. "I was thinking the same thing."

Uji crossed her arms. "You are not nearly as amusing as you believe you are."

I put a hand to my mouth and said to the physical me. "I think she's talking to you."

"You wish." I returned my attention to Uji. "I have a question for you."

"Why would I answer any of your questions?"

"Usually it's to brag about how smart you are and don't believe there is anything we can do to stop you. But you can decide if answering will cause you issues." I didn't wait for her to acknowledge. "You disabled both Hager and Ima, but I watched him take on Baldemar in an even fight."

She let out a scoff. "Neither Amram nor Baldemar are anything but average warriors. No dedication to the art. One is too concerned with dominance and the other about leading. There are few I would consider a threat."

"How about Soon-Li?"

Uji eyes flicked around as if searching the other rooftops.

"Oh, winner, winner, chicken dinner."

She blurred at us.

"Shit," we both said in unison.

She moved like lighting, attacks coming almost faster than we could see. We dodged one strike at each of us, then another. The blows came so quickly that only the fact there were two of us made it possible to evade them at all. Then we weren't. Her leg sweep came out of nowhere, followed by a palm strike as I hung horizontally in the air. This double shot slammed me to the ground. She twisted into a spinning kick that sailed through my astral head without harm. Whatever made the ghostly me solid was no longer in place.

My physical body was not as lucky. Her strike was too quick for my instinctual protection to kick in. Pain radiated through my chest like I'd been hit by a bus. I tried to inhale and pulled a ragged breath. My rib cage was shattered. Not only was she using hyper speed in her attacks, she was also using enhanced strength. But that wasn't possible. Was it?

My gift immediately started healing my physical body as my ghostly self pushed the attack. Uji dodged again and again, trying to grab the spectral form's wrist, but her hand kept passing through. She finally got wise and simply stopped moving. My astral self came in with a spinning back-kick that sailed right through her. Whatever I had done that allowed it to interact with reality was no longer working. With that thought, the image disappeared.

The ruse had the intended result of distracting her enough for my chest to heal. Now I only had the problem of being up against a vastly overpowered opponent. A level one character in a final boss fight, Glass Joe going up against Mike Tyson. Basically, I was screwed.

Uji shifted her attention away from the astral me to the physical me with a smile that said she knew exactly how deep in it I was. I switched to the defensive. I reinforced my body and relied on my years of combat training to dodge and counter. She blurred in and punched me center mass with everything she had. A crunching sound echoed off the surrounding buildings and I was tossed backwards like I was caught in an explosion, slamming into a massive air conditioning unit that crumpled.

I put a hand to my chest and took a tentative breath. There was no wheeze of a punctured lung. Plus, I honestly didn't know if I could have felt more pain than I was already dealing with. I looked up at Uji and found her on her knees, cupping her shattered hand in the crux of her arm like she would an infant. Pain and shock were etched clearly in her face.

I extracted myself from the wreckage of the AC unit; looked back at it and pulled out my wallet. I fished out one of my old business cards. The bold white lettering declared, Miser Brothers Heating and Cooling. Let us Fight the Comfort Battle, for You. It hovered above the Miser Brothers themselves, going at each other in their usual fashion. I slipped the card into one of the remaining vent slots and faced Uji.

I thought I could hear her grinding her teeth as she bared them at me. I slipped down into my best Bruce Lee stance, flicked my nose, and waved her on. She turned and launched herself over to the next building. I took off at a run after her.

I felt like I was in a scene out of the Matrix, but I was the one doing the chasing. My muscles screamed at me with every leap. Each landing was a shock wave of agony. Still, I followed. I noted, with a sense mixed emotions, that we were heading back towards the building where the rest of the team were. After a few buildings, I saw she was no longer cradling her hand. I became more wary, expecting her to turn at any moment and push the attack. I didn't have to wait long. She landed next to a massive satellite dish, ripped it off and threw it at me like a frisbee. I could see her self-satisfied smirk from my lofted position. Twisting my body, I grabbed the edge in a grip that dented the metal disk and allowed the momentum to spin me around. I released it again when my three-sixty was complete, sending it hurtling back at her.

Surprise lit Uji's face. But she reacted quickly and with a spinning kick, implanting it in a nearby wall. While she may not have expected me to return the favor, I had a feeling the satellite dish had its intended effect. My arc to the next rooftop was compromised by the attack and I came up short of the next building. I grabbed a window ledge three floors down, jerking myself to a painful stop, practically dislocating my shoulder. I thought back to Ima's statement about experience beating raw power. Uji, however, had both. I didn't know how I could defeat her. I only knew I must. The damage she could do with just one of those stashes could be catastrophic.

I looked up in time to see her launch a heavy metal bench at me from over her head. Everything slowed. I checked below me and, of course, we were dangling over a bus stop where people lingered. Not seeing anywhere to deflect it without risking collateral damage, I shifted my gift to steel myself against the attack. Everything sped back up as the iron bench crashed into me. I grabbed at it, shifted the angle and pulled it feet first into the bricks below the window I still hung from. The worst that rained down on the pedestrians below were the chips from where the legs punctured the wall.

I glanced down on my new street art and took a chance on its sturdiness by standing on it. Looking up, I waved at Uji. "Thanks! I was getting a little tired of just hanging around."

Wanting nothing more than to lie down and rest, this time, I didn't wait for her reaction before launching myself upwards. Grabbing the windowsill two floors up, I pulled to maintain my momentum.

As I came level with the roof, I threw a flurry of punches, which she easily evaded. The point wasn't to hit her, but to prevent her from smacking me back down to the pavement like a whack-a-mole. I sailed up, flipping just over her head, still throwing punches until my feet hit the ground and rolled out of range. She didn't push the attack.

As I backed up further to give myself space and time to think, I considered my options. I got the feeling she was used to opponents crumbling at her attacks and wasn't sure how to deal with me. If I were to have any chance at all, I needed to keep her off balance. I decided to try something epically stupid. I gathered myself and put all my focus on moving as fast as I could. After all, I stopped time once before, so I had to be faster than her. I blurred at her, imagining my feet leaving a trail of fire. At the last millisecond, I shifted back to putting power behind my punch to create a crushing blow.

Uji grabbed my wrist and slammed me to the ground, back first, cracking the pavers under me. This time, she didn't let go. She kicked my ribs hard enough to lift me back into the air, shattering them while still holding my wrist. Then she twisted my locked hand until I felt the crunch as both the radius and ulna snapped. Uji lifted me off the ground with my broken arm, forcing an involuntary scream from my lips. Shifting her grip, she grabbed me by the back of the collar and rammed me into a nearby wall. I slumped to the ground on my back again, pain covering me like a blanket of thorns. I struggled to breathe through my re-shattered ribs. At least one of my femurs was broken, and the pain from that alone threatened to make me lose consciousness. Her attacks were coming faster than my body could heal, which I assumed was her plan.

"The gall of your generation. You think you can come and challenge those of us who were here for the last few millennia? You think you are on my level? Me, who trained Genghis Khan." She grabbed me by the front of my shirt and lifted me to stare into my eyes. "You really thought you could beat me?"

I met her eyes. Pulled a sharp, painful breath for a last few words and wheezed, "Nope. Just trying to get in close."

I blurred with my unbroken arm and touched the side of her face.

This was the third time in almost as many days that I tried to delve into another person. My ridiculously stupid plan was to defeat the evil within her like I had done with Alex in the police station. I connected with her immediately, melding with her subconscious. Had I thought this through more, I may have considered the idea that this wasn't a demon. Nor was it a Corrupted, or even a fallen Bishop. This was one of the Tainted—an immortal being of incomprehensible power and wisdom derived from centuries of life. More importantly, the source of that power was the polar opposite of mine; a negative charge to my positive. Antimatter if you will. Scotty's words rang in my ears from the countless hours of watching Star Trek. "You can't mix matter and antimatter cold!"

A blinding light erupted from between us followed by a thunderclap. It threw both of us in opposite directions. She collided into the wall I had just been plastered against and I was thrown to the edge of the building before rolling off the edge.

I dangled from the ledge with my one good arm. Images flooded my brain; and immortal lifetime downloaded into my consciousness at once. It was like being stuck in a daydream that I couldn't pull myself out of.

I looked out of the eyes of a girl. Small fingers played with a little straw doll while she watched her father working in the rice fields. Not a care in the world. Happy.

Now older, not yet a woman, wailing over her father's slain body. The screams of her mother echoing in her ears as she is dragged off into the brush. Rough hands rip her away by the hair and drag her to a barely secluded area not far from her mother. Their mutual torment keeping each other company.

Fully grown, kneeling off to the side of her owner. The fabric she wore was of decent quality but thin enough to show all of her feminine assets and did nothing to battle the cold. She wondered what role she would play tonight. Server, punching bag, or plaything.

A ceremony. Kneeling but no longer a slave, she was revered. Her clothes were fine silks representing a fortune in themselves. A small group stood around watching the commemoration. A figure stood over her. She could feel the immense power radiating from it, like standing too close to a bonfire. He handed her a bronze dagger. She laid a hand on it and that power she had felt consumed her. The feeling was pure ecstasy.

Flashing images of death. Whole armies of foul-smelling men crashing over the enemy at her command. She stroked the dagger sticking out of her sash as she watched. The slaughter at her request was too beautiful for words. She smiled.

Hundreds of years flew by like that. The dagger always with her, though changing as time passed and the technology of war improved. Now, surrounded by Samurai, it was a tanto. Something was different this time. She was still happy, but it held a different taste; sweeter. It was the woman by her side. She affected her like none had ever done before. Her mere presence made her stomach do flips; her touch sent shockwaves through her. This happiness continued for years, until she found her bathing in the river with one of her Daimyos. The carnage she unleashed on the entire town made the river run thick with blood. She bathed in it until it merged with her skin turning it that same color.

The impact of each vision felt like a slap in the face. I struggled to keep my grip, not wanting to divert my gift from the healing it was still undergoing. I could feel the dozens of tiny pebbles in the gritty surface of the cement ledge digging into my fingers, sanding my flesh raw.

Instinctually, I knew my broken arm would be the last to knit itself. Without it, I was a worm on a hook waiting for a hungry fish to happen by. Even if I were fully healed, I wasn't sure if my overloaded brain could manage the thought process needed to climb back up. The worst Lifetime movie ever finally slowed, and I felt the damage to my ribs lessen at a greater rate. Whatever that experience had been, it had distracted my gift as well. As my vision cleared, I made the mistake of looking down. I thought maybe I had just enough strength in my fingers to hold me until my other arm could lend a hand, as it were. That was when Uji stepped up on the ledge.

"It was a decent effort for someone so far out of their depth. But ultimately you are unworthy of the station you have inherited."

Uji continued talking but I no longer heard her. I was hearing everyone else. Adam feeling he was unworthy to be a Bishop while being his true self; Ima's lack of self-worth pushed on her by her family that she felt she had passed on to her son. Krissi's experiences throughout her life that led to her ultimate fall. It all made sense. Then I remembered my mother's words from her letter. We all feel unworthy at some point in our lives. To walk the path of righteousness doesn't mean you will never stumble or stray from it. It means when you do, you pick yourself up and get back on it. You cannot change what was, you can only strive to do better today.

I looked up into the Miami sky. The sun was partially hidden behind a cloud. Light streamed through the cracks, calling to mind a renaissance painting. I fought with my own inner demons. My lack of experience. My wanting faith. The bodies I have left in my wake. I acknowledged them all and I accepted them. Another crack opened in the cloud and sunlight bathed my face. A communion prayer my old congregation repeated every week at mass came to mind.

Blinking in the sunlight, I recited them. "Lord, I am not worthy to receive you, but only say the word, and I shall be healed."

I don't know if my prayer was answered or it was the mere acceptance of my faults, but my pain melted away. I still needed to heal but I wasn't sure I would have the time.

Uji had apparently finished her monologue. She pulled a tanto from inside her sash; holding it reverently. Then she drew out the blade. The sound as it cleared the small scabbard echoed off the buildings. It called back one image from the bombardment on my mind. I realized what it was a second too late.

"Goodbye Mr. Bateleur."

Uji flew backwards off the ledge, as though yanked by some unseen force. Then I heard the shot. Another rang out, but I couldn't see the results from my position. I smiled and mumbled. "Thanks, Jelena."

I looked down at my other arm, willing it to work again. As if on cue, I felt the warmth and the strength coming back. I reached up, gripped the ledge with both hands, and set my feet. Launching myself upward ten feet over the rooftop allowed me to quickly identify where

Uji was. She was on the ground a few yards from the edge. She must have staggered back from the two shots. The tanto was still gripped in her right hand as she made her way to her feet.

I hit the ground, looking in the direction of the gunshots. I gave the international baseball sign to bring in the right hander, hoping Jelena understood the meaning.

Uji stood up. "While I applaud the effort, you are wasting your time. You cannot beat me and your sniper cannot kill me."

"She doesn't have to kill you."

I felt the bullet zip past me, hitting Uji in the wrist with such force it caused her to throw the tanto backwards. By the time the sonic boom reached me, I was already blurring in pursuit. I heard a grunt and another shot ring out. Jelena was forcing Uji to keep up her defenses. I grabbed the small sword in midair and leaped on Uji's back, wrapped my arms around her grabbing the wicked blade with both hands and driving it towards her guts. Instinctively, she tried to stop me, but I put everything I had behind the thrust she didn't know was coming. Her hands, which were covering mine, tensed as the blade dug in, then went slack.

My lips were practically brushing her ear as I whispered, "she just has to keep you busy."

I switched grips, placing my hands over hers, forcing her to hold the handle as I pulled the blade across her belly. There was minimal resistance as the razor-sharp blade sliced through her intestines. She gasped at shock and pain she must not have felt for thousands of years. I didn't wait, but twisted the blade and pulled it up into her heart.

We sat there locked in that hideous embrace of death. My legs and arms encircled her from behind. I was afraid to let go, scared it would negate what I had done. Uji was a statue, just as solid and unmoving as stone. I cautiously released my grip on the tanto and climbed down. Still, she did not move. I walked around her so I could see into her face but stayed off to the side. I was still wary that I was being tricked. Her face was an image of surprise and horror. Despite her rigidity, her skin still looked supple. Yet no blood flowed from the devastating wound in her abdomen. I looked into her eyes to see if there was any recognition and noticed the tear streaks falling from each as she stared out into nothing.

A breeze blew, tousling the few strands of hair that had come loose from her molded crown. I thought it was simply the result of being at this height, but the wind speed increased too rapidly to be natural. Clouds converged overhead, darkening the sky. Within seconds, I felt I stood in the middle of a storm. Then it was a hurricane. The wind whipped around Uji. I expected her to be lifted by the gale forces. A rumbling sound like a distant earthquake came from all around. With it, the same oily black sludge I had seen came gushing out of the wound. The wind caught the venomous ooze and swirled it around as if a giant snake living inside her had finally broken free. It hovered there, and unless I was going crazy, it considered me for a moment. I felt a sudden sense of dread and hostility and feared I might have let loose a rabid beast from hell into the world.

Another streak of light broke through the clouds and fell upon the sludge creature. It convulsed as though physically struck and started to vibrate. The rumble built up to a screech. I tried to block out the sound, but I might as well try to catch the ocean with a paper bag. The creature spun faster and faster. Then finally, in a blinding flash, blew apart and scattered into nothingness.

The winds died. The clouds parted and quiet fell. Then even the stillness disappeared, replaced by the sounds of the city that was oblivious to what had just occurred. Uji was gone. Nothing remained of her except the tanto that lay on the ground, sheathed once more.

Chapter Thirty-Five

"SHE'S DEAD?" HAGER ROTATED the tanto in his hands while Ima looked over his shoulder.

"Yup." I took a sip from the glass of scotch in my hand, looking out the window at the birds flitting back and forth between the palm trees. I had just gotten back, not too long after the rest of the team. With Uji gone, there was nothing stopping them from pulling the needed hard drives and eliminating the remaining Converted. Marie was rushed to the hospital. Fortunately, she was only hit in the shoulder. "I opened the rift back to the rooftop to give you time to get the data we needed."

"I'm still not sure how you were able to get through her defenses."

"Oh, that was easy. I caused a distraction by grabbing her with my astral form."

Ima looked at Hager. "Does he always speak so nonchalantly about things that have never been done before?"

He sighed. "Quite."

"And then you killed her?" She asked.

"It wasn't quite that easy."

"I can confirm that. I watched him take a major beating through my scope before he made her blow up." Jelena was lounging sideways in a chair in the corner, drinking a Modelo.

Ima's head perked up. "Blow up?"

She shrugged. "Not sure what else to call it."

They both looked at me and I described what had occurred. Hager dropped into a chair. The normally bombastic man looked up at me and spoke only a single word. "How?"

"I got lucky."

"I think we will need more than that," Ima prompted.

"Remember when I dealt with the demons?"

Ima's eyebrows pulled together. "Excuse me?"

I shook my head and waved away the question. "A conversation for another day. I tried to do the same with Uji."

"And?" Hager's one-word questions were making me nervous.

"Epic failure." I described the image bombardment. "I'm assuming it was because of her immensely long life." Hager nodded. "However, the process provided insight. Uji used that sword to finish me." I pointed at it with the glass. "The sight of it called the image from my subconscious." I took another sip, savoring the smokey flavor.

Hager shook his head. "Chris, if you force me to prompt you constantly for more information, this is going to take an extraordinary amount of time. What is special about the Tanto?"

I smiled at him. He finally sounded like his old self. "It was her humanity."

Jelena cocked her head. "The poem?"

I nodded.

Hager shut his eyes and shook his head. "What poem?"

"There was a French poet from the 16th century Jackie was always a fan of. He was half mad and ultimately hung himself. I remember her going on and on about him and it felt similar to what happened to Denise. I started rereading his poems from the perspective of a Bishop. One was titled The Impure. It is a long and eerily accurate depiction of the Tainted. The relevant section translates something like this.

… Separated from them at the time of their rebirth,

Cursed to carry their humanity with them,

A vessel for the vestige of what they were,

A commination for their failure,

A catalyst for their demise…"

Ima folded her arms. "And you thought to risk your life based on the maniacal ravings of a madman?"

I shook my head. It was amazing how even people surrounded by fantastical occurrences discounted what they could not understand.

"No, the poem allowed me to translate some visions. Specifically, that dagger being given to Uji as she knelt in front of formless, shapeless being of unfathomable power and menace."

"Formless? Shapeless?"

"My best description would be the hell scene from The Golden Child."

Ima stuck a thumb in my direction and asked Hager. "Is he serious?"

"You get used to it," Hager said.

"Admit it, though, it put a clear image in your head," Jelena added.

"If you saw the movie," Ima countered.

"First, I'm not claiming anything, I'm telling you what happened. Second, who hasn't seen the Golden Child?"

Ima shook her head and turned away.

Hager stood up. "I think we are getting a little off topic."

I shrugged. "I'm not sure what you're so mad about."

She looked at me again, her eyes pleading. "I am not angry with you. I'm afraid of what this all means. Of how these actions of which you speak so lightly will affect the rest of the world and the war."

"I'm confused. Isn't this a good thing?" Jelena asked. "Chris found a way to kill the things you've been battling for thousands of years. What's the problem?"

"What's the problem?" Ima looked on the verge of losing it. Hager put a hand on her arm before she launched into a tirade.

"As you said, for thousands of years we were battling the symptoms of this virus infecting our world. There was nothing we could do about the cause. As a result, many of the Tainted, especially the more powerful ones, ignored us. Or maybe a better way to say it is they never focused on us. You have just proven that we now have the ability not just to get in their way, but to cause them actual harm. You have shown them we are a threat. This so-called Tainted War has just begun."

"Seriously, how did you put up with his shit for so many years?" Jelena asked.

"I had to. I worked for his mother," Krissi answered.

"Remind me why I rescued you again," Adam asked.

"Because you felt guilty for leaving me to die. What, too soon?"

I stuck my head into Krissi's room. She was in bed with an IV drip, trying to rehydrate. Adam sat in a chair next to her. Jelena sat on the bed.

"You know a dip in the sacred waters would cure you faster than a saline drip," I said.

"Fuck that. After the last episode, I'm not eager to jump back in that pool. I think I'll give it a little time, let things work their way out naturally. "

I couldn't blame her. I still had ringing in my ears from her screams. "How are you feeling?"

"Not bad, all things considered. A hundred percent better than I was yesterday."

"Physically at least." Adam added.

Krissi eyed him like she was going to rip out his throat right there. She took a breath and the look passed. "Yeah, well. I'm as good as I'm going to get."

"For now. I will make sure she gets the help she needs."

"Let it go, Adam."

"What? I'm just saying—"

"Adam!" She was panting.

He looked at her with shock and worry on his face.

Krissi shook her head. "Sorry."

I walked into the room and tapped her on the shoulder. She looked up at me. "Don't be. You have been through more shit than anyone should have to. You will get back to some semblance of normal, but until then, you are a badass who survived hell and lived to talk about it. Don't let anyone tell you different."

Krissi nodded.

I started back to the door. "Glad you're doing better."

"Chris?"

I stopped and looked back.

"Thanks. You know for…" She cocked a head to the side.

I nodded and left the room. Jelena caught up to me a few feet down the hall and matched my pace.

"I wanted to talk, now this is all over."

"You're staying."

"How'd you know?"

"Not hard to see. You are a mother, and you are starting a new relationship. Neither of those things pair well with being on the road."

She grabbed me by the arm and spun me to face her. "Stop being a macho man. Are you gonna be good without me?"

"I'm sorry, who has supernatural powers?"

"And a habit of getting into trouble I need to get his ass out of."

"Talking about my ass again. I think I need to go to HR."

She punched me in the arm. Hard. "Moron."

"Jelena. You should stay. It's the right move for you, for Enric, and for your mother. Build a new life. Set down some new roots. If you decide you need out, you've got my number."

"What, you don't want me around now?"

"Yeah. I need the women I meet to find out I'm an ass all by themselves without you giving them a heads up first."

"You are an ass."

"See."

She made the sound again that said more than any mere words could convey. This time I grabbed her arm as she went to leave. She looked down at my hand like she was considering cutting it off but didn't say or do anything.

"Thanks for saving my life on the roof."

She smirked. "About time you acknowledged it."

"How did you know where I would be?"

"Hager gave me a heads up. John covered my six on the roof. The DEA met us halfway down and took Adam and Krissi out."

"It was a good thing Marie met with that contact outside of the Miami office."

"You're lucky the buildings were pretty close. Still, good shot though, right?"

I held out my fist for a bump. "Nobody better."

Jelena obliged my fist bump while rolling her eyes. "Speaking of Marie, did you talk to her yet?"

"Not yet. I was about to go see her."

"Try not to screw it up."

"I will do my best." I walked away.

"Bring flowers."

"I was going to." At least now I was.

"And keep John away from her."

I knocked on the hospital room door and stuck my face in the window next to it. Marie was sitting up in the adjustable hospital bed. She shook her head and waved me in. I opened the door, skirted around it, and presented the flowers I had brought with me.

"Oh fwowers, how ordinawy."

I stopped dead in my tracks. "Did you just quote Blazing Saddles?" She smirked.

"Where have you been all my life?"

"Not waiting for your lazy ass, that's for sure."

"Lazy?" I put the vase of flowers on her side table.

"You know how long I have been lying here by myself."

"I was busy saving the world."

"Talk about delusions of grandeur."

I huffed. "How's the shoulder?"

"I've had worse."

"Yeah, sorry about that."

"What the hell are you sorry about? It was my stupid reaction that gave away the plan you had going."

"I should have realized that opening up a rift in reality may come as a surprise to you."

"You know what? You're right, it is your fault."

"Why do I feel like I will never win an argument?"

"See, you're not so dumb after all."

I couldn't help but laugh, and Marie smiled back.

Then her expression changed. "I'm assuming you've come to say goodbye."

I took on a quizzical look. "Why would you assume that?"

"It's the standard trope. Hero swoops in seduces beautiful cop, saves the day, leaves to go on his next adventure. I've played the role once or twice myself."

"While I enjoy being cast as the hero, I believe you seduced me. You and your wicked wiles."

Marie frowned. "What are you, 97?"

"It's a quote from my favorite dwarf."

"Dopey?"

"Grumpy. Dopey never talked."

"Must be why he's my favorite."

"You want me to go?"

She crossed her arms. "I didn't say that. Do what you want."

"You don't care. I should just do whatever I want."

"I didn't say I didn't care, and yes, do what you want. I won't stop you."

"Fine." I kissed her. Stepped right in, leaned down before she could say more, grabbed her behind the neck and pulled her into it. There was no resistance, and I felt the tension melt out of her. When we finally pulled apart, she smiled up at me.

Cue Take a Chance on Me by ABBA. Switch to an overhead view and pull back in a slow rotation.

"What are you doing?"

"Oh sorry, was that out loud? What? I like movies."

"Speak again, and I'll shoot you."

The End

Heretic Preview

Chapter One

"*CHRIS, ARE YOU SURE this is a good idea?*" Marie asked.

"Of course," I replied. "What could go wrong?"

"*With you? Anything.*"

The wind picked up straight into my face and I had to turn. "You risk your life all the time."

"*To prevent drugs from getting on the street so people don't do things like this.*"

"Yes, but they don't have superpowers to heal them."

"Is she trying to talk you out of it?" Adam walked up behind me.

I tilted the phone away from my mouth and turned to my fellow Bishop. The title identified us not as a Roman Catholic priest of rank, but as a member of a secret supernatural sect dating back to the dawn of humankind. So we've got that going for us. "Yeah, she said it was a stupid idea."

"She's not wrong." A hawk cried out not too far away as if accenting his point.

I stuck my tongue out at him. "You're no help."

"Not trying to be."

I talked back into the phone. "Alright, I'm going now."

"Okay, have fun storming the castle."

I hung up smiling and put my phone away. My new girlfriend had a tendency to try to dissuade me from doing things she saw as unnecessarily risky endeavors. As a DEA agent, I would have expected her to be more adventurous.

"You ready?" I asked him.

"Not really."

"Then why did you agree?"

"You wouldn't shut up about it."

I zipped up my sleeves, stepping up to the edge. Adam did the same, shaking his head.

"Three."

"Two."

"One!"

We jumped off the cliff. The wingsuits caught the air as we started soaring down the mountain. The ground streaked by, becoming a familiar blur. After about fifteen seconds, trees started dotting the landscape. A few at first, which increased quickly, turning into a forest. We were skimming the top branches consistently by the height of a tall house, as the slope of the ground matched our descent angle. You can't fly with a wingsuit, nor are you gliding. Your plunge to the earth is simply elongated. For every fifty feet you drop, you move two-hundred feet laterally. The whole process gives you *a feeling* of flying.

After a few glorious seconds like this, the ground dropped and we were out in open air. I looked behind me at Adam and saw him grinning. How could he not? If I wanted to turn, I tilted my body. To slow myself I arched my back. There were no handles to pull, no motor driving me, nothing to sit on. It was just me riding the wind. Off to the left, I saw my objective. A large outcropping jetted out. The center of it had fallen away a millennium ago, leaving a gap about thirty feet wide and a few hundred long. I aimed towards the fissure.

"Chris, what are you doing?" Adam's voice buzzed in my ear through the com, just audible over the rushing of the air.

"I've got to do it."

"No, you really don't."

"You only live once."

"Yeah, and you only die once as well. I'm not sure even we can survive face planting into a mountain going eighty miles an hour."

I kept on my heading, more determined. "Relax, I've got my helmet on."

"It won't stop you from becoming a human pancake." Adam sounded like a parent trying to explain to a child that the stove was hot.

"Then why did I wear it again?"

"You're not funny."

"You can't really believe that."

"Chris veer off." An edge of panic was creeping into his voice. I appreciated the concern for my safety, but no one was talking me out of this.

The mountain side rapidly approached. The gap somehow looked narrower than it did in pictures.

"Chris, shit!"

"Tower, this is Ghost Rider requesting a flyby."

"Chris!"

I rocketed at the cliff face at inhuman speed, even from my height-ened perspective. One second I had elbow room to spare, the next I was surrounded by rock, then out in the open again. The flush of adrenaline had me buzzing, and it was all I could do to not attempt a barrel roll. I arced towards Adam as we came within sight of our landing area, a large clearing where Marie and Jelena waited for us. We both leaned back, slowing our forward momentum, then pulled our chutes. There was an intense quiet that permeated the seconds before the silk caught the air, then a loud pop almost like a gunshot. My whole body jerked with the dramatic deceleration.

Drifting slowly down, I tugged hard on the maneuvering cords and landed lightly, then turned and pulled in my chute.

Marie stepped up; giving me a hug and a kiss. "That was pretty impressive. Crazy but impressive."

I smiled at her. "If that impressed you, just wait for tonight."

"Another attempt to beat the wing record at the Buffalo Lodge?"

"I can do it this time. I only missed by four."

She kissed me again, leaned back, and looked into my eyes. "You're an idiot."

I was going to pull her in for another embrace, but Jelena stepped up. As soon as Marie had stood clear, she punched me in the stomach.

"Estúpido estás loco?"

"Glad to see you, too." I grunted. She knew I couldn't prepare myself for fear of activating my powers. If that happened, my skin would turn to iron and she would break her hand. Both she and Marie were human, with no additives. Unless you considered Jelena's other worldly ability to shoot a wart off a frog's ass at six hundred yards. I'd hired the former marine sniper as the first major violation of my career as a Bishop. Up till then we didn't solicit help from those they considered *unblessed*.

"What was the point of that stunt?" she asked.

"It was fun." My voice was still laced with pain.

"And do you think it would be fun for us scraping you off the mountainside?"

"Why are you yelling at me? Marie wasn't upset. Why are you?"

"Are you that thick? Just because she doesn't yell about it doesn't mean she's not feeling it. You are not immortal and you have a job to do. Remember the Tainted? The—" She wiggled her fingers in the air like she was playing the piano, then turned to Adam. "What's the word?"

"Puppet masters."

"Si. Puppet masters. You killed one, starting a shit storm all over the world."

"Which is why we came here," I countered, getting defensive. "To get away from all that for a few moments. To forget for a time that my actions have made everything worse." I stalked a few paces away.

"We are barely hanging on *with* you. What would we do without you?"

I faced all of them. "I don't know what I'm doing, okay? I said it. I'm clueless back there." Stepping forward again, I stood toe to toe with her. She didn't retreat, staring up at me with a look that made me think sparks were going to shoot from her eyes. I pointed at the mountain without breaking eye contact. "But that! That I know. That I can do."

"They taught you to have a death wish in the Rangers?"

"Three jumps a day for a month. I am more in control hurtling down the earth than I am battling the Tainted and their minions." I looked over at Marie. "I just needed to feel in command again."

She smiled at me. "I know, but we've been here a week." Looking closer, I could see the concern etched in her face.

Jelena yanked my head back to her. "Now that we have settled that, can we get out of this friggin jungle?"

"Forest," I corrected.

"What the fuck is the difference? There are a shitload of trees and nowhere to get good tacos."

Marie stepped up and wrapped her arms around me. "Maybe going back is a good idea."

Adam added. "It's the right thing to do."

I took a deep breath of clean mountain air and realized they weren't wrong. I nodded. "Let's go home."

Chapter Two

"You aint so bad."

Rocky III - 1982

"THIS WAS NOT MY fault." I stared down the hulk of a man in front of me. I wondered if he had been accidentally shrink-wrapped into a sack of potatoes. I had to look up at him and for me, that is saying something.

"How is it not your fault?" Marie stood next to me, holding her DEA issued Glock pointed at the monster. "He was dozing. I warned you not to wake him up. Don't wake the sleeping giant. Isn't that one of the Bishop rules?"

"Yes, but only after climbing a beanstalk. Did you see a beanstalk?" I looked around to further make my point. "Nope. Also, let me remind you that had we still been in the woods, the likelihood of running into a supernaturally drug enhanced pro wrestler would be dramatically reduced."

"You're an ass."

"You would think you could come up with something new."

"Fine, you're a giant ass."

I shrugged. "Not original, but topically relevant."

"Can you focus on the task at hand?"

The big man shifted his gaze between us, not sure who he wanted to pummel first. "Hey, Hodor!" I pulled his attention to me. "Where are the drugs? Once we get them, we will be on our way and you can return to your nap."

He roared and ran at me.

As he got in close, I side stepped with my left foot, ducked under his grab, then stood up quickly. I let the momentum launch him over my back. With the added force from my boon, the giant sailed across the gym and into the boxing ring.

"You did that on purpose just so you could get in the ring with him," Marie accused.

"Yeah, I made sure I was in the perfect position and goaded him so I could put him in that exact spot." Not for nothing, but if I could have, I definitely would have. I climbed into the ring as the big man got to his feet and faced me. We started circling each other; knees bent, hunched over, hands in claws like a scene out of the World Wrestling Federation. He must have felt more comfortable than I was because a smile crept onto his face. I went into a blur—when Bishops move faster than humanly possible—and tried to get behind him. He backhanded me when I moved in close and the blow tossed me into one corner in a heap.

This man's powers, unlike mine, were derived from a drug laced with the blood of a fallen Bishop. Another tale that you can research on your own.

In my upside-down position, I watched as the hulk-moron looked out at nonexistent fans and raised his hands in triumph. He pounded both fists in the air, then started flexing his muscles.

Marie stepped up next to the elevated ring, playing the role of my manager. "You good?"

I righted myself to sit on the correct part of my anatomy. "Oh yeah."

"Let me guess, you've got him right where you want him."

I gave her a side eye. "Of course."

"Getting bitch slapped was the plan?"

"Of course, I'm lulling him into a false sense of security."

Marie repeated the last four words in stereo with me, nodding with a corner of her mouth clenched. "How about you get up off your ass and finish this?"

"See, I knew you were always in my corner."

"Geek."

I was about to get back up when rock-brain grabbed my foot and dragged me into the center of the ring.

"Not cool, man!" I yelled. "I didn't hear no bell."

He ignored me. I planted my other foot and launched myself over his head. He turned to see what I was doing, and I ended up landing behind him. I was in a playful mood, shocking I know, so I tapped him on the shoulder. When he turned around, I landed a powered up punch to the chest with an accompanying dramatic foot stomp. It staggered him for a moment and when he came back in to grab me, I hooked one arm between his legs. Draping the other over his shoulder, I body slammed him.

The force of the supernaturally enhanced move sent out a concussive wave so that the heavy bags swung and rattled the metal weights, sounding like a cacophony of gongs. Not wanting to take any chances, I followed it up with a flying elbow to the chest. I didn't put everything I had into it, but it was a lot. The give in the floor of the ring caused his whole body to lift a few inches before slamming down again. Without hesitation, I hooked my arm around the back of his knee and hauled his bulk up so there was nothing touching the mat except his shoulders. With my free hand, I slapped the mat three times then released him, leaping up and performing my own celebratory dance where I struck a few poses and growled for effect.

Marie must have climbed in at some point because she was in the corner with her arms crossed. "Are you done?"

I stood up straight, looked around, then down at the now unconscious man, and nodded. "Yup, I'm good."

She threw me a small pen injector. I caught it and removed the cap with my teeth. Stepping over the giant, shoved it into the muscle between his neck and shoulder. It was our version of Naloxone that Dorothy, the Covenant's cranky ninety-year-old lab tech, had created to counteract the tainted drugs.

Recapping it, I tossed the pen across the room into the small garbage.

"You are a showoff. You know that, right?"

I mimed shock. "How could you say that? I am simply doing my part in this epic battle against the evil immortal Tainted who…" The rest of what I was saying was lost in Marie's kiss.

When she finally pulled back, she narrowed her eyes. "You also talk too much as well."

"Now *that* I've heard."

I leaned in for more.

There was a groan from behind me. "What happened? How did I get here?"

I turned. "Dude, timing."

Marie smacked me in the arm then extended her hand towards the man, now sitting up in the middle of the ring.

"Fine." I climbed up while hanging onto the top rope. "The drugs you have been taking were laced with a deadly chemical. We saved your life. Now, where are they?"

"I don't take drugs."

"The fugue state you were in would disagree," Marie said.

"What?"

I shook my head. "Let me guess, steroids?"

"Uhhhh."

Marie flashed her badge. "I don't want you to struggle too hard, so I'll read it for you. It says DEA, which stands for—"

"I know."

"Good, then you know the only thing that can get you unscrewed is for you to tell me where the drugs are, and where you got them from."

"Hey, that reminds me of a joke."

Marie ignored me. "What's your name?"

The big guy rubbed his neck. "André."

"Are you serious? Marie, he's André the…"

"Yes, I get it."

I asked, "Fezzik, are there rocks ahead?"

"What?"

Apparently, Andre hadn't seen one of my favorite movies of all time. I was very disappointed.

"Where are the drugs?" Marie continued prodding like I wasn't there.

He hesitated and I just couldn't resist. "Did I make it clear that your job is at stake?"

Marie pulled her Glock and pointed it at me. "Speak again, and I'll shoot you."

I pantomimed zipping my lips.

"André," Marie said. "The drugs."

Whether it was Marie's badge, her gun, or not being able to stand any more Princess Bride quotes, he gave us the drugs and his dealer's info. I followed Marie out the door, but not before peaking back in for a last dig.

"I'm going to have to find myself a new giant, that's all."

Buy Heretic to continue the adventure!

Get Exclusive Content From
W. J. Grupe Jr.

If you have enjoyed this book, I would really appreciate if you would leave a rating and a review.

If you haven't already, check out the first book in The Tainted War series, Awakening.

Sign up for my newsletter to stay up to date with everything going on.

Visit me on Facebook, Instagram, Twitter, and Linkedin.

Get the John McCaw novella and learn how he came to join the New York City Covenant of Bishops.

Available exclusively on my website:

www.WJGrupeJr.com.

Acknowledgements

As always I need to start out by thanking my family. You are my biggest supporters and I couldn't do this without you. But specifically:
Marie- Always my first reader of every version and the only person who has read this book as many times as me.
Kristina - Thanks for being my top salesperson. I hope you like your alterego.
Will - You solved my biggest plot hole. This book would not be as good without your input.

Special thanks to:
Lawrence Mangine for his help with the military elements,

my beta readers Jim, Marguerite, Jen, Lawrence, and Sarah for their insights,

my editors Mark Stay and Liv Mammone that kept me focused on my voice instead of others;

and the gang at The Best Seller Experiment - Truly the best life and craft support a writer could ask for.

www.ingramcontent.com/pod-product-compliance
Lightning Source LLC
Chambersburg PA
CBHW060528260626
47161CB00003B/806